Praise for Katie Porter's
Inside Bet

"...this racy, raunchy, hella good read...will move *Fifty Shades of Grey* to the children's section."

~ RT Book Reviews

"Every once in a while you finish a book, smile and say: *Now that's what I'm talking about!*"

~ USA TODAY

"If you are in the mood for a steamy contemporary, look no further. Katie Porter is an author to watch."

~ The Good, The Bad and The Unread

"I love reading a book where the words flow so effortlessly that you forget you are reading; you are simply living the book."

~ Guilty Pleasures Book Reviews

"*Inside Bet* is exciting, sexy, and just a bit kinky fun. It's also emotionally rich; full of regret, forgiveness, courage, and hope."

~ Fresh Fiction

"Next to all the dirty, steamy sex *Inside Bet* is a story of vulnerability. The last few chapters brought me to tears..."

~ Pearl's World of Romance

"The eroticism in this novel is exquisite, vivid and daring. Five stars and a fist pump!"

~ Book Lovers Inc.

Look for these titles by
Katie Porter

Now Available:

Came Upon a Midnight Clear

Vegas Top Guns
Double Down
Inside Bet
Hold 'Em
Hard Way

Club Devant
Lead and Follow
Chains and Canes

Inside Bet

Katie Porter

Samhain Publishing, Ltd.
11821 Mason Montgomery Road, 4B
Cincinnati, OH 45249
www.samhainpublishing.com

Inside Bet
Copyright © 2013 by Katie Porter
Print ISBN: 978-1-61921-274-9
Digital ISBN: 978-1-61921-086-8

Editing by Sasha Knight
Cover by Scott Carpenter

This book is a work of fiction. The names, characters, places, and incidents are products of the writer's imagination or have been used fictitiously and are not to be construed as real. Any resemblance to persons, living or dead, actual events, locale or organizations is entirely coincidental.

All Rights Are Reserved. No part of this book may be used or reproduced in any manner whatsoever without written permission, except in the case of brief quotations embodied in critical articles and reviews.

First Samhain Publishing, Ltd. electronic publication: August 2012
First Samhain Publishing, Ltd. print publication: July 2013

Dedication

To RJ & EG
Bad romance

Acknowledgments

We deeply appreciate our families' unflagging support. Credit for much of our sanity is owed to the Group That Shall Not Be Named. In addition, we offer thanks to Sarah Frantz, Rowan Larke, Zoe Archer, Patti Ann Colt and Kelly Schaub for their friendship, and to Kevan Lyon and Sasha Knight for their amazing enthusiasm.

Chapter One

"Tell me it's not bad news."

Heather Morris eyed her friend but found no reason to hope. This didn't look good.

Jenn slid her cell phone shut. "It's bad news."

"Devastating?"

"Well, unlike last time, there's no hospital involved. But I'm afraid our plans for the night are DOA."

Disappointment slinked between them and the good time they'd just been enjoying. The Magazine was a fabulously cool wine bar off the Strip. People with more money than sense had turned out for the bar's inaugural "Curiosities" tasting, which promised samples of exotic vintages from each continent, including a batch that had been aged at a research station in Antarctica. Another label from Malaysia boasted a pinot noir with the added healing powers of python venom, rendered inert by the bottling process.

Heather had planned to skip that one. But who could turn down the chance to taste a Tuscan merlot fermented in 24-karat-gold casks?

Jenn Kimble was the wine correspondent for an online culinary blog. She'd been the one to secure tickets, which included a complimentary sample of each selection. Then, just for fun, they were off to a new Spanish tapas place called La Rocca where reservations required a three-month wait. In appreciation, Heather had left her accounting firm two hours early to treat Jenn to a salon visit. They'd giggled like young girls, anticipating their big night out—the first they'd been able to wrangle in two months.

But now it seemed another family emergency would intervene.

"What happened?"

"Mylie can't stay with the kids past nine because her dad can take her to the gymnastics meet after all." Jenn waved her phone. "That was Rich. I thought he was just checking in to say he'd arrived, but his flight's been delayed in Atlanta. The safety lights on the aisle aren't functioning, so they have to board another plane. Of all things!"

Heather grimaced. "And now he won't be back in time to relieve Mylie."

"Bingo."

"Damn."

"Double damn."

"Call someone else," Heather said, a smidge too desperately. "Anybody. Their school janitor if you have to."

Twenty minutes passed as Jenn tried every number in her arsenal while Heather eyed The Magazine's aggressively nouveau décor. The floor-to-ceiling windows, minimalist steel fixtures and bare light bulbs hanging from strings of braided copper wire seemed the perfect sort of bizarre place to let loose.

But it was after eight on a Friday night. At such short notice, finding a sober tourist would've been easier than finding a babysitter.

"No luck," Jenn said at last.

Heather knew her friend's disappointment would well outpace her own. After all, Jenn had two preschoolers and a husband who traveled a hundred days a year. "I'm sorry, honey."

Jenn shrugged. Her gleaming blonde hair was a crime against sisterhood, especially when it was done in a princessy updo. "It was just for work."

"No way. Don't pull that with me. I know how much you were looking forward to this."

"Well, yes." Jenn let out a faint sigh. "But at least you'll be here."

"I'm not staying at this freak show if you're not here with me. Who will I point out train wrecks to? That dress, for example." She nudged Jenn, who glanced toward a woman standing at the bar. A gold lamé corset over a poofy pink lace tutu was never, ever appropriate. Except, apparently, in Vegas.

Jenn chuckled. "Double damn," she said again, more wearily this time. "Don't have kids, my dear."

"Hush. You love them."

"Okay, fine. Don't have kids until you can afford a full-time nanny."

"I'll get right on that. Maybe I can bet my retirement savings at the casinos."

"Beats the stock market." Opening her purse, Jenn rummaged until she found a pad of paper and a pen. "Take this, would you? I need six hundred words for my column tomorrow. Just take some notes on the snake venom and the Antarctica thing—the really novel ones. I already have enough about the bat-shit-crazy atmosphere."

Although Heather took the pen and paper, she wasn't ready to give up on her friend. "Are you sure? I can go relieve Mylie. You have work to do here."

"I appreciate the offer, sweetie. I do. But I haven't seen Rich in four days. That means when he finally gets home and the kids are snoring, I'll get laid. Probably *very* well." She kissed Heather on the cheek. "You stay here and go hunting."

Heather laughed outright. "Sure thing."

"I'm serious." She slipped a magenta wristband off her slender wrist and handed it over. "Give it to some halfway-normal guy and get blazing drunk."

"I don't get drunk and I don't pick up random guys."

"Are you sure you were young once?"

You have no idea.

Not even Jenn, her closest friend since moving to Vegas, had a clear picture of Heather's wild youth. Like everyone, she believed Heather to be the straight-laced Assistant Director of Internal Auditing of Hanover Financial Logistics. All true. But that hadn't always been the case. No one realized that being the only daughter of a sergeant major in the Army was shorthand for "spent my youth partying like a preacher's little girl on spring break".

The wildest part of Heather's current life was the fact Hanover specialized in casino accounts. That was enough for her mom, who continued to believe working on casino spreadsheets and quarterly reports was the same as hanging with Wayne Newton and the Osmonds.

Living in Las Vegas did, however, have interesting advantages. The Magazine was a case in point. If it could be done at all, it could be done bigger and better in Sin City. And all without the restrictions of good taste.

She waved her farewell as Jenn wiggled out toward the street-facing exit. It was entirely unjust for a mother of two to be so thin. Working out five times a week was the best Heather could manage to keep her curves from turning to saddlebags and a muffin top.

She found a table by herself. The waves propelling her evening had reduced to a flat calm, leaving her oddly restless. When the first sample was delivered by a waitress wearing an electric-blue sheath dress, Heather decided to enjoy the experience. Nothing lost.

She took a hesitant sip. Although loathe to pay $7,500 a bottle for the world's highest altitude wine, she found it imminently drinkable. In responsible memory of poor dear Jenn, she took diligent notes as another two samples arrived.

"Is this seat taken?"

Looking up, she found a pleasant surprise. A very pleasant surprise, truth be told.

A man in a smartly tailored three-piece suit stood with his hand on the back of the other chair. The pose and the suit, together with his trim physique, created a rather dashing picture. He had presence. Maybe even grace.

He was also *young*. Not young enough to make cradle-robbing jokes, maybe mid-twenties, but with an extra dash of boyish sweetness to his features.

That is, until he smiled.

Goose bumps dotted Heather's arms. Something about that smile, so slow and controlled, completely belied his youthful looks—while revealing an adorably sexy pair of dimples. Unbelievable.

He licked his lower lip, leaving his mouth slightly parted.

That did it.

"Help yourself," she said.

She watched him out of the corners of her eyes as he sat. Propping his ankle across his knee, he settled into the chair. But he didn't slouch. His odd grace meant square shoulders and a straight spine.

"So, what've I missed?"

Heather consulted her notes. "The world's highest vintage, the only vintage to be personally approved by the Crown Princess of Sweden, and one flavored with espresso."

The young man made a face. "*Toute la nuit longtemps?*"

"That's the one. What does it mean?"

"All night long." He offered a subtle sneer. "That stuff is a crime against tongues."

She didn't know which affected her more—that he automatically knew the name of a rare vintage, or how his mention of tongues dragged her attention back to his mouth. What would it take to get him to smile again? She hadn't felt that particular rush of *oh, hello* in ages.

And the French. God. Even if he was just a practiced wine snob, his low voice made love to each syllable.

"Would you like a wristband?" She assumed a guy so young wouldn't have five hundred dollars to blow on a wine-tasting event.

But he surprised her again by pulling back his cuff. There on his wrist, nestled next to an exquisite Omega dress watch, was one of The Magazine's wristbands.

"I've never been a fan of kitsch," he said, frowning at the tacky magenta thing. "But I'll endure just about anything for novelty."

The oddly suggestive timbre of his words had Heather shaking her head. He had some nerve. She'd give him that. But his Omega and fine wool suit forced her to reassess her initial impression. Either he came from money or tried very hard to look like it. In Las Vegas, one could never be sure.

Heather couldn't decide whether she wanted him to stay or hit the road. He perched smack between unsettling and interesting.

"You're here alone?" she asked.

"Not anymore."

Once more he unfurled that slow smile, dimples and all. The effect was elemental, like being chilled by the wind or warmed by the sun. This time Heather's physical reaction wasn't goose bumps but the subtle tightening of her nipples. His dark, narrow eyes crinkled at the edges, as if he knew what she was feeling.

"We'll see," she managed to say.

"Actually, I only stopped by to thank you."

"For what?"

He angled that slinky gaze toward her cleavage. "For being so generous."

The camisole she wore wasn't exactly revealing, especially not when topped by a cashmere blazer, but any time her bust line met with silk and lace, men drooled. Or...*appreciated,* as this one seemed to do.

Ha. Man. He was a snot-nosed punk who thought he could drop sexy innuendos and keep up with a woman who'd learned hard lessons about slick bastards.

Heather leaned against the table, intentionally posturing to give him a better view. "You're an arrogant little prick, aren't you?"

"It's not little," he said. "My prick, that is."

A clamped-down part of her unexpectedly relaxed. Why wasn't she creeped out? Or laughing her ass off? Either reaction seemed more appropriate than wanting to tell him to prove it.

The waitress returned, that electric-blue dress leaving nothing to the imagination. The young man, however, only took his eyes off Heather to pick up the latest wine sample. Rather than savor and consider the bouquet, he downed it in a single gulp.

Heather found herself staring and unwilling to stop. The contrast between his pale skin and dark eyes was striking. He had dark hair too, buzzed short with almost military precision. That certainly didn't fit with his suit or his smooth, angelic features, but the contradiction was delicious. No telling what was true and what was utter bullshit. He probably knew as much, using it to his advantage over unsuspecting females.

Heather wasn't unsuspecting. But she wasn't immune, either.

He matched her aggressive posture. His straight back made him look continuously eager. "No answer to that rather forward comment. I'm disappointed."

"Silence or derision were my options. It's too early in our acquaintance to discuss the size of your prick."

"I don't think that's true," he said. "I'm Jon, by the way. What's your name?"

"Heather."

"You don't look like a Heather."

"Sorry," she said tartly. "What do I look like?"

He tilted his head. She felt...assessed. Keenly aware of herself as a woman. Because of him. "More exotic. Definitely more curvaceous. Evangeline, maybe?"

Heather shivered. She was getting ticked off at this Jon character. He said everything like a dare. And it had been years since she'd been the reckless soul who indulged in dares. They always got out of hand. The hurt was never worth the risk, especially now that she had a career worth protecting.

"Sorry, no such luck," she said, trying to stay casual. His eyes weren't letting that happen. "Just the hazard of being born a girl in 1981."

"How about your middle name? Any better luck?"

"Crystal."

He feigned the disappointment of a near-miss. "Oooh, another strike. You only have one more chance."

"So if my last name is Poots or Fusty or Hogblossom...?"

"Then I'm afraid my appreciation of your breasts will be the closest we get to carnal knowledge." He shrugged. "Standards, you see."

"What's yours?"

"*My* last name? Carlisle."

"Nice one."

"It is, isn't it? But quid pro quo. Your turn." His voice was surprisingly low for someone so young, a soft rumble that tickled under her skin.

"It's Morris."

"And the damsel is saved," he said with a grin.

"You approve?" Heather almost frowned. Where the hell had that breathy question come from?

"Very much." Jon Carlisle picked her hand off the table and kissed her knuckles. For the briefest moment, she'd been sure he would bite instead of kiss. "It's a pleasure to meet you, Ms. Morris."

Chapter Two

Jon Carlisle knew women. Most of all, he *liked* women. Each possessed something unique and appreciable. Whether the curve of an elegant neck or the perfect symmetry of graceful collarbones, he had long ago made it his duty to find the special facets in each woman he met.

Heather Crystal Morris, despite her rather dated name, was the type to be savored. Rich dark hair had been barely swept away from her face and knotted at the nape of her neck, leaving her classical features prominent. Her eyes were pale blue, like the sky at high altitude, and she had a sultry way of looking at him from under the dark slashes of her eyebrows—as if she were challenging him.

Jon hadn't found enough challenges lately.

He carefully placed her hand back on the table, trailing his fingertips over her knuckles. "How is a woman like you alone tonight with a spare bracelet?"

"A woman like me? Do I want to know what you mean by that?"

"Perhaps."

She tilted her head as she rested her chin on her fist. "I have no doubt you'd answer if I asked." Dark lashes shielded her eyes. The contrast with the pale blue was rather remarkable. "So I don't think I will."

"Scared?"

Her laugh was sexy. No other word for it. Just husky enough, it evoked feelings of being wrapped in the dark with her. That would be a memorable time. He'd ensure it. "Not in the least."

The waitress appeared and presented two glasses of deep red wine. The venom-infused pinot noir.

Heather peered at the plastic cup and lifted it toward a light. "Looks rather normal, doesn't it? Like any other glass of wine?"

After a quick swirl to watch the liquid climb the sides of the glass,

Jon took a deep swallow. "It tastes like any other pinot noir too. Maybe a hint of blackberry."

She set hers down. "I'll take your word on it."

A single drop of the rich liquid lingered on his bottom lip. He licked it off, not missing how Heather's gaze tracked the small movement. Again. "Don't tell me you're going to chicken out."

Her spine went slightly stiff. The move pushed her glorious chest toward him. The straight slashes of her brows lowered. "It has python venom in it. Choosing not to drink it is the prudent choice."

Jon couldn't help but lean forward. Suddenly he knew her type. Quiet. Cautious. Restrained. Not quite the challenge he'd been hoping for, but he would persevere. "Do you always make the prudent choice? Even *saying* that feels like too much effort."

"I like my life orderly." She said it as if she'd needed to make the same defense time and again.

Before Jon could poke further, pull back more of her layers, the waitress in the too-tight dress bumped the back of Heather's chair. A plastic sample cup bobbled and tipped.

Heather jerked forward, but it was too late. Dark red wine spilled down the back of her jacket. "Blast," she hissed.

"Oh!" the waitress squealed. "I'm so sorry. Let me get you something to wipe that up." But the tray wiggled again when she reached for napkins.

"Forget it." Heather waved her away then yanked off the jacket. "Damn, it's cashmere."

"Here." Jon grabbed a few cocktail napkins from a stack beside a bowl of palate-cleansing cracker crisps. Even as he handed them over, his mind surged to Mach two.

Perhaps he didn't have Heather Crystal Morris figured out after all.

In taking off the dark blue blazer, she'd revealed the pale white camisole underneath. A deep border of lace dipped over the swells of her cleavage. Her breasts were beautiful, with a nice heft that would feel marvelous in his palms. He'd already expected that. He was something of a master at peering beneath the layers women wore. Practice made perfect.

No, the surprise was Heather's nipple ring.

His body tightened. He became a predator scenting a vulnerable rabbit.

The barest hint of metal was visible under layers of silk and a thin bra. A perfect out-of-place circle—something to swirl with his tongue while he buried his face between those beautiful breasts. Something to tug with his teeth as she rode him, her lush body working his cock.

That nipple ring was a hint of wickedness waiting to be unleashed.

Jon was just the man to unleash it.

He pushed away a genuine smile that threatened. No sense in revealing his true desires so soon. "Is it ruined?"

"I'm not sure," she said with a sigh. "But whether it is or not, it's the perfect end to an awful evening."

"That's unkind."

She glared as she tapped at the stain with a napkin. "Is this where I'm supposed to say 'present company excluded'?"

"It would be appreciated."

"Sorry. I'm not in the mood for placating anyone." She hung the jacket on the back of her seat. "My friend Jenn and I were supposed to have a girls' night out. We even had reservations at La Rocca, but she had babysitter issues."

"Nice place." Jon had dined there a week after it opened. His mother and father would weep themselves to the grave if he didn't occasionally use the pull of their family name and fortune. His need for novelty had propelled him, not his parents' expectations. "I'm not convinced it lives up to the hype."

Dark brows lifted, and a disbelieving smile curved her lush mouth. "Oh, you've been, have you?"

He made a sound of agreement, low enough that Heather leaned forward to catch it. As she did, she provided a flawless view down the shadowy valley of her cleavage. Jon was swept over with the image of pushing his cock between those full tits while she darted her tongue to lick his head. The thought began to cultivate the first stirring of a hard-on.

He pushed her glass of pinot noir closer. "Here. Try it. If you do, this will be the night you drank snake-venom wine rather than the night your jacket was stained."

"That's the best argument I've ever heard for drinking animal toxins." She circled the lip of the plastic cup with her forefinger. After a nod, she picked it up and drank. Her throat worked over a swallow. "Not bad."

He liked women who gave hesitation the middle finger. He liked them very much. "I won't be gauche enough to tell you I told you so."

"It would be appreciated," she said, echoing his words from only a moment ago.

"How much?"

She licked a drop of wine off her bottom lip—again, it seemed an intentional echo. Was she teasing him? He enjoyed that idea, almost as much as he enjoyed imagining what she could do with that mouth. Dirty things. Delicious things.

Her fingers brushed the line of her collarbone. "What do you mean?"

"Do you appreciate it enough to let me go with you to La Rocca?"

She shook her head on another husky laugh. "I don't think so."

The waitress dropped off another round, these containing a nearly colorless white wine. A whisper of condensation clung to them. Cool and dry, it carried the cold kiss of Antarctica, where it had been pressed.

Heather's quiet moan upon finishing her sample sent a shock point-blank to Jon's dick. "Oh, that one's good." She scribbled something in her little notebook. "Maybe not 'a year's mortgage payments' good, but definitely my favorite."

He watched her over the rim of his glass. "Invite me to dinner with you."

Pale eyes flashed. "Why in the world do you think I should do that?"

Taking her hand once again, he traced the inside of her wrist. Her mouth made pretty protests, but her frantic pulse said otherwise. He drew his touch over the fleshy base of her thumb, down into the soft valley of her palm. If he'd known her even a little bit better, he would have used his nail to scrape a pale red line over her soft skin.

"Because you want to," he said quietly. "You've been good for a very long time, haven't you?"

She nodded silently. Her neck moved so jerkily that she seemed to be agreeing despite good intentions.

Kink that he was, he liked that. He relished helping a woman find her boundaries—just before blasting through them. "Then invite me because you deserve a night of being bad."

Her breath had gone shallow. Full breasts rose and fell. "You're supposed to be my reward?"

"I could be."

The crowded wine bar disappeared. Voices fluxed around them but only as background noise. Jon kept his gaze on hers, willing her to agree. There was something about this woman in particular...

He rather thought she'd be a novelty.

Her lips parted on a soft breath. She nodded. Swallowed visibly. "Let's go."

Jon escorted her to the parking lot in no time, their wine-tasting bracelets abandoned on the table for any lucky patron to find. Sweltering air slicked his neck. He rubbed his nearly bare head. Wearing a suit in the late July heat of Las Vegas took dedication, but again, he had standards.

His pace slightly faster than usual, he didn't want to risk that Heather would back off. Back down. Despite a streak of wildness, she obviously tried to bury it deeply. He wondered how deeply she'd be able to hide it if he got her on her hands and knees, that curvy ass in the air. The treasure would be dipping his fingers into her pussy to discover just how wet she was. For him.

Her steps slowed. "Jenn and I didn't drive. We planned to take a taxi all night."

"I brought my car." He slung his thumbs in the pockets of his slacks. She would agree or she wouldn't.

Heather studied him from head to toe. "Do you promise you're not some freaky serial killer?"

His laugh was abrupt and real. Another novelty. "I've been called a freak a time or two, but I swear I'd never intentionally hurt a woman. Unless she asked for it."

That line probably wouldn't put him in safe company with puppies and kittens and guys who waited for an invitation. But he wanted to see her reaction. A quiet inhalation was his reward. Her tempting nipple ring pressed against the thin restraint of silk.

She nibbled her bottom lip. Goddamn, but he'd like to put those teeth to work nibbling him. Wherever she wanted.

After digging a BlackBerry out of her purse, she pointed it at him, then clicked away. "All right. Let's go."

"What did you do?"

"I sent myself an email with a picture and description of you. Just in case."

Placing a hand at the small of her back, he escorted her toward his car. Soft muscles jumped. "You're full of surprises, aren't you?"

"I'm really not. I've got very little to hide."

He bent low over her ear. She smelled of expensive perfume and the berry kiss of fine wine. "Then we'll have to make sure you develop some secrets."

He thumbed his key fob. The lights of his Aston Martin flashed. In the dusky light of evening, the DBS was a deep, dark beast. All power and growling strength. The car was worth every cent he'd paid. The only machine he loved more was his F-16, but that was property of the US government.

Heather's high heels clicked to an abrupt stop on the asphalt. "Did you borrow it from Daddy?"

"No. Daddy drives a Bentley."

She looked from him, to the convertible, then back again. "Just who are you, Jon Carlisle?"

His smile built slowly from somewhere deep inside. Pure enjoyment of the moment. The gathering excitement of night. A beautiful woman on his arm. A sinfully fast car waiting to whisk them toward the unknown.

"I'm a fighter pilot."

Chapter Three

"Bullshit."

The profanity leapt out of her mouth before she could stop it. She hardly ever cursed, especially not at the office where decorum and steadfast dedication would earn her a promotion to full director. Someday soon.

But his outrageous claim was just too much.

"It's true." With a casual shrug, he slid his hands into his trouser pockets. "I fly an F-16 with the 64th Aggressor Squadron out of Nellis."

"I don't believe you."

His implacable expression was one of the best poker faces she'd ever seen. "We should establish this up front, Ms. Morris. I never lie." Blankness gave way to a boyish grin. "Well, not to real people. Sometimes it makes life easier to tell COs what they want to hear."

Heather refused to be charmed. Her dad's twenty years in the Army meant she'd grown up knowing military men of all kinds, learning how they acted, how they thought. Eventually she'd learned to avoid them as she would an oncoming freight train.

Jon Carlisle wasn't one of them.

She leaned against the passenger-side door. A gleaming finish suggested it had been recently waxed. "That's the second unbelievable claim you've made tonight, the first being the size of your prick. This one, at least, you can substantiate in a public parking lot."

"I wouldn't impose such limits on either of us."

"Proof, please."

She knew it was the truth even before he pulled out his wallet because he didn't hesitate.

She examined his Air Force-issued ID, particularly his photo. A different version of Captain Jonathan Carlisle stared back at her. No sarcasm or teasing there—only the proud, solemn expression of a serviceman in full dress. To know he was capable of both personas messed with her ability to breathe.

"Satisfied?"

She offered the barest smile as she returned the ID. "Not yet."

"The night's still young. Get in."

Heather slid into the passenger seat. He closed the door behind her, which enveloped her in luxury. The Aston was *gorgeous*. She'd been in her share of expensive cars, but they were vehicles of understated elegance. BMWs and Mercedes. The tools businessmen used to impress their colleagues. This sleek, expensive convertible was a rich boy's toy.

Jon slipped behind the wheel and fired it up. A sound unlike any she'd ever heard purred from the engine, powerful yet restrained. A perfect fit for its owner. The slow, tedious flow of Friday-night traffic as they edged down the Strip was downright cruel. She wondered what the car and the man could do if allowed to go flat out.

A delicious shiver skated up her arms.

Jon didn't seem tense at all. He downshifted as they hit another red light. She found herself watching his wrist, his hand, his tapered, elegant fingers. Everything about him was efficient, with no wasted effort, while still maintaining that easy grace.

She wanted to talk, if only as a distraction against her sudden fascination, only she didn't trust her voice.

He pulled up to The Palazzo's valet stand. La Rocca's was located inside. "And here we are."

Heather reached for her cashmere blazer. Even slightly stained, it was more appropriate than wearing her camisole to dinner.

"Leave it," Jon said.

"No way. You know why I can't."

"Oh?"

She met his innocent gaze head-on. "You haven't been able to take your eyes off it."

"Not true." He leaned across the armrest, edging into her space. "Your mouth is just as erotic as your nipple ring."

Heat sizzled in her lungs and between her legs. Her nipples tightened, as if simply saying the words aloud had roused their curiosity.

"Heather, c'mon. You know Las Vegas. No one will be paying attention...except for me." He pulled back and shrugged, as controlled as when he'd driven the convertible. "You decide."

Two uniformed valets opened their doors. Jon handed over his keys and slipped away, leaving her behind. Heather sat there, the blazer in her lap.

The valet cleared his throat. After one last deep breath, she emerged into the desert night. The blazer lay in a heap on her seat.

Jon's mouth quirked as he offered his arm. She took it, knowing that a very different woman had stepped out of his Aston Martin—some version of herself she hadn't been in a long time.

La Rocca's was not what outsiders might expect of Las Vegas, where glitz skirted so near to tasteless. The lobby was elegant almost to the point of invisibility. No touch shone brighter than the rest. The result was understated, even soothing. The décor said that any patron deserved to know true luxury. A beguiling idea.

"Mr. Carlisle," said a man in a flawless tuxedo. "Good to see you again."

"Mr. La Rocca. Out mingling with the serfs, I see." Jon extended his hand. Heather could only watch as the two greeted one another with such familiarity. It seemed Jon hadn't been lying about dining there. "I love the new watch," he said.

"Thanks," said the restaurateur. "How's your father?"

"Nothing changes back home. You know that. Same grumpy bastard as always."

Heather did a double take. At the mention of his father, Jon's voice had taken on a brittle edge, so different than his otherwise cultured cool.

Mr. La Rocca checked the reservation book. "I didn't see you on the guest list."

"I'm Ms. Morris's plus one."

Mr. La Rocca turned his eyes to Heather, cataloging her assets with far less polish than Jon had. "Enchanting."

Jon's forearm tensed beneath her hand. "Isn't she, though?"

"But now that you're here..." Mr. La Rocca's expression turned solicitous. "Perhaps I can beg a favor?"

"Beg away."

Heather caught his bemused smile and stifled one of her own.

"There's a diplomat in town from Paris," Mr. La Rocca said. "He's at the bar with his, ah, companion. They didn't have a reservation, and of course we're booked full…"

Screwing up her mouth, Heather figured out his angle. The dirty old man wanted their table.

She was ready to protest when Jon covered her hand and squeezed. "Make it worth our while, Mr. La Rocca."

"Fifty dollars in house chips?"

"I don't know. What do you think, Ms. Morris? Is fifty dollars enough to assuage your disappointment?"

Heather looked at both men in turn. This was an opportunity to take a stand. "Make it one hundred. And have your best dessert ready to pick up when we call it a night."

Mr. La Rocca grinned. "A fellow snake charmer, Jon? I'll tell Patrick to set you up."

As the restaurant's owner went to settle the details, Jon leaned close. His breath touched her ear a moment before his nose brushed her temple. "Well played."

Her heart rate doubled, giving lie to the idea that she'd made the demand to spite Mr. La Rocca. Jon's whispered appreciation had been the goal all along. It wasn't enough to pick up the gauntlets he threw down. She felt compelled to impress him while doing so.

Jon Carlisle was, quite simply, dangerous.

Chips in hand, they wove back through the resort. Heather felt dwarfed by soaring ceilings and Italian-style columns. Her eyes were drawn to touches of gold and columns of pure white marble. The main casino floor was busy, as always, full of countless conversations and the sounds of games in full swing. However, like the rest of the hotel's high-end décor, there wasn't an ounce of tacky in sight, not even in the powder room she ducked into. This was the playground of adults with taste.

She handed Jon the stack of ten-dollar chips. "Your choice."

"Isn't that a privilege usually reserved for the lady?"

"This *is* my privilege. Your choice." Curiosity had her mentally wagering what game he'd choose. Poker, maybe? He certainly had the expression for it. "On one condition."

Fathomless eyes narrowed, which would have seemed sinister if not for the amusement dancing in their dark depths. "That doesn't sound promising."

"You haven't heard it yet. Only one chip at a time." She paused, then added the phrase sitting on her tongue. "Make it last."

"I'm good at that."

He led her across the casino floor to one of the roulette tables. A small crowd had gathered, as diverse as any in Las Vegas. Businessmen, elderly couples, guys on the prowl, obvious tourists—all watched as the croupier gave the wheel a spin and dropped her ball.

"Roulette, eh?"

"Pure chance. One can calculate the odds but not defy them. And I have a condition too."

"Oh?"

Jon turned her until they faced belly to belly. Those elegant hands settled at the tops of her hips. His thumbs rested on the waistband of her skirt, as if reminding her how little effort would be required to strip it down. The casino's clear, bright lighting allowed Heather a good look at his eye color. They were a rich honeyed brown, like brandy. Expensive and decadent.

His voice was surprisingly serious when he said, "I want you to pick a safe word."

Heather flinched. She couldn't help it. The host of images and scenarios and positions evoked by that simple sentence caused her body to jump.

She swallowed thickly. His lips parted in silent reply.

There was no brushing this off, but she felt compelled to make the attempt. Any good woman would. "I need a safe word to play roulette?"

"You need a safe word to play with me." He was staring at the base of her throat where her pulse drummed.

"Panda," she blurted out.

He smiled on a sudden laugh, showing off those dimples. She'd caught him out again—risk followed by reward.

She was in huge trouble.

"Panda," he repeated. "Got it." The croupier had cleared away the chips and opened another round of betting. "Now what's your favorite fruit?"

"Strawberries."

He counted on his fingers as he spelled the word. "Twelve it is." But instead of placing one of their ten chips on the table, he stashed them in an inside coat pocket. In their place he withdrew a chip marked $100.

"Where did you get that?"

"The exchange," he said. "While you used the ladies' room."

"That's not what I meant by one at a time."

Jon edged between gamblers at the table and made room for Heather beside him. It was a tight fit, her hip pressed flush against his. "Don't worry. There's more where this came from. I'm just trying to make it more exciting."

More exciting? Gambling ten dollars at a time was rich enough for her blood. She could quote to the second decimal the balance of her checking account and various retirement plans. Her most recent promotion to assistant director had nixed the last of her student loans. Her net worth wouldn't be achingly small for long, but that only added to her fiscal discipline.

The idea of laying a cool hundred on a single spin was like Jon and his dimples and his wet dream of a sports car: glorious excess.

He found her ear again with his rumbling whisper. "We'll make it last as long as we want." Then he placed the $100 chip on red twelve. "For strawberries."

"An inside bet?"

"You know roulette?"

"I know gambling," she said, not bothering to conceal her pride. "Hanover Financial Logistics concentrates on accounting for the casinos. Knowing the lingo is a business requirement."

Only belatedly did she wonder how dull that might sound to a fighter pilot. Auditing soft count procedures, even for casinos, wasn't exactly dogfighting over the desert.

He only lifted an animated eyebrow, giving no hint of his true assessment. "Then you might know that the odds on an inside bet are 37-to-1."

"I'm impressed."

"I like numbers. My professional specialty, actually." Then for her ears only he said, "I also like seeing what you'll do next. So tell me, Ms. Morris, what shall we do if that ball drops on twelve? Make it good. I know you enjoy surprising me."

Oh, but she did. He was a man who, by all appearances, grabbed life by the balls. She wanted to give *his* balls a good grab just to remind him that not everything—or everyone—was as it seemed.

"The odds are too long to make that any real fun. How about if it drops on any red?"

"Too easy. You'll hedge and give me something common."

Her hip molded against the roulette table. If he looked down, he'd have a clear view of the cleavage he found so fascinating, but his gaze didn't budge from hers. He was waiting, just as she was, to see how much daring she could drag into the light.

Taking the chance, Heather indulged the first of her many fantasies involving this man. She cupped the base of his skull. He smelled of something like Obsession or Pierre Cardin. Rich. Classic. Masculine. She pressed harder, rubbing a little, enjoying how his cropped hair scoured her skin.

"Not common at all, Captain Carlisle. If the ball drops on red, I'll show you my tattoo."

Chapter Four

Reflexively, Jon clasped the soft swell of her hips before he could discipline himself. Finger by finger he forced himself to ease off. Tipping his hand had never been his style.

"It seems you're keeping secrets after all."

Even her smile was a secret, wrapping layer upon layer like a present. "It won't be much of one if I show you."

"But what's a secret without the temptation of sharing?"

They watched the mesmerizing spin of the ball. Jon stacked her in front of him, surprised by his unwillingness to give up the degree of contact she'd accepted—even though it meant revealing his gathering hard-on. Pressed against the sweet swell of Heather's ass, it was only going to grow stronger.

The thin silk of her top allowed her skin's heat to sink into his hands. He spread his fingertips over her taut waist.

The wheel slowed. The ball bounced freely and dropped on twenty-two. While Jon would've preferred the number twelve, red would certainly do.

Heather tensed. He brushed a kiss along the curve of her ear. Silken hair slid over his cheek. "Didn't think you'd have to pay up?"

Nerves wove through her soft laughter. "No one ever really wins in Vegas."

"That's not true at all." He spread his hands wider, moving to her stomach. His middle finger circled the shallow dip of her navel, vulnerable beneath her thin camisole. "I'd already won before it even dropped on red."

She shivered. "I suppose you want your prize?"

"Certainly."

He'd almost expected her to hesitate, until she slanted him a look from under her lashes. All challenge and readiness. She lifted her shirt a few inches along her right side. A slender green vine with tiny purple buds climbed up from her skirt, curving around her waist and disappearing up the back of her filmy camisole. He peered closer. The delicate shading within the vine was script, though he couldn't make out the words.

This was no drunken-sorority-girl tat. It was a work of art. Carefully chosen. The delicate outlines and coloring must have taken hours of patience under the tattoo gun.

Jon's fingers tingled with the need to touch. So he did. Her skin was as fine as any he'd ever encountered. Softer. He'd love to trace that delicate line with his tongue, then nibble his way back down.

He followed the twisting vine to where it ducked beneath the snug waistband of her skirt. There he discovered another hint of lace and silk.

She hissed in a breath. "I said I'd show you my tattoo, not my panties."

"Yet."

"You're rather self-assured." Heather faced forward again, but nothing in her posture suggested that he should remove his hand. She dropped the hem of her top so that lace simply draped over his wrist. Brave girl. He rewarded her with a teasing, kneading motion along the dip of her waist.

"Why shouldn't I be?" he asked against her throat.

"Has anyone ever told you it verges on arrogant?"

"Once or twice. Or more."

"You don't care?"

He didn't really like talking to her without seeing her eyes. Considering her measured, careful voice, she was more difficult to read without precise physical clues.

"Arrogant is what frightened people call bold." He didn't need to bend far to speak directly into her ear. In her heels, she was nearly his height. Good thing his ego had never been fragile. Actually, he rather liked the advantages. It made a whole host of sexual positions easier to contemplate. "When am I going to see your panties?"

"Lay another bet, flyboy."

The croupier had gathered all the chips, paid out the few winners and opened the table for more bets.

"What's your birthday?"

That earned him a sidelong glance over her shoulder. "The seventh of August."

"Not long off."

She laced her fingers over his, across her stomach, with the layer of silk in between. "Plan on buying me a present?"

He leaned their bodies forward to drop another $100 chip on the black square marked seven. Her ass tucked neatly against his cock. Just as he'd thought. They would fit well together.

"What do you want?"

"Everything I'm worth," she said. "So maybe the sun and the moon?"

"I'll throw the stars in too."

"You think you're pretty slick." No question there. Just bemused humor. "But I'm still waiting on our side bet."

"How slick *you* are. That's my reward if I win."

"What?"

A fine trembling had taken over her limbs. He was perversely proud that she didn't back down, despite obvious jitters.

"If I win with a black seven, I get to find out how wet your panties are."

"Here?" Her swallow was an audible click. "How?"

He slid his pinkie under the band of her skirt. Not far enough to brush the top hem of her underwear, but enough to make her think of them. "I'll leave that up to you."

Suddenly she laughed. The tension drawing her shoulders tight against his chest dissolved. "You know what? Fine. At 37-to-1 odds, the chances I'll have to pay out are slim."

He hid a real smile against her nape. So many to tuck away that evening. "But there's still a chance."

"You like chances?"

He darted out his tongue and claimed a taste of her skin. Soft peaches and rich cream. "I live for them."

The uniformed croupier declared the table closed and propelled the roulette wheel with a flick of her wrist. The white ball bounced twice before settling into a smooth counter-roll against the wheel's movement.

Heather's breathing went shallow and fast. He spread his hand over her stomach, the better to feel the fast rise and fall of her diaphragm. She'd breathe like that on her way to orgasm.

Enjoying the lustrous feel of her skin against his lips, Jon didn't lift his face. He didn't need to. Her lush body's sudden jolt told him the exact result.

The ball had landed in the number seven pocket.

"Are you going to pay up, Ms. Morris?"

"I'd never welsh on a bet."

"Like I said, the method is up to you." He brushed a lock of dark brown hair away from her ear. Although he didn't want to give her an out, neither did he want to hear the word *panda* yet. If pushed too far too fast, she would back off entirely. "You can whisper the answer, if you'd rather."

She turned slowly. The crowds around the table meant they stayed pressed together. No way she could've missed the brush of his stiffening prick across her hip. Maybe now she wouldn't doubt its size.

Pale blue eyes evaluated him, as if he were an impossible equation. Good. He enjoyed being that tough to read.

She patted his shirt along the line of his vest. Lovely hands. Her long fingers were tipped with a fresh French manicure. He imagined how they'd look when clawing linen sheets as he edged her nearer and nearer to coming. How long could he sustain her there without letting her go over?

"Stay right here," she said, her voice huskier than ever.

"Going somewhere?"

"Yes."

"Are you going to be back?" He didn't like that question after hearing it said aloud. Too…undisciplined.

"You'll just have to wait and find out."

She disappeared into the crowd. Jon watched her as far as he could. She didn't wiggle as she walked—more like she slinked along. Her hips telegraphed every sensuous intention. Unfortunately, a stream of Japanese tourists following a tour guide's up-held umbrella closed off his view.

He turned back to the table. While accepting his winnings and handing the croupier a nice tip, he tried to regulate a flush of pure excitement. He had an inkling of what she was up to. If Heather managed, he'd be very proud of her—and more intrigued than ever. She was the kind of woman who tasted risk carefully. The tip of her tongue at first. Not a deep swallow. That made every tiny step all the more valuable.

He gambled too much while she was gone, dropping four hundred dollars on a single spin. Seven again, since it had already brought him such luck. His parents would be appalled if they could see him, so it was a good thing he didn't answer to them anymore. Grandfather's trust fund remained excessively handy for pissing them off and for killing time.

When she returned, she slid under his arm as if she weren't tormenting him with every movement. As if she belonged there. Her fingers ducked into his trouser pocket and out again in a wickedly fast move.

She carefully faced the roulette table as she spoke. "I think you'll be happy."

Slipping his hand into his pocket, Jon found lace and silk. If he weren't careful, he'd come to associate the combo with her. The tiny scrap of panties was unmistakably wet. Not drenched—not yet—but now she was bare under her tailored skirt. Any stray breeze could curl beneath the hem to stroke her skin. He wondered if she waxed or kept a delicate thatch of curls.

"Good girl," he purred.

That earned another backward glance. Black irises swelled to deep pools. "Time for another bet."

He pulled her flush to his hips. "What age did you lose your virginity?"

Hot, bright red flushed her high cheekbones. "Fourteen."

Ignoring a jolt of excitement, he placed a single chip onto the number. "So young. Was it worth it?"

Her laugh this time was awkward. Rough at the edges. "It depends what you mean. Did I get the validation I was looking for? Sure."

"That's not what I meant." He wrapped his arm all the way across her belly so that he clutched her opposite hip. Her curves fit the body he'd forged through years of discipline. "I wanted to know if you came."

She shuddered then shook her head. "No."

"That is a damn pity."

"Can't expect that much when you're so young and stupid."

"Ready for our next wager?"

She let her head bend back to rest on his shoulder. "Lay it on me, flyboy."

"If I hit, I want to see you make yourself come."

"An inside bet?"

"Yup."

"Again, the odds are on my side."

"And look where that logic got you last time." He chuckled against her loosely bound hair, catching the light scent of roses. "The house edge is just over five percent. Five point two six, actually. You should know, I lost two rounds while you were gone. Don't play it based on numbers. Agree because you want me to know exactly what makes you break apart—the way you touch yourself when you're all alone."

She slicked her tongue across her lips. "You think I want you to know that?"

"Maybe. Maybe you don't. But you do want to be wicked."

Chapter Five

Heather had taken only two lovers in the three years since moving to Las Vegas. In those three years, her contact with erections had been limited to the moments immediately before and during sex. A furtive knowledge.

Jon had been pressing against her for the last twenty minutes. Constant. Insistent. But oddly…polite. They both knew he was aroused, just as they both knew she was. It was a strange comfort to be on the same page.

"Heather." The low rumble of his voice was no less powerful for having become used to it. She drank in the sound of her name. "The ball's dropped. Give me your answer."

"Yes. I'll do it."

"Yes is my favorite word."

She watched the spinning colors and a flash of white as the ball rounded and bounced. How much longer could they play this way? She'd wanted it to last, but that was before her body had gone liquid and hot, keyed up beyond anything she could recall. The future of their evening hung in the balance as the wheel began to slow.

Jon slid his fingers inside her waistband, up to the second knuckles. She softened against his chest. He was slender but very fit, easily accepting her relaxed weight. The tip of his tongue wet her nape.

Heather gripped the edge of the high table, but that wasn't what her body needed. She reached behind her and laid her palms flat on the backs of his thighs.

"You're giving the guy across the table quite a show," he said, his voice rougher now. "Your breasts lifting. Your breathing ragged."

"He doesn't know the half of it."

She squeezed. Jon matched it, tensing his fingers above her hipbones. He thrust ever so gently. Heather bit the inside of her cheek to keep from moaning.

The ball dropped. Number eighteen.

Jon chuckled. "Had you been a good girl and waited till college, we'd have won."

"I get the feeling you like it better this way." She punctuated the statement with a subtle wiggle of her ass.

He pressed his forehead against the back of her neck. His breath was faster too. "Do that again."

Smiling, she did as he instructed, only slower this time, more deliberately. She relished knowing how she affected him.

While the croupier cleaned up the losing bets, Heather turned in Jon's arms. His pelvis wedged against hers, with his hands slipping down to cup her ass. His eyes were tight, narrowed, very dark. His temple pulsed. She reached up and smoothed her fingers into his short hair.

Turning his head, he found the inside of her wrist with his mouth. He kissed her once. Then he licked.

She whispered, "One more bet."

He sucked. The sudden shock of sensation almost made her gasp. His gaze never left hers. Only the slight graze of teeth against that sensitive skin made her retreat. It was too much, too public.

She slid her hand down his chest before dipping inside his suit coat. The wool was warm, holding his heat. The pocket bearing the chips from La Rocca's was easy enough to find.

"Place your bets," called the croupier.

Calmly, despite her hammering heart, Heather leaned over the table to deposit all of the ten-dollar chips. If she managed to brush her rear against Jon's hard-on a few times, all the better. He lifted her silk top, just over her tattoo, and petted her there.

"No peeking," she said, straightening.

He glanced over her shoulder to survey the table. And he *laughed.* Not a chuckle or a snicker, but a full-bodied laugh that caught her by surprise. She loved the rich sound of it. Unchecked. Amusement accentuated his youthful features.

Heather grinned. "What?"

"You've covered a lot of possibilities, Ms. Morris."

She had. On purpose. Ten chips waited for any number of

Inside Bet

possibilities—odd, even, red, black, zero, double zero. Then she'd chosen inside bets—her current age, and to commemorate that evening, the day, month and year.

"The house may win financially on this spin," she said, turning back to face him. "But we win. Whatever we want."

"The possibilities are staggering."

"They are."

"Your bet. Your call."

She loosened his tie. As she worked, she was surprised to see the distinct wine-colored red of a hickey on the inside of her wrist. He must've sucked harder than she realized.

The tie slid off with one tug, its silken snap like a whip. She held it between her teeth as she undid the top two buttons of his dress shirt. He watched her with a curious expression, lifting one very animated eyebrow in silent question.

Tie in hand, she said, "That's better. Not so formal."

"I like being formal. It holds the barbarians at bay."

She smirked, her attention drawn to the notch at the base of his throat. "The barbarians would club you with sticks and rocks."

"The government trusts me with automatic weapons and live ordnance. I can handle myself."

"I have no doubt. Now, if it pays out only one-to-one, we get a room and head upstairs."

That quirky eyebrow lifted again. "Oh, really?"

"The catch is that it's straight missionary position and we don't spend the night. Just a good time to take the edge off this foreplay."

"I thought you wanted memorable." His hands inched higher along her ribs. He could graze the underside of her breasts if he stretched those long fingers.

"You think it won't be memorable?" Against his cheek she whispered, "My tattoo, my nipple ring, my breasts. All yours."

He cleared his throat, his Adam's apple working. "Point taken. But if one of the inside bets win? What then?"

Heather stuffed the tie in his hands, flashing her most audacious smile. "Then you spend the weekend hunting for pandas."

"They're rare."

"You hope."

"No conditions?"

"Other than condoms and respecting the safe word? None."

He brushed a kiss across her forehead. "I have a hard time believing you're that brave."

"You'll just have to try me."

The ball was already spinning. Heather lost the ability to breathe as she turned back to watch it clatter and roll. A fine tremble overtook her shoulders.

"Relax." His whisper sent a shiver down her throat. "You don't know what to root for, do you?"

She shook her head.

Rather than tease, Jon merely rubbed her upper arms. The gesture did nothing to banish the anticipation. "*Je le ferai bon pour toi,*" he said. "*Je le promis.*"

Breath catching hard, Heather tightened her thighs against a surprising rush of desire. "Say that again."

He complied before translating, "I'll make it good for you, Heather. Promise."

That answered the question of whether his French came from wine snobbery or a knowledge of the language. She wasn't going to last an elevator ride with this man, let alone a whole weekend.

Two final rotations of the wheel were enough to end the agony. The ball dropped into the pocket of the number thirty-two.

The word "Damn" slipped out of her mouth.

"You bet on thirty-one, didn't you?"

"Yes," she said. "My current age."

"That is a crying shame."

"But not a complete loss."

She was surprised by her disappointment. Bad enough that she already planned on sleeping with this sexy, terrifying jet pilot. Really, that should've been enough. As the croupier handed over the paltry sums for winning on black and odd, Heather thought the whole thing a near-miss.

A regret waiting to happen.

Jon took her arm but said nothing. They exchanged their chips, then split up. He went to reserve the room while Heather retrieved the dessert from La Rocca: a sumptuous slice of cheesecake drizzled with dark chocolate and topped with fresh whipped cream.

When reunited at the concierge desk, he handed her a glass of champagne. He kept another for himself.

"What's this?"

"Came complimentary," he said.

"A nice touch." She showed off her cheesecake prize. "I don't know what you're having because this is all mine."

Jon sipped his champagne. "That's hardly fair, Ms. Morris. I insist on the whipped cream, if nothing else."

She was already beginning to realize his pattern. He called her Ms. Morris when he was playing games. His slip-ups were becoming more frequent. When convincing her to leave the blazer, or when reassuring her as that final spin wound down—then, he'd used her given name. The former ratcheted her anticipation while the latter kept her from panicking.

Deciphering even that small facet of his behavior should've been enough to break the spell. Instead she wanted to hear which he used next.

The elevator was crowded at first, but they were alone together after the eleventh floor. Jon leaned against the mirrored wall, arms crossed, apparently lost in thought. Until then she realized his gaze was fixed on her ankle.

He shouldn't notice so much. Not about her. Not beyond the intentional mysteries she'd dangled in an effort to set him off balance. That he could be studying something as innocent as her ankle seemed far too intimate. Wiggling her ass against his cock was positively gauche compared to his deliberate elegance.

He saw her looking. A smile touched his lips. "You're thinking, aren't you?"

"Yes," she admitted.

"A good friend of mine does that way too much. You know how he found a way around it?"

"I have a guess."

Jon looked up, his grin devilish. "Tell me."

"Fucking."

"The lady wins a prize."

The elevator opened to their floor. Jon escorted her down the hall. He smoothly inserted the keycard and opened the door. "After you."

Heather stepped inside...and dropped her jaw. The suite was *massive*. To the left of the marble entryway was a half bath and a coat closet. Beyond there waited a full dining room and living room. The far wall was made almost entirely of windows. She walked deeper into the white, cream and gold opulence. The bedroom and master bath adjoined the living areas, with a graceful chaise situated beneath another bank of glass. They overlooked the pool deck far below.

She'd seen such suites as part of her work. The casino heads liked to show off their properties as a special treat to her firm.

To stay in such a place...?

No, she reminded herself. She wasn't there to stay the night. The wager had been for a quickie. It seemed such a waste.

Jon shut the door. The click barely registered over her racing pulse.

"Sorry," he said casually. He still carried his tie. "The penthouses were booked."

"You can stop showing off now."

"I like to."

"So I've gathered."

She realized then what had cooled the fire. She'd fastened them with restrictions. The play that had flavored their turn at the table was gone. *Straight missionary*, she'd said. *We won't spend the night*, she'd said. That meant curtailing every impulse to do more, to go further—to lounge in bed until noon tomorrow and start all over again. It seemed a crime to hamstring their potential.

For the second time, she felt she was living in the midst of a future regret.

Heather kicked off her pumps. A sigh escaped her as she dug her toes into the carpet. Jon missed none of it, his poker face in place as he lounged against the entryway wall.

Such a waste on so many levels.

After placing the cheesecake in the fridge and downing her

champagne, she returned to where he stood. Taking the tie from his hand she said, "You remember how I said my birthday is on the seventh?"

"Uh-huh."

"So we missed that particular inside bet by, what, thirteen days?"

"Looks like." He reached around her nape and let her hair down. That was nice—gentle, even. Then he knotted his fingers, tugging.

Her decision made, her breath suddenly calm, Heather draped his tie over her shoulder and began to unbutton his suit vest. "Seems a shame. But the nice thing is that it provided some inspiration. Now I know what you can get me as an early present."

"Oh?"

"Forget the moon and the stars, flyboy. I want to pretend we won that inside bet."

His nostrils flared on an inhalation. He tightened his fist in her hair. "Be sure, Heather."

"I am sure. I want this weekend. With you." She stood on tiptoes, ready to kiss him for the first time. "With no limits."

Chapter Six

With one hand loosely twisted in Heather's hair, Jon wondered if she had any idea what a gift she'd handed him. Limitless possibilities that spun out before them. So many directions they could go. So many choices.

For example, she expected him to kiss her. Her lips had parted and her pale eyes smoldered from under dark, thick lashes. In the hollow of her throat, her pulse fluttered wildly. Her gaze had fixed on his mouth.

Jon would kiss her. Soon.

First he wanted to taste her anticipation.

He bent his head slowly, dragging the tip of his tongue over that throbbing pulse. Her quiet gasp was an aphrodisiac of the highest quality. She tipped her neck to the side to allow better access.

That seemed the theme of the night. Access. How far she'd let him push in search of her limits.

He sipped along her throat toward the curve of her jaw. Behind one delicate ear, he fastened his mouth. Sucked slightly. She shivered when he grazed his teeth over her. This time she didn't pull away, not like when they'd been at the table. There, it had required all of his self-control to release her graceful wrist.

He dragged his cheek over hers, purposely scoring her with five o'clock shadow. She shivered again. Her fingers clenched his open vest, and her thumbs brushed the top of his abs.

So, the lovely Ms. Morris liked a touch of danger with her arousal. He would gladly provide that.

He kissed the corner of her mouth first. Gently. A promise.

He shouldn't have expected her to be passive. She turned her head, fighting the fist in her hair and the sting it must've caused. And she kissed him.

Their mouths slid together slowly. Open, but no more—until he bit the swell of her bottom lip. She released a delicious gasp into his mouth. Her hips surged, brushing his groin.

He tightened his hand in her hair, then forcibly released that fierce grip.

Deliberation was as much a part of desire as the actions themselves. Each movement should be choreographed for maximum response, or someone might go home unfulfilled. Unacceptable.

Pulling his mouth away, Jon drew her hair down over her shoulders. He smoothed his knuckles across the tops of her bountiful breasts. "Will you do something for me, Ms. Morris?"

She looked up at him from under her dark brows. "I plan to do many things for you."

Damn, he needed to get it together.

He knelt briefly and picked up his tie where it had slipped from her shoulder. Lacing his fingers through hers, the tie dangling from his other hand, Jon led the way to an overstuffed chair that faced away from the wide bank of windows. The lights of the Strip twinkled in an omnipresent glow.

He released her hand and sat, hitching his ankle over one knee. Alive with possibilities, he draped his favorite silk tie across his lap. "I want to see your tattoo."

"You already have." The way she smiled said she knew what he meant but intended to make him ask.

That was fine with Jon. He had no problem asking for what he wanted. Things were simpler that way. Cleaner. No entangling strings. He'd never enjoyed how they pinched.

"Strip, Ms. Morris."

Her eyes twinkled. "What will I get in return?"

"Immediately or eventually?"

She pushed her hair over her shoulders. Undoubtedly she knew what the move did to her up-thrust breasts. "Let's go with both."

"In the immediate sense, you'll get my tongue licking your skin." He dropped his ankle from his knee and leaned forward. He slipped his fingers in the waistband of her skirt then tugged her between his knees. "Eventually, I'll make you come so hard you'll forget the color of your pretty blue eyes."

The smooth curve of her belly twitched against his knuckles. "You make a lot of promises."

"Only what I intend to do."

Heather studied him. Her hands covered his against her stomach until she encircled his wrists. Deliberately, she transferred his hands to his thighs.

The silk top went first, stripped over her head. Thick hair settled around her shoulders in a dark cloud. Her body only got better with every inch revealed. A scrap of cream-colored lace held her breasts up to be admired. The tiny circle of her nipple ring gleamed gold through the sheer material. Then the bra was gone too. Odes should've been written to her waist, all curvy femininity. Color streaming in from the grand windows dotted her lustrous skin.

She reached back toward her ass. A zipper sounded. Her gaze never left his, not even when she lowered her skirt with a shimmy. Her mound was gorgeous, with dark hair groomed and trimmed to a narrow strip. Standing with her feet barely apart, she provided a glimpse of her bare lips.

Jon dug his fingers into his knees. He blew out a shaky breath. "Christ, you're beautiful."

She lifted her chin a few inches but said nothing, only withstood his intense scrutiny.

Oh, he liked that.

The tattoo began at the gentle bump of her hipbone before crawling up the right side of her waist to disappear behind her back.

"Come here." His hands were already reaching for her, to curve around the hot skin of her hips.

He turned her body and traced the beautifully worked vine. The ink wound its way up to where it teased beneath the sharp edge of her shoulder blade. His fascination with it was…surprising. Maybe it was the image of Heather patiently draped over the tattooist's chair for hours, biting her lip against the sting. Maybe it was the perfectly fashioned hourglass shape it adorned. He wanted to spend hours learning every detail.

"What does it say?"

She looked over her shoulder. A light pink blush stained her skin. "Things without remedy should be without regard: what's done is done."

"Lady Macbeth? So, Ms. Morris has a tragic side."

She shrugged as if it meant nothing to her, but her hands covered his once again. "It's really more about *ignoring* tragedy."

"Ignoring? Funny. I hear someone trying very hard to forget." Starting at the deep curve of her hip, he licked up the slender vine. Along the way he paused to nip softly at a bud or two. Or five. "And the flowers?"

"Morning glories."

Jon only traveled as far as he could from the chair. He was unwilling to give up his place. A pull at her hips turned her back to face him. Her lips were parted, eyes glassy, when she faced him again. She bowed her head forward.

Such a treasure.

"Touch yourself." He kept his voice silky smooth. "I still want to see how you make yourself come."

"Here?" She sounded doubtful but began to. Elegant fingers smoothed over her stomach. "I don't think I've ever tried while standing up. Without at least something to lean against."

"I'll catch you if you fall."

"Will you?"

"I will, Heather."

He didn't give promises lightly. He meant every one—if only to stick his middle finger to those who'd broken faith with him. No way would he let her crumble, unless that referred to her defenses. Those would be nothing but rubble by the time he was through.

Heather started without hurry, first cupping her breasts. Her nails scraped the heavy under-swell, then circled her nipples. She wound her pinkie through the tiny gold circle of her ring and twisted softly. The entire time, she kept her gaze locked on his—not meekly accepting the challenge, but rising to it.

She was beauty and grace personified. Old-school classic, but the tattoo and nipple ring added tantalizing spice.

One hand glided down her body, pausing to dip into the shallow bowl of her navel before continuing. She covered her mound and, with her middle finger, delved between her lips. Aching pulses. Her mouth opened. Pale eyes drooped with near satisfaction, but she never dropped his gaze.

Jon found his own mouth slipping open. His hands draped loosely on her hips until he lowered them to her thighs. Her muscles jumped. He couldn't determine whether his touch or the measured strokes over her clit caused the tiny twitches. Her chest lifted on fast gasps. The warm sweetness of her arousal was there with his every inhalation.

Letting go of her breast, Heather curled her hand around the back of his head. Fingers wide, she brushed her palm over his hair. Tingles worked down his neck, over his spine and centered deep in his balls. God, he was hard. His cock throbbed, begging to come out and play.

Like the touches she bestowed on herself, her orgasm was restrained. Quiet. Though it seemed no less powerful for it. Her belly twitched and her thighs locked beneath his touch. He filled his hands with her ass, providing extra support as her knees dipped. Only then did she release his gaze, her eyes sliding heavenward before slipping shut. Her chin dropped to her chest as she released a deep sigh.

"Beautiful," he whispered. "Perfection."

He pulled her hand from her pussy. A single finger gleamed with her juices. When Jon sucked it into his mouth, flavor burst over his tongue like the rich bouquet of an expensive wine. Her other hand tightened over his skull and her eyes flashed open.

"And now?" She spoke with that husky tone he was coming to recognize. "Have you learned how to make me come?"

He stood slowly. "I had no doubt I could do that."

"Then why this?"

He scooped up his tie. After drawing Heather's arms behind her back, he wrapped the silk over and around her wrists. Her arms formed a box shape. She didn't protest, only watched him over her shoulder, her expression surprisingly blank. He soothed her with a lingering stroke over the line of her tattoo.

"I asked because I thought it would be beautiful to watch. One of those once-in-a-lifetime things, like the Egyptian pyramids or flying straight into the sun at dawn." He kissed the delicate nape of her neck, dragging his tongue over three bumps of her spine. "I was right."

She shuddered. "And now?"

He gently pushed until she knelt on the chair, facing away from him. Jon held her upper arms and levered her forward until her shoulders rested against the padded back. The placement of the chair meant her forehead brushed the window glass, and her gorgeous ass was vulnerable to his whims. Her knees spread outward, but Jon didn't miss how she linked together her big toes. Nerves, despite her stoic front.

Breathing steadily to calm his anticipation, he moved around the room to douse the lights. One by one they winked out until the bright city provided most of the illumination. The only lamp he left on shed a perfect circle of white over the artistic tableau he'd made of Heather.

"Las Vegas glows at night, doesn't it?"

She made a humming agreement. "I love cities at night. Maybe Las Vegas most of all."

"Do you think anyone can see you?"

"I don't know," she whispered.

"Do you *want* them to see you?"

Heather didn't answer, so he gave her ass a quick slap. She gasped. Then, caressing with exquisite care, he touched her neck with soft strokes before skimming down to the deep curves of her body.

He pressed his mouth to the dip of her lower back, right above the swelling peach of her ass. He placed a kiss on the skin turned slightly pink by his slap. His voice vibrated along her back as he said, "You're going to have to listen to me, Ms. Morris. Or risk the consequences."

Chapter Seven

Heather pushed back against him and spun around.

This was getting out of hand, but not how any good woman would fear. She was *losing*. Every challenge was a high-stakes wager. Jon would take every hand if she didn't put a stop to it. He was a Svengali with no fear of being bested. She wasn't going to let him have her that easily.

"Who said you could turn around?" he asked, his eyebrow lifted.

He was still *clothed*, for Christ's sake.

"I used my natural-born free will," she said.

"Overrated."

"I want to see you naked too."

Another guy might've turned her back over the chair and fucked her. She'd been with men like that. Jon kept his gaze steady, his body tense, his mind firmly in control. He was even smiling, complete with dimples—the tempting smile that had first hinted at his true nature. The game was still on and he was still winning.

Even the way he undressed was a series of calculated moves. The buttons. The fabric parting. The zipper sounding so very loud as her breathing accelerated. Heather soaked in every movement just as he had with her, until he stood naked.

Lean and toned, he had a street-fighter's body and an angel's face. Tendons and ropes of muscle covered long, graceful bones. Even his cock matched the rest of his physique—long, arrow straight, and as hard as a glass dildo. He didn't have an ounce of softness on him.

"Come here," she said.

She wiggled forward on the chair, hoping he'd give in just this much. With an indulgent smirk, he met her there. Their nearness put her mouth right at the level of his navel. She nudged his cock aside with her cheek, flicked her tongue along the shaft, her eyes gazing upward.

"I want you to give me what I want," she said against the skin of his stomach.

"You have my attention."

"I want you to fuck me," she whispered. "*Really* fuck me. Enough teasing now."

"You make teasing worth my while. I love seeing the war on your face just before you give in."

Heather nuzzled the trail of hair that led down from his bellybutton. The best she got was an involuntary shiver along the backs of his legs.

That's it, flyboy.

She'd already come. Even if she didn't come again for the rest of the weekend—which seemed *really* unlikely—it would still be the best in recent memory. Now was the time to take a chance and drag him along too.

Slowly, she rose from the chair. Her breasts glanced against his chest, and his erection burned her stomach. The curiosity in his eyes was encouraging. She'd win another fantastic orgasm *and* memory of the moment when he cracked.

"Captain Carlisle, do you know the business definition of compromise?"

He lifted an eyebrow. It was comical and sexy and terrorizing all at once. "Not my forte."

She brushed her lips along his upper arm, circling, kissing the taut flesh between his shoulder blades. Another shiver from him. Her body clenched in response. She started mid-spine and licked all the way up. The base of his neck was tight with cables of muscle. She found a place to nestle her teeth, then sank deep.

He groaned.

Heather smiled against the bite marks. "It's where each party walks away satisfied while giving up as little as possible."

"What are you willing to give up?" He sounded hoarse now. She wanted him to keep talking, to let that low silky voice coil under her skin, but she didn't trust herself.

Naked, peppered by the lights of Vegas, they stood face-to-face. She glanced down her body. With her hands still tied behind her back, her breasts pushed out more boldly. Her nipples, one topped by the shining gold ring, seemed to be reaching for him. "That should be obvious. I checked my modesty at the door."

Jon's nostrils pulsed with each breath, so much less steady now. "And what is...untouchable?"

"My self-respect," she said plainly. "I need to be able to look myself in the mirror come morning."

His narrow eyes pinched. Heather wanted to look away—he probed that deeply. Taking notes. Making plans.

She chose her words carefully. "Whereas you believe your self-control is beyond reach."

He chuckled. "You want me to lose control?"

"No," she whispered. "I want to *make* you lose it."

"I must say. You are *fascinating*."

Yes, fascinating now. All of her secrets would be his, if he had his way. Then their games would be over. She knew that through hard lessons. Men tired of girls who had no mystery left to offer.

Heather pushed that inevitability away and slipped past his side. Jon padded behind, his footsteps silent on the plush carpet. He was elemental at her back. She was being hunted. This time she would not be caught unless she allowed it.

As Jon followed her into the bedroom, however, she doubted her resolve. His expression was so self-assured. He had no doubt as to how this would end—on his terms. That confidence was unnerving, especially considering how masterful he'd been thus far. She knew it would only get better, which was as intimidating as hell.

"So this will be our field of battle?" His smug tone settled it. They were absolutely *not* going to start on the sumptuous king-sized bed. Likely he knew such a space as well as he did his posh sports car.

He reached for her waist, but she edged away. A husky laugh twisted out of her chest. "Not here."

He grinned as if accepting the dare while Heather took the opportunity to scan the room. Possibilities. *See it the way he sees it. As kinky as you wanna be.*

Her eyes were drawn back to the windows. She'd had such a thrill looking out over the city, high on the possibility that someone could be watching. The chair had been her shield. A safeguard.

A safeguard she no longer needed.

Inside Bet

She licked her lips. "That war you like to see? Just before I give in? That's what I want from you."

A strange expression passed over his face. His lips parted in the way that sped her blood and wet her thighs. The tension around his eyes faded. He looked nearly as young as his features insisted. "I almost believe you could do it."

Without saying a word, she strolled the length of the bedroom, drawn to the windows like a bug to a light. Jon's gaze sizzled along her spine. She could almost hear his curiosity, almost taste it.

After stepping around the long chaise, she faced the city. Entirely nude. Her arms still loosely bound. Anticipation wiggled under her skin. She stepped forward until her nipples touched the window. The ring made the smallest *clink*. She pressed, kept pressing, until her torso was flush, her thighs spread.

He could leave her there, she realized with a tremor of dread. Jon Carlisle could leave her pressed against the glass, her body exposed to the whole Strip.

That would be devastating.

But then his heat pushed against her back. Such a contrast to the cool window. "What a picture you make." He traced a finger along her side. "This tattoo says more and more about you with every passing second. You push it away, don't you?"

"Yes."

"And what fear are you pushing away right now?"

She turned her face so that her cheek touched the implacable glass. "That you'll leave me here."

"Standing against the window, with no one to come play?"

"Yes."

He brushed his fingers along the backs of her thighs. "That would be an incredible waste. Because, my dear Ms. Morris," he said against her shoulder, "I cannot recall a more erotic sight."

Relief coursed through her, a reward for her daring. His appreciation was the strongest aphrodisiac. The sound of a condom wrapper jacked her need even higher. So wet now, her inner thighs slick, she shifted to try to relieve the rekindled ache. Soon he would touch her. Soon he would be inside her.

His hands gently spread her open. He was so deliberate, even now, pushing up and in with a long, slow thrust. Sensation surged from that contact. He filled her completely, stretching her, radiating fiery sparks of pleasure out from where they joined. His groin nestled flush to her ass. Heather moaned again as he pressed her flat against the window. Her breathed fogged the glass.

"What must you look like," he said near her ear, his voice strained. "I can only imagine."

"And you like that."

"God, yes."

His pace quickened much faster than she'd expected. Perhaps the man had limits too. His cock was gloriously hard, so long that each driving thrust reverberated toward her belly. The rhythm he established was just...perfect. Quick, steady, deep. He found her hips with tense hands, gripping in time with his strokes.

Heather lost herself in that rhythm, pounding and building so strongly that it blotted out thought. Only sound and sensation remained, climbing. Jon's breathing rasped. She had to hold on a little longer, resisting an orgasm that threatened like a tidal wave.

He unexpectedly withdrew but didn't leave, didn't tease. Instead he cupped four fingers up inside her and scooped away her flood of moisture. He slid his hand down her thighs, painting her own arousal on her skin.

Heather shook with want as he pulled her back from the glass and bent her at the waist. Untying her arms, which tingled with a rush of returning sensation, Jon pressed her hands against the glass. Slippery masculine fingers twined with hers.

His thrusting return was all the more powerful for the fresh friction. Their bodies slapped and pulsed, working at finding their rhythm once again. Jon teased her nipple ring, her clit, but then settled his forearm lengthwise along her spine. He pushed. *Hard.*

The force arched her back, bowing her deeply, and reared her ass up to meet his assault. He grunted softly with each ramming thrust. His forearm pressed a counterpoint pressure to his cock. Pain gathered along her spine, just as immeasurable pleasure built where he worked. It was all too much. She wanted him to stop, wanted to use the safe word.

That thought made Heather clench her teeth. No way. *No way* was he breaking her so easily. She knew he was that powerful, that dangerous. The only escape was to come before she gave in.

Her body burst apart. A fiery climax sizzled up from her cunt. She clenched and trembled. The blinding haze nearly obliterated her plan, but she nudged it away just enough—just enough to shove Jon back.

Free of him, Heather turned against the window. She pushed her stiff fingers hard against her clit, pressing, as the waves continued to crash and throb. Knees soft, she slid down. The sweat on her back squeaked along the glass. All the while she watched Jon's dazed, bewildered expression. She landed on the carpeted floor, her knees splayed. The angle of her crisscrossed forearms thrust her breasts forward.

"Come on my tits," she gasped.

Jon blinked. "Fuck it."

He stripped his condom with a quick snap. Dick in hand, he closed the scant distance between them and jerked. Faster, faster, he worked his cock from balls to head and back again. He panted through his open mouth, eyes black. The tendons along his wrist and forearm bulged with the strain until, at last, he groaned long and loud. Hot come shot across her breasts.

He sagged to the floor, kneeling between her open thighs.

Heather leaned her head against the glass, smiling. She grabbed the back of his neck and pulled his face between her breasts.

"Clean me up," she whispered.

He stroked his tongue over skin sleeked with his hot release. Lapped it up without hesitation. She held him there as he finished, moaned and collapsed against her body.

Chapter Eight

Jon pushed his forehead against the cool window, but nothing could wipe away the slide of his chest over Heather's. Neither would he want it to be otherwise. Her body was everything lush and wicked.

And her mind...

Being pressed against her was worth every moment. Their night had been nothing short of remarkable.

He'd mapped it out from the moment he bent her forward over the chair in the living room. He'd meant to get the cheesecake out of the fridge and put the whipped cream to delectable purposes. But Heather...

Heather had taken the wheel and jerked them into another lane. Jon flew jets and drove an Aston Martin. Giving up the wheel was not comfortable. But it was certainly interesting.

And she hadn't stopped at his orgasm. Forcing him to lick his come off her breasts had been nothing short of nuclear—an element of kink he'd never tried. The ultimate novelty.

His face hidden by the window and tucked against the crook of her neck, he let his defenses drop. No plastic grins and calculated moves. Just satisfaction. A slow breath eased the tension in his chest.

Before he crushed her, he pushed off and rolled to the side. The glass slid against his back, further cooling his skin. His knees felt suspiciously loose as he stretched straight. The carpet rubbed his ass.

He spun out a slow smile, as if his chest wasn't still heaving with one of his best orgasms in years. "What would you estimate that payoff at?"

The curl of her mouth was mostly contented, but he thought he saw a gleaming blade of challenge. Maybe that was only his surprise. Or his determination not to let it happen again.

"Thirty-seven to one," she said. "Easily."

He pushed to his feet and held out a hand to help her up. He almost expected her to pass, to stand on her own. She seemed determined to come at him from an equal footing.

But surprise was among her most potent weapons. She gracefully slipped slender fingers into his.

After the last hour, he ought to have been spent. The soft slide of her skin proved otherwise. His continued interest was stoked by the Las Vegas lights gleaming off wet streaks crisscrossing her magnificent tits.

She followed his gaze down then laughed huskily. "I suppose I should get cleaned up."

He nodded, intending to let her walk past him toward the bathroom.

Instead, one sharp tug yanked her close. He was quickly coming to relish their near-perfect match in height. Her hips nudged his groin and her breasts pillowed against his chest. He angled her face.

By all rights, their kiss should have been easy. Relaxed. They'd already taken the edge off.

But it wasn't.

Teeth clicked together. Lips claimed and took. Her mouth stole every thought out of his head until he devolved into the rough, rude kid he'd never been. Their tongues fought. In the swirling cloud of heat that swept between them, Jon probably gave away too much of his surprise. He was verging on confused.

That would never do.

Heather pulled away first. Silvery-blue eyes studied him. The shield of her lashes kept her thoughts tucked down. She lifted a hand to curl over his jaw. For a second he thought he'd won the round, but then she stepped away with a soft pat to his cheek and another of those fucking secret smiles.

The bathroom door closed with a quiet *snick*.

Jon stood in the middle of the bedroom. He rubbed a hand over his crown. He didn't find anything close to the tingling effect he'd felt when Heather did the same thing.

Shaking his head, he ducked into the half bath in the other room to clean up. With any other woman, he'd have followed her into that bastion of marble and brass and potential sin.

He needed a moment.

After wiping up and pulling his boxer briefs back on, he grabbed a miniature bottle of scotch from the minibar to pour it into a glass. It was no Glenrothes, but it would do. The sharp burn of the liquor slipped down his throat, chasing away his lingering...confusion, he supposed. Putting a name on something so ephemeral was difficult, but he would.

Somehow he was drawn back to the wide bank of windows. He'd get her propped on that chair the way he envisioned, one way or the other.

A quiet step was almost muffled by the thick carpet. Heather had wrapped her body in one of the plush white robes that came complimentary with the suite. The belt was tied in a firm knot, but her fingertips grazed back and forth over her upper chest, as if she still thought of his release on her skin.

Setting down his drink, Jon met her in the middle of the room and brushed a kiss over her cheek. "Are you hungry? I find I'm starving." Her wrists were surprisingly slender for the richness of her body. Tender. Damageable. He looped his grip lightly around them.

She pulled back to look him in the eyes. "How easily you shut it all down again."

"The highs and lows are part of the fun."

For a moment he thought she'd call him on his bullshit. The decision to let it slide was a visible tug on the corners of her mouth. "I'm starving too. I assume a place this nice has concierge service."

"Of course." He crossed to the phone on the desk that served most travelers as a business center. "Anything you want, from French fries to *coq au vin*. You have only to name it."

She twiddled the robe's belt through her fingers. Her toes curled into the carpet. "Will you do me one favor?"

"Of course."

"Don't make it all sound so...generous. I don't want to feel like I'm being bought."

After returning the phone to its cradle, he crossed back to Heather. Her pulse was racing again, but not for any reason he liked. Jon had never needed to buy a woman. The thought that she might feel so shabby was an anathema.

"You may have noticed my tastes, Heather? Believe me when I say that even if you weren't here, I'd be indulging however I liked."

Her erotic mouth curled into the lush smile he much preferred. "When you put it that way...I think I'd like a chicken salad."

"That's it?"

She leaned forward and nestled against his jaw. A quiet shiver tightened the back of his neck. "What can I say? I save my appetites for other arenas."

Now that was a rallying cry he could certainly get behind. He ordered her salad, plus the chef's tasting menu with wine pairings for himself. For both of them, he added oysters.

"No oysters, sir," the man said.

"How can you have thirteen kinds of bottled water and no oysters?"

"Sorry, sir."

"Fine. The cheese assortment instead."

As soon as he'd hung up the phone, Van Halen's "Hot for Teacher" screamed from his trouser pocket.

Heather lifted her eyebrows in silent question.

He grinned as he dug out his cell. "It's a long story, and very little of it's mine to tell." He stepped nearer to the windows for a modicum of privacy. "Yo, Fang. What's up?"

Major Ryan "Fang" Haverty's voice was as sharp and clear as it was during staff meetings. "I just got a call from Leah."

Jon glanced at his watch. "It's a weekend and it's after midnight. Of course you did. Where is she?"

"Some dive bar. The bartender who took her phone for a minute sounded really pissed."

That was Princess Leah, all right. Fellow pilot Leah "Princess" Girardi should've made major a year ago, but she was too reckless. Wild. She still lived like a sorority girl on spring break. None of it impacted her impeccable, graceful flying techniques, but she was a hot mess once she touched the ground.

"If she's been fighting again, she's going to get her ass hemmed up by the CO."

"Where are you?" Ryan asked. "Can you go get her?"

Jon looked back over his shoulder. Heather had taken a half

bottle of red wine from the minibar and was industriously working at the cork. The white robe engulfed most of her body, but a sleeve had slipped down to bare her shoulder. Pale skin glowed in the soft light. He rubbed his hand over his bare chest where a lovely tension clawed back to life.

"No," he answered slowly. "I don't think I can."

The quiet hum in the background of the call was Cass, Ryan's girlfriend. It was still bizarre that Jon's friend seemed on his way to breaking up their triad. He, Ryan and Leah had been friends from the moment Jon's boots touched Nellis Air Force Base soil almost two years earlier.

They'd always be friends, but it wasn't going to be the same. It shouldn't be, now that Fang had found someone who made him happy.

"You going to tell me what you're up to?" Ryan asked.

"You going to tell me what Cass is wearing?"

A long silence followed, which was more generous than Jon probably deserved. "No worries," Ryan said at last. "I'll go get her. Drag her ass home."

Jon exhaled a long breath. He'd learned loyalty at a very young age, mostly from watching what not to do. His family had splintered after his older sister had died—right when they should have drawn closer together. He'd lost his parents as clearly as if they'd been victims of the same car accident. They'd made cold and closed off an art form.

He didn't like abdicating his responsibilities as a friend, but circumstances made it necessary. Heather and their night together was a one-time-only event. Jon didn't know how to do long term, even if he had any inclination. Best to enjoy moments as they happened. Ryan could handle Leah, with Cass there to welcome him home after he'd done his good deed.

Plus the hard truth remained: at some point they were going to have to let Leah sink or swim.

"Let me know if you need help," he said.

"Naw, I've got it covered." Cass's quiet giggle came over the line before it was muffled. Probably by Ryan's hand. "I just figured it was worth a shot."

They hung up after quick goodbyes. Jon tossed his phone onto the desk.

Heather wandered nearer. "Problem?"

He shook his head then touched her shoulder. Soft skin was still warm from the cuddling comfort of the robe. "No, shouldn't be."

"A friend?" She sipped her wine, watching him over the rim of the glass.

He was glad he'd been able to get a decent room at such short notice. Watching her drink wine from little plastic cups at the tasting had been simply...wrong—like serving twenty-year-old scotch in a Dixie cup.

"Yes. But it's his turn. He owes me a few."

"Turn?" Her eyebrows lifted. "To do what?"

"To pick up our other friend, Leah, from whatever trouble she's up to this time." His gaze flicked over her face. "You look surprised."

"Maybe a little. You have to admit it doesn't jibe with your self-indulgent playboy act."

Something uncomfortable slid down his spine—a surprising measure of chagrin that he'd been caught out so easily. But then, Heather seemed particularly astute.

He forced an indulgent chuckle. "I'll have you know that I don't have to try very hard."

Graceful hands slid around his hips. Heather traced the line of muscle that arrowed from his waist into the band of his briefs. She looked up at him from under her brows. "I'll understand if you have to go."

"Not a chance."

He took her wine and set it on the desk next to his phone. After weaving his fingers through the dark fall of her hair, he scraped his nails over her scalp. She bent her head back as he traced soft nibbles up the vulnerable skin of her throat. The kiss he drew from her lips was charged. Expectant.

"Because I haven't found any pandas yet."

Chapter Nine

Heather studied the arrogant flyboy as she stabbed another strip of grilled chicken. She'd been ready to lounge on the gorgeous sectional couch, eating dinner on her lap just as she did at home. Before she was able to make the suggestion, Jon had laid out their room service on the dining table. He'd placed the silver, napkins and glasses as if reproducing a manual on blueblood etiquette. Was that because of his upbringing, or had the military influenced his need for order?

Etiquette, however, generally required wearing a shirt to the table. Jon was still beautifully naked except for his close-fitting boxers.

So instead of the couch's luxurious comfort, she sat at the table and watched him. A fair trade, by any standard.

"I'm glad they didn't have oysters," she said, breaking the silence. "They're disgusting."

"But a purported aphrodisiac."

She grinned. "Do you really think we need one?"

He eyed her over the rim of his wide wineglass, giving the rich red liquid a swirl. "You know, you don't look like you'll be thirty-two in a week."

She narrowed her eyes. "What, exactly, do you expect a thirty-two-year-old to look like?"

"I'll get a plate of food in my lap if I say 'withered crone', yes?"

"And then a fork to your testicles."

A chuckling smile renewed his dimples. "Can't have that. No, you look...fantastic." As if that compliment were too spontaneous, or maybe too normal, he slanted his gaze toward where her robe gaped slightly across her breasts. "Fantastic everywhere."

"You can't help it, can you? The innuendo."

"Why would I want to?"

Because there's a time and place for sincerity, she wanted to say.

Inside Bet

Maybe she would've exposed herself that way had she been fifteen years younger. Or even five. Heather had no qualms with slinking gracefully into her thirties if it meant having the presence of mind and confidence to keep up with someone like Jon. Demolition men simply didn't do sincerity.

She'd learned that the hard way.

He used a piece of bread to mop the last of the beef juices off the plate. Definitely not one hundred percent Mr. Manners.

"So how old are you, then, smartass?"

"Twenty-six," he said.

Though his demeanor was that of Casanova with decades of experience under his belt, his features were obscenely smooth. Perhaps twenty-six was an appropriate compromise.

"Did they let you in the Air Force as a tween?"

"Might as well have," he said, leaning back. "Let's just say I have an aptitude for numbers that only registers on the charts of very special assessors. The physics of trajectory and velocity—none of the calculations ever fazed me. I can see them in real time, like a movie reel, even when flying faster than the speed of sound. I studied aeronautics and hopped into the first plane Uncle Sam let me have."

"Have you been in combat?"

He slid her an unreadable look. "The Aggressor Squadron is a teaching tool. We simulate enemy dogfighting styles to train pilots from around the world. We wouldn't be much good to them if we hadn't taken a tour or three."

A funny lurch thumped beneath her ribs as Heather sipped her wine. She was trying to reconcile the idea of Jon in combat, not liking that picture at all.

So little about him added up. She could imagine him being a genius. That didn't seem out of keeping with his arrogance or how he walked ahead of life—not running after it as most men did during their twenties. But just because one had a penchant for numbers and studied aeronautics didn't mean volunteering for the Air Force, let alone going to war.

She wanted to ask why. Instead she took another bite of salad.

"More wine?" he asked, as if he hadn't just implied having flown combat sorties.

When Heather declined, he set aside the small bottle rather than pour more for himself. She realized he'd switched to water since finishing his food.

That was oddly reassuring. She wouldn't have been able to trust him had he indulged to excess. Drunken fucks hadn't been her style for years. A notice that her pending enrollment at Penn State was threatened by high school discipline problems, as well as a sexual near-miss during one particularly risky weekend, had put the fear of God in her.

Now if she couldn't wrestle at least half the power back from any relationship, she didn't want it. No more waking up on the floor of a room she didn't recognize, and no more shying away from what she desired—at work or with men. That explained why she'd been so choosy with her lovers. The potential for pleasure simply hadn't been worth the consequences to the sense of self she gripped like a tether.

Jon was different. Everything about him screamed *limited time only*. He was fast becoming a special treasure to stuff into her box of memories—decadent memories worth savoring.

He was watching her quietly, probing again.

Her stomach unsettled, she pushed away the remaining few scraps of her salad. Upon swallowing the last of her wine, she made herself a vow. When she looked toward the future with Jon, even to the next morning, she would imagine a wall of red brick. Slamming expectations against such a wall would hurt like hell. Best not to have any.

She pushed away from the table and walked to the fridge, retrieving her hard-fought piece of cheesecake. Jon's gaze followed as she made herself comfortable on the couch. His dark eyes were mysterious in the soft lamplight, as if pupil and iris were one and the same. That brandy color was only for daylight and bright places, not their private retreat.

"I don't care if you are all silverware and cloth napkins, rich boy," she said, flipping open the takeaway lid. "I'm not eating my dessert at the table."

"Are you going to share?"

"If you're good."

He rose from the table, a grin crawling across his lips. The times she'd seen him laugh spontaneously could be counted on only a finger

Inside Bet

or two. She hoped he found things amusing on the inside, at least, even if he tramped down the reflex. It would be a sad life indeed to live at the expense of real humor, always calculating the worth of putting it on display.

She knew that for a fact.

"Ms. Morris, you may have noticed that being good is not my specialty."

He flopped heavily onto the couch, his grace abandoned. Heather lifted the cheesecake out of the way as he did. The tactic was a diversion, apparently, as he parted the folds of her robe and settled the back of his head in her lap.

"You don't do anything by half, do you?"

Jon shook his head, which rubbed the bristles of his short hair against her inner thighs. His smile told her he'd done it on purpose. Impossible man.

"Now feed me," he said.

Heather placed the plastic container on his work-of-art abs. One forkful at a time, they traded bites. The cheesecake was utterly amazing, just tangy enough to counter the sweetness. The texture was so thick that it clung to the tines, no matter how slowly she dragged the fork past compressed lips. Subtle citrus flavored the chilly whipped cream, which was an unexpected surprise. It blended perfectly on her palate with the dark chocolate sauce.

Watching Jon eat and being watched by him—that was the real treat. Every lick. Every swallow. Every blissful moan of appreciation.

"You know what I'm going to do to you," he said casually.

Shivers raced across her skin. Goose bumps. "Perhaps. But I think you should tell me."

"Why?"

"Because being blunt about erotic things is arousing."

A muscle on his cheek twitched. "They can be. True. But what about the mystery of the unknown?"

"You've already suggested that I know what you're going to do."

"You know, Heather, if you flew as well as you spar, you'd be a hell of a pilot."

She trumped his chuckle with an outright laugh. "I'd pass out before I made it into the cockpit."

He placed the cheesecake on the coffee table and turned onto his stomach, supported by his elbows. He blew a warm breath against the bare skin of her thighs while offering a remarkable view. Beneath his clingy briefs, his ass was taut and firm, just rounded enough to provide shape. The twin divots at his lower back were tempting enough to lick.

"I doubt that," he said. "I have firsthand knowledge that you're a brave woman." He turned his head to grin up at her. "But you'd plow into something if you managed to take off."

"In what life do you get to insult a woman while making plans to go down on her?"

"Who said I was going down on you?"

"I did."

"Duly noted. And I wasn't insulting you. You know full well that Heather Morris and an F-16 were not meant to be." He nudged the robe open to her navel and dipped his tongue inside. "But Heather and an F-16 *pilot*? That's perfection."

"You think I'd be here with just any flyboy?"

"Since you'd already agreed to dine with me before discovering my panty-wetting profession, then no."

"Your ego is plated with titanium."

"Safer that way."

Before Heather could process that enigmatic comment, he pushed up on his hands, levering as if preparing for pushups. The movement rippled across the muscles of his back and shoulders, bunching his triceps into fierce, powerful knots. She caressed that flex and play of flesh. He was lean, solid, so strong.

Jon brought the cheesecake back within reach then opened her robe. Deliberate. Controlled. Already she'd learned to expect pleasure when his words dried up and his eyes turned sultry. The anticipation alone was enough to make her wet.

He scooped a finger of whipped cream and painted it along her inner thighs, up to her stomach. With patience and slow moves, he made her into his own personal dessert. Shivering, Heather forced her muscles to relax. She had no doubt, *none*, that he would make this amazing.

Inside Bet

Jon dipped his head. Where his tongue would go first was a mystery. Only a glimmer of warming breath gave away his intention, just before he licked her thigh. Heat surged through her limbs. He consumed her. Teeth and tongue explored, lips sucked—all the while opening her thighs with implacable hands.

He murmured low and soft against her skin, words in French she couldn't understand. Knowing him, it was probably filthy. The sublime and the sordid together. That was Jon. And he made her crazy.

Heather's hands were restless. She rubbed her inner wrists against his buzzed hair, then petted up the length of his spine as tension built in her belly. He feasted, he teased, but he never got close to her clit.

Soon it was all she could think about—that place he hadn't yet touched. She wanted his mouth there, firm against her sizzling nerves. She gave her body permission to beg. A moan started low in her throat, lengthening to a sound like a plea. She tensed her nails into the striated muscles of his shoulders and along his scalp. He hissed against her skin.

"Wider," he said simply.

No talk and no sweet sentiments, just a quiet command Heather couldn't help but obey. She spread her legs as he slipped around to the floor, kneeling. He parted her lips, leaned low and sucked.

Her hips clenched, but she forced herself to hold still. Part of her knew this was a gift. No matter how he teased and nibbled, he was being rather generous—giving, making no head-game demands. She felt the need to save her strength.

Jon was having none of it. He tensed his tongue, thrusting softly into her pussy. Heather bracketed his head in her hands. Desire swept over her in seeing him that way. His smoky eyes watched her. He judged every gasp, every twitch, as he dragged out her body's secrets.

She couldn't stand much more.

Seeming to sense that, he balanced an elbow on the couch, which freed his other hand. With his lips firm on her clit, he shoved two fingers into her cunt. No warning. Just that hard drive. Her body snapped back, the sudden orgasm like the quick crack of a whip.

"Oh, *God*," she groaned.

For long moments Jon remained kneeling. His tongue laved and caressed, soothing her back into herself. Or perhaps he just enjoyed her taste. Heather could only lie there, momentarily spent, watching him work as she stroked circles over his bristly head. His attention ensured that she couldn't tune out and call it a night. Her body—the greedy thing—still wanted more.

Then, rubbing the back of his hand across his mouth, he slipped out of his briefs and returned to the couch. Gloriously nude, he spread his knees. That animated eyebrow quirked as he glanced down at his renewed erection. "Heather love, be a dear and bring those beautiful lips over here. It's my turn."

Chapter Ten

Jon stretched his arms along the back of the couch and waited. As much as he wanted Heather's mouth on his cock, he wasn't begging for it. She seemed entirely capable of making up her own mind. About everything.

Besides, when Heather eased off the cushions to kneel between his thighs, the payoff was more satisfying. She ran her hands up the insides of his legs. Everything they did verged on slow motion, like they'd been dipped in spun honey. It was the tinge of competition. Neither wanted to be the first to snap.

Jon had already given up the first round when he'd ground his forearm along her spine as he slammed in to her, all for the pleasure of feeling her lovely back arch into his touch. Forcing him to come on her tits, at her command, had given Heather the win.

She looked up at him, pale eyes flashing. Suddenly he realized why he liked that coy move so much. It was this moment. This possibility. Her thumbs grazed the sensitive skin of his balls. She slid her cheek down his shaft. He'd been picturing his prick in her mouth every time she looked at him that way.

He gathered her dark brown hair and smoothed it all over one shoulder so he could see her face. The pink tip of her tongue darted out to slick his cock, from the base on up. She engulfed his throbbing head. He hissed in a breath and clenched his hand in her hair.

Earlier, he'd made himself back off from the same motion, but no more. He wound his fingers more tightly through the strands. "You didn't seem like a tease earlier. In fact, I distinctly remember how you insisted that I fuck you immediately."

Pure challenge gleamed in her blue gaze. She circled her thumb and forefinger around the base of his dick. Tugged. "Time and place, I suppose."

He smiled, a little unwillingly. "More like you're trying to drive me nuts."

"That too."

Pulling the hair tighter he said, "Suck me."

Even when Heather bent her head and circled those lush lips around his cock, he felt...off. Like he was still losing. The shock down to his balls was exquisite—a sensation worth any sacrifice. She coiled her tongue over his head as her hands slid up and down his shaft.

Letting his spine curl, he shifted his ass to the edge of the cushion and sank into her tender mercies. Perhaps she noticed his hint because she took him deeply. Her mouth was a wet, fiery furnace. Her cheeks hollowed with the suction.

Jon traced the shadows under her cheekbones. "Has anyone ever told you how pretty you look with a cock tucked between those luscious lips?"

A slurp heralded her mouth's pop off the end of his dick. She lapped a dot of moisture from his slit. "Not in a long time."

His attention returned to her throat, as if dragged back to that vulnerability. She was so well armored everywhere else, including her thoughts, that he sought any way in.

"But you've been told that before?"

Something dark and unpleasant filtered across her features. She ignored his question. Again.

Instead she bobbed her head over his cock, her tongue grazing the underside of his shaft. Her thumbs crisscrossed to massage beneath his balls. Pure pleasure jerked his hips up. He wound silky strands between his knuckles.

She took every bit of it. Her mouth angled over his shaft again and again. The combination of wet pressure and suction was driving him up over the edge faster than he would've liked. He'd had plenty of blow jobs—some of them damn good. Nothing compared to the wicked pleasure of watching Heather's classic beauty do something so dirty with so much enthusiasm.

He latched his fingers behind her head, applying pressure. She only pulsed deeper, until the head of his cock brushed the back of her throat. When she returned to lick the ridge around his head, she grinned.

"Bedroom," he growled. "Now."

The even playing field of the bed was somewhere he knew well.

There, he'd have her spread out for his pleasure. Turn the tables.

"I think we're doing just fine here."

Slow and controlled, he tucked her hair behind her ears. "Sure, we are. If we stay here, I get to come hard in your pretty mouth. But if we go in there...I get to make you come as well. I can work with either."

She opened her mouth one more time, and she clenched the tendons of his inner thighs.

"If you put it that way." In a flash she was up on her feet, running for the bedroom. Her words trailed over her shoulder along with a stream of dark hair. "Last one to the bedroom comes last."

He laughed. Full-out laughed, even as his dick throbbed with wanting her ripe peach-shaped ass, even as he grabbed a condom out of his suit coat, even as he plotted how he'd make her crack. The adventure of that task was obvious now, so much more challenging than he'd expected when finding her all alone at the wine bar.

Stepping into the bedroom offered more proof of that. Heather had sprawled across the mound of pillows at the head of the bed. The robe was just a pile of white tossed to the side. Nothing hid her curvaceous body.

She'd started without him. Her knees were splayed. With one hand she stroked her clit and with the other she cupped her breast, tracing patterns with her nails over the soft flesh. "You lost," she purred. "I get the first orgasm."

"Greedy."

She murmured a wordless agreement.

Jon crawled up the bed. His arms shook as he levered over her, though he was nowhere near muscle failure. Just plain eagerness.

She didn't stop circling her fingers over her wet pussy as he slipped on the condom. "Sometimes it's good being a girl."

He wrapped her wrists in his grip, then pinned them to the pillow. When he kneed her thighs wider, his touch was rougher than he'd normally use for the first night with a woman. But something about Heather made him feel rougher. Harsher. More on edge.

She didn't seem to mind. Her tits rose and fell on fast breaths, pressed up by her stretched position.

He kissed her. Poured his intentions into her mouth.

Then he slammed his cock home.

She gasped. Her chin lifted, baring the tender length of her pale throat. Her pussy clamped over him—welcoming at the same time. Long legs rose to hook over his hips.

Damn how he fucked her. Jon let go of her wrists to grip her waist. He lowered his head to that tempting circle of gold adorning one nipple. When he tugged it between his teeth, he soaked up the quiet moan that spilled from her throat. Finally.

He thrust into her again and again. Her hips rose to meet every push.

He hadn't expected her to shove his shoulders. Her legs wrenched tight as they twisted. Then he was flat on his back, watching her body work over his. She lifted on her knees, palms flat to his stomach. Her eyes drifted shut as her head fell back. Dark hair tangled over her shoulders.

Jon slipped his hands up to cup her breasts. She rode him, eyes closed, as if he weren't there. She used his body. He hooked his fingers over her shoulders. Muscles taut, he yanked her down onto his thrusts.

His hands kept going—almost of their own will.

Eager to reclaim her attention, he pressed his thumbs against her throat. His arms trembled as he held back the impulse to clamp tighter. Such a technique would skyrocket her orgasm.

Heather's eyes flashed open. He expected her to relent. Call *panda*. She didn't. She pinched a stronger grip on his stomach, kept working her hips. Her sheath pulled at his cock. Delicious, hot waves clawed up his spine.

Pale blue eyes almost dared him to do it, to squeeze, to cut off her air.

Jon backed off.

Unbelievable.

He'd never been the one to yield. He fucked. He took whatever his partner was willing to give. And he went home happy.

This was more.

Instead he shoved off the mattress, flipping Heather onto her back. Their bodies pressed together. Her clit ground against his pubic bone. He squeezed her ass and jerked up into her. With his face buried between her gorgeous breasts, he took bite after bite of soft flesh.

Sweet Jesus, it was all he could do to hold back his orgasm until her pussy tightened over his cock. His reward though... That was worth every delayed moment of gratification. She moaned quietly in his ear, her fingers twisting across the base of his skull. Sharp nails scored his neck.

Jon let himself go. He tucked his face into the curve of her neck and bit down. Hard. A pure, primal need to claim. His orgasm shocked him with its pulsing power.

They collapsed onto the bed as one, Heather plastered over his lax body. Sticky sweat cooled on their skin.

Jon kept his eyes closed as he tried to figure out when he'd lost the thread. When he'd lost control. Again.

Half of him wanted to get all twisted up over it, but that wasn't worth the energy. Not when it would take only a little rest before they could have another go. Heather was a fleeting gift he would enjoy until he found her breaking point.

He ditched the condom then pulled down the comforter. Heather protested, but her voice was quieted by the slide toward sleep. She wiggled under the sheet anyway.

After dousing the single light burning in the other room, he hung the *Do Not Disturb* sign and secured the lock. He didn't want them bothered. Not until they were good and ready to go.

He pulled the curtains shut and froze. He'd unconsciously been planning to settle in for the entire weekend, which was definitely not his style. They'd both gotten their rocks off. By all accounts, he should be halfway to gone.

Heather was already asleep. He slipped into bed and wound a lock of her hair around his finger. Tomorrow he'd break down her shields. All he needed was a plan of attack.

Chapter Eleven

Heather blinked at the sound of a bath being drawn. Lying on her stomach, she stretched slow and deep. Pointed toes tangled in the far-flung sheets. A shiver brought her around toward consciousness. She was nude, of course, but realizing that so forcefully was a full wake-up call.

She tossed the hair out of her eyes and pushed off the mattress. Jon stood in the doorway between the bedroom and the huge white marble bathroom. He wore an appreciative smile and a robe tied loosely at his trim waist. The sight of his bare feet was a priceless daytime intimacy—a bit of commoner from the man who wore a three-piece suit as if it were skin.

"It's nearly noon," he said.

"Too early, then."

"Up now. I want to watch you ride me in the bathtub."

A smirk edged her lips, her token protest. The rest of her body fizzled to life with his blunt words. "Do I have time to brush my teeth first?"

He rolled his eyes. "So finicky."

"Bet you already brushed *and* flossed."

After a quick double take, he shrugged. "Make fun if you want, but I'm not the one with rotten cheesecake breath."

Heather licked her lower lip and made a face. He was right about that. She met him in the bathroom and brushed her teeth as Jon stripped the robe. So insouciant. As if men built like him just walked around all over the place. He seemed to have neither modesty nor pride when it came to his body. It was just a vessel to help his brilliant mind find pleasure.

Heather had no such nonchalance when watching him. He was relatively pale for a guy living in a desert, but she couldn't imagine a fighter pilot having too many free hours to sun himself. Dark hair feathered over his forearms, thighs and calves, not to mention the thatch that started at his belly button and trailed to his groin. His morning erection was wide awake.

With her thighs a little sore from the previous night—and from the hour just before dawn when they'd found each other through a foggy veil of sleep—Heather relished the idea of a bath.

"Come on," he urged, feasting on her nakedness. "I'll sit your pussy over one of the water jets."

Around her toothbrush she mumbled, "You'd let a tub do your work for you?"

"Miracles of modern technology."

Heather rinsed. She ran a comb through her hair to make it easier to wash. Then she joined him in the steaming hot water, taking the comb with her.

Scalding sensation grabbed at her ass and thighs. She hissed softly. So tender there, the skin so thin. Jon supported her with his strong hands as she settled in. Their legs alternated. The vanity light bathed gold over their bodies, making her think of beautiful angels with filthy minds.

Maybe she'd harbored the delusion of wanting to talk. Daylight was for getting to know one another, right? Heather didn't bother. *Limited time only.* Jon's proud hard-on was just too enticing to resist.

She soaped a washcloth and smiled as she washed, rebuffing his attempts to "help".

"I do actually want to get clean," she said.

"You'd get clean. Just some places more than others."

"I'm an equal-opportunity bather."

"Hippie."

Laughing, she splashed his chest. He grabbed up the cloth and quickly mimicked her, tugging away when she wanted to wash his chest. Or his back. Anywhere. The pull and bunch of his muscles as he worked to reach between his shoulder blades was enough to dry her mouth. His sudsy pectoral stretched to accommodate the movement, revealing a wet streak of hair beneath each arm.

While Jon finished, she dipped her head between their tangled legs and wet her hair. She lathered slowly, taking her time because it felt so good to indulge. She lathered, arms upstretched, while he practically panted over her breasts. Whatever he'd been doing with the washcloth stopped mid-motion. Heather bent low again. Her nose nearly touched the water's surface as she swished the shampoo away. Conditioner. Scrub. Rinse again.

"Get over here," he growled, catching her wrist.

She flipped the wet hair behind her back, knowing it must look stringy and ridiculous. But Jon's mind was obviously elsewhere. He pulled her to her knees, angling their bodies so that she straddled his lap. She reached out to grab the condom he'd left on the closed toilet seat. Rolling it on was tricky in the water and with how eager he seemed. Maybe time and familiarity were beginning to wear him down. He was no longer quite so intent on drawing out every moment to its most torturous limit.

With a lift and a shift, she found the right angle and slid down onto his long length. A groan slipped from her throat. She'd been with men whose penises were wider, but never one so long or so damn *hard*. He was absolutely rigid, as if wanting her any more would cause them both physical damage.

She scooped water onto his head and laughed as it dripped into his eyes.

He blinked, his eyelashes dark and spiky. "What are you doing?"

"Washing your hair."

His hands gripping her hips, he initiated their rhythm. "Go ahead and try."

Heather poured a dab of shampoo and lathered his short, bristled hair. The coarse texture scraped her palms. His expression was a coy mix of passion and happily pampered. With more scoops of water, she washed him clean. He kept his eyes pinched shut. The pattern of his thrusts had slowed, feeling all the more intimate for just being *in* her, still waiting.

When she'd cleared away all the soap, she kissed each eyelid. "You can come out now."

She was done cleaning him, not done teasing him. Taking comb in hand, she pressed it hard against the base of his neck and scraped up to his crown. A hard shudder shook his shoulders.

"Again," he rasped.

Heather complied. His features tensed at the first bite of the comb's teeth, then eased and relaxed as the pain washed over his senses.

"God, Jon, that's sexy."

"No shit."

With a growl he found her hips again, guiding a faster fuck. Water lapped the tops of her thighs and the curve of her ass. Heather braced her hands on the marble wall behind his head. Her breasts hung forward, swaying, their weight so noticeable in that position. Every bounce radiated down to her nipples.

She reached around and turned the water back on, which started the jets. High-pressure streams of hot water burst against her legs. Jon grunted as two jets powered around his lower back and burst against Heather's kneecaps.

"Damn hot."

"Suck it up, Captain."

He grabbed her hair in retaliation, twisting the wet strands into a knot at the base of her neck. Christ, he had fierce hands. Lean and strong. She couldn't move her head unless he wanted her to—which he didn't. The force of his pulsing cock picked up. She could only brace her upper body in a way that didn't pull too far from his unforgiving fist.

Even as his mouth opened to drag in quicker gulps of air, he wore a beautiful, depraved smile. He hadn't given up his need for control, only decided to exercise it during a new phase of their encounter— while fucking, rather than before. Her every dirty thought was reflected in his eyes.

Still he tested her, dragging her hair back, harder, arching her body. Jon lifted away from the sloping wall of the tub and caught one of her nipples with his lips. She was trapped by his hands, his mouth, his cock. The water streamed over her in hot, torrid jets. A lash of his tongue sent jolts from her breasts to where he pounded.

He snagged her golden ring between his teeth. Each thrust forced a tug. He sucked deeper, taking the whole nipple into his mouth. His tongue looped and swirled until she winced against that beautiful pain.

Her orgasm was like the sunrise, slow in coming but visible for a long way off. She reached for it, her body tense and greedy. The rhythm, the water, the heat...

"Heather? Heather, come on. Stay with me."

But Jon wasn't inside her anymore. He was sitting up, with a solid grip on her forearms. His face was pinched with an intense look of concern. The water was off, but steam hung in the humid bathroom.

"Hey, good." He exhaled heavily. "There you are."

She blinked. "What?"

"Heather, you about passed out."

The seriousness of his expression said he wasn't lying. Worry furrowed his forehead, the first time she'd seen him truly upset.

"That's it," he said tightly. "You're clean enough. Come on."

Despite Heather's protests, he would not be deterred. He hauled her gently to her feet then toweled her off. His actions were so innocent that she gave up trying to fight. Being on the receiving end of his concern was a surprising luxury. The world still spun, the edges dark, but her breathing slowly returned to normal.

Jon led her to the bed and pressed her back. He smoothed wet hair away from her face, his caress whisper soft. The length of his body nestled alongside hers. His penis, at half-mast, tucked against her thigh. Tension in his arms and belly had yet to disperse.

"You were really worried," she whispered, smoothing his cheek.

Apparently reassured, Jon leaned close and touched his lips to hers. Small kisses. Delicate kisses. She wanted to shout at him for such unexpected tenderness, to stop him from unleashing a wholly different sort of danger.

"A woman with her eyes rolling back into her head is not sexy."

Nope. Didn't help. Even his quips didn't take the edge off how badly she'd spooked him. And he was spooking her. Wanting real warmth from a guy like Jon was like wanting cuddles from a porcupine. Eventually she'd bleed and cry.

"I'm fine, Jon. Really. I'm sorry I scared you, but I was having a good time."

"*Too* good," he muttered, sitting up halfway. "If you're going to gasp for air when getting fucked, at least do it safely."

A memory from their previous night quivered over her. His hands had been at her throat. The feeling of being under his control, with her safety his to dictate, had been as intoxicating as any drug. He'd hesitated, then backed away from a boundary that was apparently too remote.

Heather never would have considered such an act. Ever. Not with anyone else.

That heady rush of sensation as she'd climbed toward orgasm would not leave her. The thrum and beat of their rhythm still fired her blood. Neither had found satisfaction. It wouldn't take much to get them right back to that moment, on the brink of completion.

Part of her was, frankly, a little freaked by his solicitude. She wanted Jon back. Freaky, pervy Jon with his delicious sinfulness. He could seduce her mind and her body a thousand times in a row and she'd never complain—as long as she got to fuck with his head in return.

The concern that was almost caring...? That strayed near real emotion.

Time to remind them both of what their weekend was about.

"I'd need an unspoken safe word, don't you think?"

Confusion twisted his brow. "What?"

"Like, a safety signal instead?"

"Heather, what are you talking about?"

"You said we'd have to do it properly, so let's be safe."

His confusion cleared away with a quick inhalation. Eyes the color of brandy turned dark on a rush of desire. His mouth opened. His tongue darted out, as if tasting the possibility in the air.

"You want my hands on your throat?" he asked, his voice low and horse. "While we fuck?"

Heather nodded.

"And you're serious?"

"Completely."

"Have you ever done it before?"

She shook her head, the pillowcase damp from her hair. "Have you?"

"Not..." He exhaled. "Spontaneously, yes. In the heat of the moment."

"Like last night." With a little pout she added, "Had you gone through with it."

77

"Believe me, most women don't go for strangulation on their first night."

"I don't doubt it."

Jon pushed his jaw sideways, his expression beset with reservations. But his erection had gone into overdrive. It pressed hard and hot at her hip. "And you'd trust me with this? Why?"

"In there, just now, you could've kept going. A selfish bastard might have. But that's not your style, is it? You want a girl to know every single thing you're doing, everything you want to do." She slid her hand down to his hip then around to his ass. The forceful curl of her fingers was rewarded by his nudging thrust. "Now it's like that snake-venom wine. When else would I ever have this chance?"

He'd turned solemn, despite the heavy pulse in his dick.

Maybe he reached a decision. Maybe the temptation was too great. The desire in his eyes turned vivid. "You're right. A spoken word won't work. Hold up three fingers over your face like this. Got it? And if you look ready to slip away again, I'm stopping."

She nodded as a fierce tingle of anticipation started in her toes and wiggled all the way up to her scalp.

Because Jon's wicked smile had come out to play.

Chapter Twelve

Jon started slowly, as if his prick weren't already throbbing. As if his mind hadn't been utterly and completely blown. He gathered Heather into his lap and hooked her legs around his ass. Silently promising to make it good, he slipped his hands into her hair and stole a long, hot kiss. He cupped her full breasts to feather kisses across them, licking down the center of her cleavage.

He'd seen how she shied away from softness. Instead, Heather wanted breath play. Far be it for him to deny her.

If she noticed the tremble in his hands when he put on a new condom, she graciously ignored it. She kept stroking his body. Graceful fingertips traced his pecs and the lines of his tense abs. Shit, he'd be a lot more nervous if the person planning to wrap hands around his throat kept shaking. The fire in her pale eyes spoke only of anticipation. A sharpened sword of want. Need. Temptation.

He fucking loved that he'd done that for her. By agreeing.

It wasn't as if he wouldn't get off on the idea.

His body was screaming for hers.

Once he was sheathed, he angled her back so his cock slipped through her lower lips. She was soaked. Dripping for him. He speared his fingers through her folds, circling her tight opening. She gasped quietly.

Wouldn't be long until she was gasping a lot louder. Choking for breath.

The trust she'd blithely handed him was obscene.

He tucked his swollen head into her as she leaned back on her hands. Took him in deep.

Jon dropped his forehead to her breastbone. He wasn't hiding. Nope. He just needed a second to adjust to the tight grip of her cunt and the grasping need she seemed to be indulging in, reveling in.

He didn't have that luxury. Not this time. He had to be sharp.

Careful. Because she didn't want to be.

"Last chance," he said, a hoarse growl in his voice.

"You're not getting out that easily."

Curling one hand across the back of her neck, he kissed her again. Lingering, pushing as deeply as she could take him. He stroked his tongue across hers in the same rhythm of his cock in her pussy—her hot, wet pussy clinging to every inch.

He shunted that thought away. Had to. She felt so good. *Too* good. He might lose control or, hell, even come too fast. Focusing on her safety—her enjoyment—was paramount. For the time being, she was the center of his goddamn universe.

He meant to work her up to the edge of coming before wrapping his hands around her long, lovely throat. Heather had other ideas.

Even as her curvy hips thrust, she gripped his wrists and forced him to caress her breasts. Higher. His fingers trailed across her collarbones. Her sly gaze never left his. The challenge in their pale depths marked a bar he'd have to vault—or he wouldn't make it. She released his hands and grabbed her fill of his back and shoulders.

Jon took over from there.

With his thumbs, he caressed the softness under her chin. He hooked his index fingers behind her ears. She was as smooth as handspun silk. Tender. Luscious. Vulnerable.

She was wide open for him.

He lowered his thumbs to the lovely curve where her chin blended into her throat. He pressed. Gently at first, then deeper when her eyes brightened.

Parted lips made no sound while her pelvis jerked in his lap.

Fuck, he had to get his brain out of his dick. Nothing could block her tight grip. Or the wetness dripping between them. Or the shivering rolls of her sleek hips.

He let up for a second, so she could gasp for breath. Then, with fire curving her mouth into a dangerous smile, she leaned her chin forward into his hands. Daring him to go further.

Jon wrapped one hand through the tumbling mass of her hair. That it was still damp at the ends was shocking to believe. They'd gone so far so fast.

He curled his other hand over the front of her neck.

Inside Bet

Heather leaned into his grip. He squeezed harder. Tighter. And still they rocked together in a slapping crush. Her face pink, she was striving for her orgasm. Tense heels wedged against his ass, as Jon fought the towering wave threatening to crush him.

More. Faster. *Now*.

For all the perversion, this was more than a fuck. Trust spun out between them. Tangible. He could taste it in the sultry air.

Heather yanked back, gasping. Her throat worked over a gulp. He locked down his limbs, readying himself to hear "panda". It would be hard as hell to retreat from the violent precipice she'd encouraged, but he'd manage. He'd have to. Her trust was everything.

Instead, she clamped her hands even tighter over his, helping him choke the air from her own throat. A sheen of sweat filmed her temples. And still she smiled at him. Wickedly.

A stream of curses poured out of him. French and English. Rough and filthy. "God, you're gorgeous. Your face red. Your body covered in sweat. Fuck me, Heather love. Take what you need."

That seemed to be enough. Their fingers laced together and wrenched. So fucking tight now. Her hips twitched once, twice. She made no sound as she came, but her lips blew wide on a silent scream. More than enough. She'd lost control. Wide open to him.

His conquest.

Jon's body exploded. His orgasm crashed down his spine, out through his prick in harsh pulses. His entire brain went black in swift streaks of *gone*.

He cranked his fingers off one by one. Her throat was red. Angry. But she melted over him, arms wrapped around his shoulders. She nuzzled his neck as his lips brushed her shoulder. Her soft laugh was both husky and hysterical at the edges.

Jon's skin was too sensitized. The hard buds of her nipples against his chest sent shivers up and down his limbs. He lowered her slowly, until her hair spread over the pile of gleaming white pillows. His mouth had run dry.

Carefully, languidly, he combed his fingers through her hair until it smoothed around her shoulders. "You okay?"

She blinked then licked her lips. Nodded. She curled a hand over the back of his head and rubbed. Her throat worked over a tight swallow. "I probably shouldn't tell you this..."

"I'm sure I can handle it," he said, knowing what would come next.

She regretted it. There was wild, and then there was goddamn insane. They'd treaded into territory even Jon hadn't mapped.

"It'll only make your ego bigger." Her mouth curled into a surprisingly sweet smile. "But that was the best orgasm of my life."

He forced a chuckle. Damn, she was full of surprises. "I'm not even sure I can take credit for that."

"Trust me on this. I trusted you."

He pushed back damp tendrils that clung to her cheeks. "You did. That was...amazing. You're a precious woman, Heather Morris. What you gave me was a gift."

Pale blue eyes darkened. Something pulled her mouth down at the corners. "Don't bullshit me, flyboy."

"No bullshit. I don't lie, remember?"

She pushed up and shot him some serious side-eye. "That's what you said."

"So, more trust then." He traced the line of her tattoo. Bending down, he pressed kisses over the pattern, stopping at every flower. He touched the tip of his tongue to the words. *"Le passé n'a aucun prise a toi, quand meme amoureuse."*

"Hm?"

"The past has no hold on you, lover."

She cast a smile over her shoulder. An enigma.

Jon wiped a hand down his face, which was damp with sweat. He dropped against the pillows. "God, I need to rest," he said on a soft laugh.

"About that." She swung her legs over the side of the bed and stood.

He couldn't believe she had strength enough to do anything. Hell, he had only done the choking, and he was spent. Half of that was the wiggling sludge of his brain. He loved numbers, but planning and strategy were beyond him. Even with women.

He needed time to find his feet.

Heather picked up the robe he'd tossed over the chaise then

wrapped it around herself. She tied the belt like an infantry grunt strapping on body armor. Short, sharp moves.

"I was thinking."

"Haven't I warned you about that?" His words were light, but something tremulous ate its way down his spine.

She grinned, but she'd closed off again. There was no hint of the openness he'd seen only minutes ago. "I think we should call it done."

He dragged his torso off the bed. "Done?"

They'd barreled past fun and games when she almost passed out in the tub. The worry he'd felt had been shocking, something he'd only experienced for his closest friends. Not for a weekend fling.

She was wearing a damn good poker face though—a soft smile, eyes widely innocent. As if he hadn't just clamped her throat while they fucked senseless.

Heather returned to the bed and placed a nearly chaste kiss on his lips. "This has been wonderful, Jon. I want to make sure... I think we should end on a high note."

His mouth opened on a protest—and snapped shut just as quickly. The thought of begging a woman to stay set his back teeth to grinding. Hard. Jon hadn't needed to beg for attention in years, and he sure as hell didn't intend to start with a one-night stand.

"By all means." The smile he slipped across his face was one of his sharpest. Most dangerous. "This was the high note to top all high notes."

Never mind how he'd meant to lay her down and lick her from head to toe until she came in a slow wave—something softer to remember after their violence.

He lounged in the bed while Heather cleaned up and re-dressed in the same lace camisole and tailored skirt.

The strange—very strange—part was that he'd done this before. Chilled out while a woman prepared to leave by herself.

It hadn't bothered him before, and it didn't bother him now.

He'd make sure of it.

Chapter Thirteen

A midweek birthday could never compete with one that fell on a weekend.

Heather and two colleagues, Kyle Yu and Grant Pickerel, went out to lunch with Mr. Quinn, President of Hanover Financial Logistics, which was the best she could expect from the day she turned thirty-two. Jenn and her husband's responsibilities meant partying on a Wednesday night, no matter how modestly, was out of the question.

The intimate French bistro was classy and very busy, and it had the advantage of being almost entirely devoid of tourists. Mr. Quinn was buying, which was always a plus—and an especially rare treat from a notorious tightwad—but she didn't feel comfortable drinking in front of him. Work meant her professional self.

Which had been difficult to maintain since her weekend with Jon.

Likely no one would notice, but Heather did. The little things. She'd missed an email from a client, requiring a follow-up reminder. She'd been all but ready to sign off on an attest engagement when she realized she'd forgotten to outline the casino's recording procedures. She'd been late to work two days in a row. Twenty minutes. No huge tragedy.

Only she knew her lateness had been caused by fitful nights filled with devastating dreams. Some were touch-for-touch recreations of encounters she'd shared with Jon. Others were pure fantasy, her unconscious mind tormenting her with the pleasures they had yet to sample. They could get lost again, together, in the dark or in the full light of day. It would be bliss.

She'd awoken aching and unsatisfied...and late.

So no alcohol at lunch, even if she could've used the means of relaxing. Work was work. She kept her personal life and her professional ambitions well apart, having renounced trusting her judgment if the two collided.

When the waiter announced the day's specials, all of which were in French, Heather found herself back on that couch in The Palazzo, with Jon murmuring against her thighs. God, he'd sounded amazing, his voice rough with passion. She crossed her legs under the table.

Le passé n'a aucun prise a toi, quand meme amoureuse.

The past has no hold on you, lover.

She spent long hours trying to blame him. Had Jon kept their play wholly sexual, she wouldn't have had a problem seeing him again. She might have even sought him out for her birthday evening. The best present was one that could be enjoyed over and over again.

He'd changed, subtly. Nothing she could pinpoint, nothing she could explain. All she knew was that his brief bout of tenderness had been too much to take—when he'd combed her wet hair, his hands so gentle after having just been wrapped around her neck. Such unexpected compassion had thrown her blind, idiotic heart into overdrive. Hoping. Making plans.

Not with a man like him.

"Here's to Heather." Mr. Quinn raised his iced tea. "Many happy returns."

Kyle and Grant echoed his toast, with a particularly attentive smile on Grant's face.

She should just be happy. Enjoy this. Her colleagues trusted her and respected her. The bottom line in her various investment accounts, though not untouched by the market's volatility, was still solid. She would have money for her parents' future, paying them back for all they'd done to get her through tough years. The future was hers to determine, not a brick wall waiting to crack her open.

The office was only two blocks away, which was manageable in the August heat, but only just. Even three years in Vegas hadn't acclimated her to the oven-strong temperatures. College summers in Pennsylvania could get warm and sticky, but not like a blow dryer frying her face. Sweat dampened her forehead as the hundred-plus heat wilted her hair.

Grant walked beside her, his broad shoulders hunched against a nicely cut suit. "Do you have any plans for your birthday?"

Heather kept the rhythm of her walk, although the question caught her off-guard. Grant was in his mid-forties, recently divorced, well-established with the firm. She liked his salt-and-pepper hair and easy smile. The possibility of going out with him was rather unnerving, though, because thoughts of him were still colored by his ex, Tina, and their three sons.

And no mingling sex and work. She couldn't afford to slip. Her promotion and her reputation were simply too important.

"Probably not," she found herself saying. "I think a rental and too much chocolate."

"I could join you, if you wanted company. Maybe bring a bottle of wine?"

He held the door as she slipped into the cool lobby. Air conditioning was such a miracle. She faced Grant, looking him over with an attempt at fresh eyes. He kept good care of himself, which apparently had been part of the trouble behind the divorce. Too many hours at the gym...followed by one too many late-night cocktail parties at the clients' casinos.

He was a nice-enough guy, if one didn't have plans to get involved. The ex, the kids, their status as colleagues—all too complicated.

The trouble was, Heather had already found her good time. She tried to imagine Grant's teeth on her nipple ring, Grant's cock pressed against her ass, Grant's hands on her throat. She couldn't do it. Jon had left a mark on her sex life. She only hoped it wasn't indelible. The idea of comparing future lovers to what she'd shared so briefly with one particular Air Force captain was just awful.

"That sounds...nice, Grant," she said cautiously. "Really, it does. But I think I'll have to pass. For now. I've been out of sorts lately."

He managed a wan smile and was sweet enough to change the subject. Heather didn't breathe normally until she made it back to the safety of her private office, which had a maddeningly perfect view of the Strip. When emails piled up and she didn't know where to start on the tasks laid out before her, she located The Palazzo along the skyline.

Snap out of it.

Leaning her elbows on the desk, she held her head. For the first time she wondered if she'd made a mistake in leaving him.

What could it hurt?

No.

There was nothing more to be had from her fabulous hours with Jon Carlisle. He was her early birthday present—one she'd remember with a naughty smile for the rest of her life. Everyone in Sin City knew how the house operated. With each successive bet, a person reduced his odds of earning a profit. It was Las Vegas 101. The theorem of the gambler's ruin—one of the oldest formulas in mathematics. Any game of chance based on a negative expected value would eventually exhaust finite resources.

Such was the equivalent of time spent with a hedonist like Jon. Each return would become more dangerous than the last. Hearts got involved. Hearts got broken.

She wanted her bets to be as safe as possible. One day she would find a stable, normal guy who treated her with love and respect. He would reinforce her hard-earned restraint, not encircle it with dynamite. There would be mutual trust and sharing.

Like you trusted Jon? Like you shared one another?

Nope. Brick wall.

She tried to work, but her thoughts were a jumble. Worse, she was physically edgy, tense in a way that could only be described as *horny*.

Heather was just about to head home early, intending to cite her birthday as an excuse, when someone knocked on her office door.

"Come in," she called.

A woman in a white T-shirt and a pair of bright blue dungarees opened the door. The logo on the shoulder of her T-shirt read *Lilies of the Field*. "Are you Ms. Morris?"

"Yes."

"Got a flower delivery for you."

The woman produced a slender vase. Gold filaments wove through the delicate glass, subtly catching the light. Curved like the spine of a woman, it held a single purple morning glory that exactly matched those of her tattoo.

Heather could only stare at the gift, knowing exactly who'd sent it. They had parted almost anonymously, but Jon had sought her out.

After signing for the gift, she watched the delivery woman close the office door. Heather was alone. Her fingers trembled slightly as she opened the tiny cream-colored card. Its gold filaments echoed those in the vase. Every detail bore his stamp—meticulous, classic, designed to pry underneath her skin.

What's done is done?
Your call. Happy 32nd.
Jon

And his phone number. That was it.

She shivered at that reminder of *Macbeth.* Leave it to Jon to turn a bit of Shakespearian tragedy into the classiest come-on of all time. Her nipple ring tugged against her bra, suddenly too sensitive to bear. She pushed the card against her lips, as if she'd be able to smell him there, but it was just printer ink on cardstock.

Closing her eyes, she fought a battle that had no good outcome. No erotic images came to her. No pictures of Jon's body or their bodies together. Instead she was stuck on the idea of how she'd spend her birthday evening. Alone in her house. Sick on chocolate. Hoping the rental was good enough to hold her attention. Then what? A sex toy and early bedtime?

The voice she heard in her mind was Jon's as he'd ripped off his condom, losing control, ready to come on her breasts. *Fuck it.*

She grabbed her BlackBerry and dialed before she could think. Her fingertips were numb, her thighs hot. Every gulp of air reminded her of his hands controlling whether she took another breath. The phone rang and rang. Would she leave a voicemail or simply hang up?

"Yo, this is Carlisle."

She spoke past her dry tongue. "Afternoon, Captain."

A long pause followed. She counted her heartbeats as they sped past. Her thumb hovered over the button to switch off the call.

"You got my present," he said.

"I did, thank you. It's beautiful." Her slingback heels fidgeted up and down until she forced them to still. "What do you have in mind?"

"Dinner."

"Where?"

"Haven't decided."

"Any place nice will need reservations."

He chuckled softly. "Don't worry about that."

The scream of an airplane's engine forced Heather to hold the phone away from her ear. Something primal knotted in her gut, timeless and needy. He was a fighter pilot, for Christ's sake. He lived for danger and novelty, a connoisseur of fine, rare things.

And he wanted her.

That tugged her spine a little straighter. She deserved to be desired by such a man on her birthday. She needed this. Again. For herself.

"Sorry about that," he said after the plane had passed.

"You're still at work?"

"Just paperwork now. I'm done flying."

Another shiver. Jon sweaty and rushing on adrenaline, his lean welterweight body climbing down from a fighter's cockpit. God, he would have such a swagger.

"Can you pick me up?" she asked.

Another long silence. Was he trying to teach her a lesson for dropping him? Was he regretting having sent the flower? She curled her fingers into her palm, ready to pierce her own skin out of anticipation.

Finally he cleared his throat. "I need time to clean up here. How about your place at seven?"

"Seven." She glanced at the wall clock. Four hours away. Now that she'd given herself permission to indulge, that time was agony. "Make it six, Captain."

"Very well."

Heather recited her address, breaking down another barrier between them. He would see where she lived. That intimacy made her pulse quicken.

"But you should do something for me," he said, almost offhandedly.

She soaked in the rumble of his voice. Low. A little scratchy. He sounded just as he had when they'd fucked. With Jon, sex and desire had a particular timbre.

"Tell me."

His voice dipped again, as if there was a possibility he would be overheard. "Touch yourself. Right now."

A denial leaped to her tongue. Of course she couldn't.

She swallowed her protest. After a quick trip to the door, locking it, she returned to her desk. What was the use of a private office if she didn't make the most of it?

"Do any of your colleagues speak French?" she asked.

"Not that I know of." She heard the smile in his words. "Shall I?"

"Yes, please."

She swiveled in the chair, turning until she could reclaim her view of The Palazzo. Just that glimpse was enough to set her blood alight, as Jon's whispered French slinked past her defenses. Heather lifted the hem of her brushed-silk skirt. Her hand became his hand, the feel of his fingers caressing, circling, dipping inside.

From the phone she heard the sound of a car door closing. "Now we're alone," he rasped. "I want to hear you come. Let me hear you."

"I can't."

"You can. I don't need loud, Ms. Morris. I know how you sound. Just close your eyes and let me hear you breathe."

Heather pulsed her fingers in faster circles. The finish was close now, her lungs heaving. She sucked in a hard breath as a slow, honeyed orgasm filled her world, all blazing color and hot light. She stayed quiet, only permitting a slow, controlled exhalation. He could have that.

The rest was hers to keep.

"*Merci*, Heather love. I'll see you at six."

Chapter Fourteen

Sweltering, Jon sat in his car. He hadn't wanted to take the time to kick on the engine and let the A/C roar. He'd been too focused on hearing Heather. More specifically, hearing her come—the soft hitch in her breathing, then the gusty exhalation. Just listening to those sweet sounds was enough to get him going.

He tapped the phone against his closed lips as he stared out the window. Technically his only view was the side of the 64th Aggressor Squadron's headquarters, but that didn't stop his imagination. Heather's graceful fingers, tipped with the tasteful French manicure and dipping in her wet pussy, still layered across his vision.

Ordering the flower had almost been impulse. Almost.

He'd spent a little too long determining what to write on the card to fully merit that level of insouciance.

He'd decided to go through with it because he hadn't been able to unravel Heather. Was she the bold, fearless woman he thought her? Or something less…intriguing? He'd believed he would know from the tone of her voice—if she even called—but an air of mystery still surrounded her.

The only thing he'd confirmed was that speaking French got her hot. At least that was something he could work with.

A sharp knock clicked on the driver's-side window, only inches from his head. He kept his reaction down to a fast jerk.

Major Ryan Haverty and Captain Leah Girardi stood outside his door, wearing matching expressions of amusement.

Sighing, Jon pushed the ignition button and lowered the power window. "You two have a problem?"

Ryan leaned a forearm across the top of the car and bent to bring his head low. The man was such a beef-fed All-American. Tall as a house and almost as sturdy. "No, *mon ami*. Not at all."

Leah grinned and blew air kisses. Her dark hair skimmed straight back from her face and wound into a bun that met regulation. For now. Off-duty hours would find it a mess. "*Oui, oui,*" she whispered like a breathless Marilyn Monroe.

Fuck. They'd heard him.

He kept his posture loose in the leather bucket seat, then smiled. "If your only intent is to give me a rash of shit, can we get on with it pronto? I've got to turn in my inventory. I'm getting out of here on time, hell or high water."

"Got plans, Dimples?" asked Ryan, a smirky grin on his face.

The major had earned that one, probably a couple times over. Not that long ago, Jon had busted Ryan's balls about his plans—or lack of them—one night when Cass had shown up in a very interesting costume. "As a matter of fact, I do. Hence my need to get out of here."

"Aw, damn." Leah leaned down to look in the window. "Does that mean no karaoke tonight?"

"It's Wednesday, Princess," Jon said on a sigh. "Don't you ever slow down?"

"Come on. It's more fun if everyone's there. Bring the chick."

"What makes you think I'm seeing a woman tonight?"

Leah only rolled her eyes. "Gee, because you're not gay?"

"Heather's not the karaoke type." But as soon as he said it, Jon realized he had no idea if that was true. He could picture her onstage, in a pool of white light as she sang some ballad. She'd do it with her eyes closed, ignoring her fear and getting lost in the song.

That would be amazing to see.

"Children, children," Ryan said with a laugh. "Can we please get back on task?"

Leah grinned. "Giving Tin Tin crap is my primary directive."

Her insistence on using the call sign he hated was another of her special gifts. Ryan lightly cuffed her on the shoulder, but his expression sobered.

Jon sobered back. "Was there something you needed to talk to me about?" The faster they got business over with, the faster he could get to Heather.

"Definitely. Today's classes did *not* go well, and part of it was your fault. You can't keep dogging the new guy. Kisser's earned his place here, same as anyone."

Captain Eric "Kisser" Donaghue. The bane of his recent professional existence.

Jon clenched the steering wheel. "He deserved it."

"We're here to train incoming pilots. Not hand our own squadron mates their asses."

"Kicking that hotshot's ass *is* good training." He managed to infuse his voice with a parody of humor, but it was tough. Calling the man a hotshot was an understatement. He was all short dick and big ego. If allowed to continue, he'd get someone shot down. Odds weren't good he'd do the world a favor and make sure it was himself.

Jon knew he was still touchy about his right to be in the Aggressors. He was probably too young, too green. Most folks were good enough to ignore how many strings his father had pulled to land Jon at Nellis. But he'd made members of the 64th into his second family. He'd never really be versed in how to trust a *real* family, so they were the best he'd ever have. Putting up with shit that risked their lives was a fucking no-go.

"Agreed," Ryan said with a slight smile. "He's arrogant and needs a little…seasoning. But not by you. If the CO gets wind of it, your ass will be hemmed up. Prove you can do him some good rather than just flinging trash. Otherwise I'll pair you with another pilot for the next week of sorties."

"And then there goes my fun. Are we done?"

Ryan's gaze was steady and unwavering as he probed. His unwillingness to back down was one of the qualities that made him a good leader. "For now," was all he said. He patted the roof of the car as he stood and walked away. Leah followed, tossing a wave over her shoulder.

Fucking hell. Jon drummed his fingers on the open window of the Aston Martin. He'd been still riding high on the frustration of trying to teach Donaghue a lesson when Heather's call came through. Talking her through her orgasm, spilling dirty French words out as quickly as he could think of them, had been a hell of a way to unwind. Now that outlet had dissolved.

He'd just have to see one of her orgasms in person and work on a few of his own.

Jon wasn't sure why he was taken aback that Heather lived in an actual house. He'd assumed she was just like him, efficient and modern and living in a condo.

Instead, the tidy Craftsman bungalow on the outskirts of Vegas had plenty of character. The walls were stucco. A porch made of dark-stained wooden beams clung to the front as he walked up the path.

When he rang the doorbell, he heard no response from inside. He checked his watch. Six on the dot. The Air Force had taught him punctuality, even if it had failed to help him ignore dickweeds who put his friends at risk.

He shoved the memory of Donaghue and his air jockeying away. Tonight was about Heather and her birthday. He rang the doorbell again.

This time came the quiet clatter of high heels across wooden floors. The door swung open.

"You look gorgeous."

"That took you somewhere around three-fourths of a second to say." Her smile was secretive again—teasing him, sure, but with a darker edge. "I'm supposed to believe you?"

He tugged her close. The kiss he stole was slow. Careful. Hopefully tantalizing as hell. "It doesn't take me any longer than that to see you."

Pure truth, just like he always spoke.

She wore a dark green wraparound dress that dipped low across her cleavage and clung to her tiny waist. Red lipstick turned her mouth into a lush pout of eroticism—and reminded Jon to wipe their kiss off his lips with a linen handkerchief. She'd swept her hair up again, baring the smooth line of her neck. His skin twitched at the memory of his hands there.

He shoved that away too, along with the beginnings of an erection. Oh, he planned to get to that, but later. He wanted to pick her apart, figure out what made her tick.

He wasn't exactly the relationship type—lack of shining examples and all that. But even he saw the appeal of sticking together for another time or two. What made her able to walk away from their single night together when he'd relived so many moments?

Inside Bet

He liked tucking her into his car. Heather was a woman to be pampered, whether she knew it or not. She looked up at him as she gracefully swung her legs inside. "Where are we going?"

He rounded to the driver's side before answering. "La Rocca. I still owe you dinner."

"You were able to get reservations that easily? You *have* to explain that one. Jenn and I waited three months."

He kept his speed down as the powerful car rumbled through Heather's quiet neighborhood. At some point he intended to get them out on the open road and let it rip. He wanted to know if she'd love it as much as he did.

"My parents were one of Mr. La Rocca's earliest patrons. They staked his first restaurant in Hyannis."

She twisted in the bucket seat, watching him. "Hyannis? As in Kennedy-compound Hyannis?"

"Near enough." He smiled at her. "Impressed?"

"Surprised is more like it." Pale blue eyes narrowed. "Carlisle and Hyannis. Why does that sound so familiar?"

"Because my grandfather was a post-war financial pioneer. Pretty sure his theories are still taught in the universities."

"He certainly was in mine. Not just for his aggressive investment strategies but for shutting down his firm."

"Turned out my father had absolutely zero interest in working. At anything." Jon rolled stiff shoulders. "Grandfather was rather disheartened. Always said he should've waited around for me."

"How in the world did you end up in the Air Force?"

"It's the only way to fly fighter jets." He lifted her hand and kissed her knuckles without taking his eyes off the road. Then he nibbled softly on the pad of her thumb. "And ladies love a fighter pilot."

She shivered, but she was too smart to be put off the scent. "No," she said, drawing the word out. "That's not it. Not all of it, at least. You'd never be hurting for female companionship."

He blew out a tight breath. They were halfway to the restaurant. If he worked it right, he could distract her, but he found himself talking anyway—part of Heather's strange magic. "It's the rush and the challenge. My older sister died when I was in my freshman year of high school."

She made a soft sound of sympathy, but he shook it off.

"It was sad," he said, keeping his tone even. Just facts. "But it also helped me find flying. After...that, I spent a lot of time with the pilots who flew my dad's private jet. As soon as I stepped in the cockpit, I knew where I had to be."

"And you had to be the best of the best."

"Of course," he said glibly. This wasn't how he'd meant to start their evening. His ribs felt compressed. "What's the point of doing anything if you're not the best?"

Silence filtered through the cabin of the car, broken only by the steady rumble of the engine and some idiot honking two lanes over. Jon slid his ass an inch or two in the seat. Uncomfortable wasn't even the word. He couldn't remember the last time he'd mentioned Sara, not even in passing. His parents didn't like to talk about her, and Jon's closest friends knew only the barest details.

Heather's hand smoothed over his thigh. The muscles he'd inadvertently flexed suddenly eased under the touch.

"I know one thing you're the best at," she finally said.

He allowed himself to chuckle. "I thought you were worried about my ego."

"Maybe I've decided I deserve another birthday present."

"That's a certainty."

"Jon?" Her voice hit that husky timbre he was coming to know—and to anticipate. "You should know something."

"Oh?"

She scraped her nails over his slacks. "I didn't wear panties tonight."

He slanted her a long, hungry look despite the traffic on the Strip. Heather, bare under that clingy dress. Any arousal would paint the tops of her thighs with moisture.

She was playing dirty pool. Jon had no idea how he'd keep his hands off her through dinner.

Chapter Fifteen

They weren't going to make it to La Rocca. Heather had started to think of the restaurant as her own white whale. Roadblocks closed off main avenues as police directed traffic onto side streets. The lights of two ambulances and a fire truck in the distance meant this was no ordinary evening snarl.

"I have an idea," she said. "Pull off here, into the Wynn."

Jon nodded and smoothly took advantage of a momentary break in the oncoming traffic. He zipped onto Wynn Avenue. More cars. The line for the valet was backed up to the street.

"Forget it." Heather pointed. "Drive back to the self-park."

His dubious expression, with an eyebrow arched in blueblood disdain, made her smile. Such a snob she'd found. Not for the first time she wondered what he would make of her upbringing. But then her thoughts strayed toward what he would think of her parents, should they ever meet—and that stopped her quick.

No future. No plans.

She rummaged for her BlackBerry as Jon navigated toward the self-park garage. After scrolling through her contacts, she placed the call. "Hello, Peter? It's Heather Morris. I wonder if you could do me a huge favor?"

Peter Bloom was her main contact at the Wynn. The confirmed workaholic was probably still at his desk in the corporate offices on the north side. Sane people stayed away from the Strip, even if it was their business.

"Anything, Heather. I can't recall you ever asking."

"Never had the need." She liked that she used her favors judiciously, hoarding them like a squirrel with acorns. "Could you snag me a table at The Country Club, maybe the corporate table out by the falls?"

"No one has it this evening, that I know of. I'll do what I can."

"And phone in a temp tag too?"

"Of course. Any chance you can do my visit a week early in repayment?"

"I'm sorry, I can't. We have half your prep work to do yet."

"What, you can't bend time and space?"

"One day I'll get it right. Thanks again."

Heather switched off the call as Jon pulled the DBS around to the parking structure. She directed him to an upper level reserved for professional visitors. Unlike the lower ramps where cars jockeyed for any available space, the guest area was nearly deserted. Heather chatted with the security guard, who called in to confirm their temp tag.

"That's good news." She took Jon's arm as they crossed toward the pedestrian exit. "Peter works fast and he never takes no for an answer."

"Peter?"

"My contact here at the Wynn. We do their audits."

"So, Ms. Morris can pull a few strings of her own? Nice."

She smiled, inordinately proud of being able to swing this. Jon was rich as Croesus, but she'd worked too hard not to benefit from her dedication and skill.

The resort was abuzz with activity, regardless of it being a Wednesday night. Sin City had no regard for days of the week. Heather pressed more deeply against Jon's body as they navigated through the corridors. Tourists queued for an evening show.

If anything, his attire was even more immaculate than what he'd worn to the wine tasting. This was Jon making an effort. His vest was a striking silk brocade in colors of deep blue and charcoal gray, flecked with silver threads. The suit itself was a classic wool blend in matching charcoal. Its trim, tailored cut was almost mod, accentuating his lean strength. A midnight-blue tie and a crisp white collar circled his throat. The tendons along his nape looked especially powerful, revealed by his buzz cut.

She didn't know how she could stand it. The urge to tug him into a dark corner and hitch her legs around his hips was almost too powerful. Only the knowledge that they were in a casino, with the universe's most intense camera and security systems, kept her on good behavior. For now.

The Country Club was themed with Scottish décor, as if they'd traveled across the Atlantic instead of across town. Jon eyed the place with a satisfying degree of approval. She had to stop hoping to impress him. It gave away the power she fought so hard to keep.

"Ms. Morris," said the maître d' as they arrived. "Mr. Bloom told us to expect you. Right this way."

Minutes later they settled at the table reserved for wining and dining the Wynn's various subcontractors. Situated on a golf course, the forty-foot waterfall off the eighteenth green created a white-noise backdrop. Conversations felt almost private, with the sounds of the Strip washed away. The idyllic, lush setting seemed so far removed from the sparse desert just beyond its obsessively tended limits.

"Nice," Jon said, his gaze lost over the rolling course. "Very nice."

Heather swallowed a heady bubble of fulfillment. Her birthday. Her little magic trick.

"May I take your drink order, ma'am?"

"Scottish milkshake," she said without hesitation.

Jon shot her an incredulous look then returned his attention to the fresh-faced male waiter. "*Cuvée Speciale Cent Cinquantenaire.*"

The waiter nodded and provided menus before turning away.

"Show off," she said to Jon. "You could've just called it Grand Marnier like a normal person."

"It's *special* Grand Marnier." He grinned. "Besides, I've resolved to use French whenever possible. One must practice to maintain fluency."

"I'm convinced you memorized some tourist tape. When you speak to me, you're reciting how to ask for a doctor or the location of the nearest payphone."

"*Où se trouve le téléphone public? J'ai besoin d'un médecin.*"

Heather's thighs tensed. He was teasing her, talking payphones and doctors, but it didn't matter. The intent behind his eyes was the same as if he'd been discussing plans to duck under the table and eat her out. An easy prospect, considering her secret state of undress.

"What did you wear to work that Monday morning?" His gaze heated her throat.

Another sudden jump in her arousal.

She *had* been able to look in the mirror, luckily—mostly because she'd been the one to initiate so many of their encounters. The enormity of what they'd done together only increased with the passing days...until seeing him on her front porch. Then she'd just wanted more.

"I have a silk blouse with a Mandarin collar."

His lips tugged into a lopsided smile.

The menus were a welcome distraction. She realized she wasn't *playing* cool—merely trying to maintain it. Her eyes lurched along the complicated list of ingredients in each dish, the hallmark of a high-end restaurant that still made her smile.

"It's never simple," she muttered to herself. "I mean, what's wrong with a pulled-pork sandwich? I can't even hazard a guess at what chimichurri is." Jon began to explain, but she waved him off. "Don't bother."

He set his menu aside. "So, what do you consider a luxury?"

"Anything I didn't have as a child."

The answer was so automatic that she suffered a fast blush. He was underhanded and sneaky. She should've seen it coming.

"Such as?"

"Juice boxes. Pop-Tarts. Velveeta."

"Velveeta?" Jon shook his head, his smile a touch confused. "You're going to have to explain."

"To the alien from Planet Hyannis?"

The waiter returned with their drinks. Heather asked for a filet, rare, while Jon ordered the rack of lamb. Only when the waiter had departed did Jon nod to her milkshake. "What's in it?"

"Whiskey. Glenlivet twelve-year, actually."

He borrowed her straw to take a sip. "Damn, that's not bad. Too bad I'm driving. One-drink limit."

"And flying tomorrow?"

"That too." His fingers on his crystal tumbler, he met her eyes. "Now back to the Velveeta."

"I see how your mind works," she said. "I grew up just how you'd imagine where brand-name anything was a luxury. My mom would volunteer for the city when they'd get a delivery of government-issue cheese. At the end of distributing it for a day, she'd get to take home a few of the five-pound blocks."

"I had no idea."

"It freezes, you know. Cheese. Keeps for a long time that way. You hardly notice the difference in texture if it's in casseroles. Velveeta was better." Heather sipped her decadent milkshake, if only to convince herself that those days were behind her.

"What did your parents do?"

"Mom stayed at home. Dad retired a sergeant-major. Army."

Jon's eyebrow lifted. "Ah. A sergeant-major's daughter. That explains a great deal." Leave it to him to read between the lines, making assumptions about how she spent her wild-child youth. "Then you went to college. Chose a sensible major."

"With a guaranteed career afterward, yeah. Now I'm angling to be director. Dull, right? But do me a favor?"

"Hm?"

"Don't turn that into a point of martyrdom," she said. "I love my job."

Their food arrived, bearing with it the fragrant aroma of rich living. Heather's steak was a decadent creation, full-flavored and tender. She let the taste lure her away from difficult memories, basking in the moment. The desert night air, the sound of the waterfall—and Jon across from her, looking for all the world like modern-day royalty.

Except for the buzzed head.

She licked salty juices off her lower lip, enjoying how he watched her. Always. "Why in the world did you join the military?"

"I told you. The planes."

"But why not...astronaut?"

Leaning back from the table, his lamb half devoured, he affected the casual air that insisted all was well. He might not admit to lying with his mouth, but every calculated movement created an alternate version of the real Jon—whoever that was. Heather had to remind herself that she preferred him this way. The hedonistic young prince. Her heart would trip on any more honesty.

"I'll admit to a certain degree of youthful rebellion," he said.

"You did it to spite your parents?"

He shrugged. "They could brag me up joining NASA."

"Not serving your country?"

"Not so much." Elbows on the table, he pitched his voice to a conspiratorial whisper. "But do me a favor?"

Hearing the echo of her words, she smiled. "Hm?"

"Don't turn that into a point of heroism. Someday maybe I'll fly commercial liners, or even design new aircraft. For now it's the speed."

"How did you manage to keep access to your bank account, what with pissing off Mummy and Daddy?"

"My grandfather. He flew fighters in WWII, over Sicily and Italy." He skewered a bite of lamb. "Back when rich men's sons still thought it their duty to go to war. He lost his leg."

"I'm sorry."

Jon grinned. "Don't be. He parlayed his father's industrial fortune into scads more and made the most out of his injury. Even there at the end, he had the sympathy of lovely young women."

"So you take after him, then?"

"All I know is that I'll still be irresistible at eighty."

He pushed the plate away with a slight groan. Heather felt the same way, stuffed full of indescribable fare.

Jon's attention went somewhere far away, looking out over the shadowed golf course. "I went home on leave between tours. He wanted to see me. There he was, in the medical suite in his mansion, surrounded by a cadre of gorgeous nurses he'd personally chosen. He told me three things...the first being that he was proud of me."

His voice choked off. Heather couldn't look away, no matter how his sudden emotion messed with her respiration. She'd felt the same aching pang upon learning that he'd lost his older sister. Puzzle pieces were aligning to make him into a rational whole, not the enigma she'd assumed. That made him even more vulnerable. Human. Dangerous.

"I didn't join up to make anyone proud," he said after clearing his throat. He was Jon again, wearing a cocky grin. "Second, he told me I was set for life, and that I'd become an irredeemable punk because of it. His words."

"Nice."

"But his last point was that the choice was mine. I could make something of myself or...coast." He looked out toward the waterfall. "My old man had the last laugh, though. I finished my second tour and found out I'd been transferred here to the 64th. Mom was tired of me in harm's way. They'd made a few calls to secure the transfer then appealed to my ego." He threw back the last of his Grand Marnier, rather than sip. "So here I am. The best of the best. Like you said."

Mommy and Daddy pulling strings. It didn't sit well on him, no matter his obvious pride in his job. The casual calm he'd maintained so well throughout dinner all but disappeared. He fidgeted with the tines of an unused salad fork.

"You'll have to show me your fighter sometime," she said.

His lips pressed together. Heather realized what she'd done. Plans. A future. She'd invited that possibility, when even hazarding a guess about the next evening was a bad idea.

"We'll see."

His words should have been a relief. He was letting her mistake slide. But Heather didn't like being cast adrift by his locked-down expression.

"Come on," he said, standing unexpectedly. "Let's get out of here."

Chapter Sixteen

Jon had not told Heather about his grandfather in order to garner some twisted sympathy.

But that's what it had felt like when she suggested seeing his jet. Her voice had been soft and her eyes dark with compassion. He'd been on the receiving end of plenty of that bullshit his freshman year when kids told him how sorry they were while whispering behind his back about Sara's car accident. Reaching out to his parents had only revealed cold automatons. At least he'd found a measure of quiet in the air—peace, while the speed screamed through his mind.

For fuck's sake, he wanted Heather to ask to see his jet because it got her hot. Because she wanted to know more about him. Not because it was a bone to throw him when he was being maudlin.

Yet even as his steps quickened, weaving through the lower levels of the Wynn, he realized what a prize Heather was on his arm. Smart, beautiful and incredibly astute. Any man would be proud to keep her attention.

If only she didn't have that way of prying inside him.

They approached his car in the nearly empty ranks of the parking garage. Heather tugged on his suit coat. "Where are we going?"

Shit. He hadn't planned anything, meaning to get her talking. He wanted any clue about her, to make sure this was a birthday she wouldn't forget. Instead she'd gotten *him* to talk.

They turned to face one another. Jon leaned her against the passenger-side door. "It's your night. Why don't you tell me?"

Her hands slid around the back of his jacket, flirting with the bottom hem of his vest. She looked perfectly at home lounging against such a wild beast of a car—like she could tame it.

"Don't tell me wicked Jon Carlisle is out of ideas." She stretched up on her toes to whisper in his ear. The soft wash of her breath tingled over his neck. "I think you've forgotten one important fact."

Inside Bet

"What's that?"

"I'm still not wearing panties."

His body dropped into overdrive, like when his F-16 screamed off the runway. "Trust me, Heather love. There hasn't been an instant I've forgotten. Your beautiful pussy bare under your dress—and how easily I could slide my hand up your leg. Touch you."

She flicked her tongue across his earlobe. "But you haven't done it. I thought even you didn't have that much restraint."

He had restraint. Buckets of it. Enough to turn her inside out with want, even in the yellow-lit cave of the parking garage.

Stroking gently, he traced up her sides until he grazed the full swell of her breasts. Just a glancing touch, enough to make her think of potential.

"You like to play with fire, don't you, Ms. Morris?"

"I used to. And then I got burned."

Tilting his head, he touched his mouth to the bend where her chin met her throat—the exact place he'd clamped while fucking her. "But here you are. Again. You couldn't have been *too* singed."

Her eyes went dark as her irises widened. "I thought I got over it."

"Over what?"

"The recklessness." She laced her fingers behind his neck and pressed her chest against his. "But you're right. Here I am."

Too many layers of cloth between them. He loved dressing finely. There was a certain skill in putting forth the impression he wanted others to see. He would quickly come to regret his hubris if it meant restricting contact between him and Heather.

"We're not being that bad," he said, keeping his voice low. "This is barely a hug. This is what kids do after dates at the movies."

"I don't feel like a kid." She'd hit that husky tone again—a promise of delights to come.

Jon dipped low to stroke her hips in a languid caress. "No. No, you don't."

"Anyway, I don't think you'd have liked me when I was young. No challenge."

"You certainly are a challenge, Ms. Morris." He wove his fingers into her hair and tilted her head back. "Luckily I'm the kind of man who rises to the occasion."

He kissed her, intending it to stay slow. Tempting. But fuck if he wasn't quickly losing the reins. Again. She wrapped her arms around his shoulders and pressed up on her toes. Their mouths slid together hard. Fast.

He drew her tongue into his mouth and sucked. Sharp fingernails dug into the back of his neck.

And then he lost the next sortie too. With his hands under her skirt, he found the long expanse of her thigh—and the moisture that dampened the crease of her sweet pussy. He cupped her smooth mound, gratified when her arms tightened.

She pressed up into his touch, until he slid a single finger between her lips. Slick wetness was his reward. Her clit was already swollen and hot.

The moan started in her chest and released into his mouth, barely more than a breath.

"You're already wet for me, Ms. Morris," he said silkily. The tender line of her throat was practically begging for his teeth. So he indulged, locking tight over the cord that stood out in stark relief. Then he soothed the area with long, deliberate licks. "Tell me what you want and it's yours."

Heather bent her head to the side, allowing him all the space he needed to nibble her sugar-sweet skin. "I want your cock," she whispered. "Fucking me so deep that I feel it all the way through me."

He bit her neck—hard enough to leave a red mark. When had he come to enjoy seeing his brand on her skin?

"*Here*, Ms. Morris?" He kept circling her clit. "You're even braver than I thought."

She drew back to look in his eyes. The parking garage was almost empty of cars, and he'd chosen a space at the far end of the row. But that didn't completely ameliorate the possibility of discovery.

"Maybe I just want this more." Her hands worked at his belt then slid down his zipper. "Do you have any idea how reckless you make me feel?"

It couldn't be half as insane as she made him. He kissed her hard, taking that anxiety from her, letting it ride him to a fine edge of control.

Inside Bet

He dug a condom out of his inside coat pocket. Their hands fumbled together as they both tried to roll it down his cock. The touch of her soft fingers on his shaft made his balls draw up with anticipation.

Her skirt rucked between them with a couple fast grabs. Jon bent his knees a fraction, thankful once again for their almost matching height.

Then there was nothing but the hot welcome of her pussy. Clench and suck. The way her hands delved beneath his suit coat to wrap around his back.

He thrust slowly, quietly, not wanting to make a spectacle of them both. God, she went to his head. Got under his skin. He pushed harder. His hips knocked into hers until her head dropped back on a groan. Her dark hair brushed against the roof of his convertible.

He slid his hands around her hips to cushion her from the metal. They were *wild* together. Explosive. Straining like they wanted to meld into a fiery ball.

A stream of French poured out of his mouth against the curve of her neck. She shuddered, pinned between his deep thrusts and the unrelenting car door. "More," she gasped.

He'd gladly give her more. Everything.

The gathering haze of his climax almost concealed the clatter and hum of approaching voices. Almost. His breath choked in his lungs as he tried to get his bearings.

"Shh," he whispered in her ear. "Someone's coming."

Heather froze. Her eyes went wide. But then that sultry, secret smile curved her red mouth. She licked her lips and spread her fingers wide under the bottom hem of his vest.

Swiftly, he tugged her skirt down around her ass, covering her. He moved his hands to the sleek line of her back, just a man and woman embracing. He didn't withdraw. His open coat concealed how they were sealed together.

He bent low to her ear. "Do you want to be caught, Ms. Morris? Because your cunt is clenching down on me so tightly that I think you do."

"Not particularly."

"But the idea? That's enough." He wound through the silken mass of her hair and cupped the back of her head. "You're so hot, you could come like this, couldn't you?"

Her breath was shaky. "And you? You're not immune."

The voices drew nearer, but the concrete walls meant he couldn't tell their direction. "Not at all. But be quiet. Don't come."

Her hips jerked against him. He kept pushing in tiny, miniscule twitches, his cock moving gently inside her. She bit her lower lip.

"Don't come, Ms. Morris," he purred. "Don't moan. They'll catch us. See you so hot. So horny you're going to explode all over my dick. So wanton. Like a slut so hungry for it she can't even wait to get somewhere private."

Her hands gripped his back even as her sheath clenched his cock.

Then she drew her head back to study him. "Who, exactly, has more to lose in this scenario, Captain Carlisle? Hmm?" Slipping her hands into the back of his pants, she gripped his ass. Squeezed. "What do they call it? Behavior unbecoming?"

Goddamn it. He mashed his face against her shoulder and beat back the orgasm threatening to take him down.

Her mouth slid over his throat, along the line of his collar. She licked. Long and slow, likely leaving a bright trail of red lipstick.

She was winning. Again.

Deep breaths didn't get his head together. But it was enough. Barely.

Somehow he managed to pull out of her. She made a soft sound of protest, and her hands clenched his ass cheeks. He tucked himself back into his slacks and zipped them up—condom and all, for Christ's sake. Another few swift motions tugged her skirt down to cover her wet pussy.

He spun out one of his slow, special smiles. "You're right, Ms. Morris. By all means, let's not get in trouble."

He handed her into the car, ignoring the confusion in her eyes, which was rapidly turning to annoyance. Maybe even anger. As Jon shut the car door, her lush, erotic mouth plumped into a pout he'd never seen but dearly relished.

Only when he stalked around the back of the car, crossing to his door, did he scrub a hand over his face. He was shaking. Wanting her. Needing to be back inside her.

"You have got to be kidding," she said as he climbed into the driver's seat.

Jon only popped the convertible top and fired up the ignition.

Driving took extra effort as he peeled out of the parking garage. The purring rumble of the engine shook into his bones. He pushed the speed limit, edging faster and faster.

He aimed the Aston Martin out of Las Vegas, deep into the desert. And floored it.

Chapter Seventeen

Heather sank into the leather bucket seat as the desert night whipped against her face. She glared absently at the dashboard. The lights of the city faded into a glow in her door mirror, with nothing but open road stretching ahead of them.

She'd wondered what Jon and the sleek black Aston Martin could do if unleashed. She was in no mood to appreciate either. Her body still hummed and spun itself inside out while her mind grappled with the impossible.

Jon had stopped. Stopped cold.

The embarrassment she expected to feel didn't come. Getting caught in that parking garage would've been a professional disaster for both of them. Where was her sense of self-preservation? Her sense of shame?

All gone.

Only a petulant sort of anger remained. She was actually *pissed* at her spoilsport date.

Her birthday. Her body. Her rules.

The alternative, that he'd already claimed so much of her, was too frightening to consider. Pushing away fear was considerably easier when all she risked was the physical. Jon had proved remarkably considerate on that score.

She wanted her lover. Not this odd pinched feeling in her chest.

A semi's distant lights drew nearer as the amazing DBS ran it down. Predator and prey. Jon popped it into fifth, his grip tense on the gearshift. The tendons running up the back of his hand and wrist snapped taut with the motion. The ease he usually displayed when driving was gone.

Closer now, and closer still, he hadn't changed lanes to overtake the lumbering truck. Heather gripped the armrest on the passenger side door. Night air scored her cheeks as the Aston punched up past ninety. Her heartbeat tripled. At the last possible moment, Jon smoothly dove into the outside lane. They darted past the semi as the driver blasted his horn.

"Are you *insane?*" she yelled over the whip of wind.

Jon merely glanced her way, that depraved smile twisting his lips. Maybe he was only enjoying the thrill of the ride. Maybe he was inviting her to return to their former play. All Heather knew was that the sight of him handling that powerful machine with such ease was more than she could stand. Her body was already so keyed up, so overheated, that it clamored for more. More of him.

With nothing stretched ahead but flat blacktop, he shifted up to sixth. Hundreds of horsepower growled under the hood. The vibration sank into her skin, like the steady bite of a hot, hot shower. Sensation built, gathering, almost numbing, but constantly raising the stakes. Release, when it came, would be overwhelming.

Heather reached across the chasm that had opened between them. She wanted to touch him. Needed to. She started with his hand on the gearshift, unwilling to distract him too much. Their speed was up to one hundred now. Threading her fingers over his, she felt the humming vibration where man met machine. *He* controlled that power. The thrill shot a bolt of heat between her thighs.

Trailing her fingers higher, she worked up to his shoulder, his nape, the top of his head. Jon made a rumbling noise in his throat, one she could only feel. Sound had been claimed by the rushing flow of air, which cooled but didn't remedy her flushed skin.

Eyes still on the road, he darted his tongue to lick the inside of her forearm. Heather slid her hand to press her index finger along the seam of his lips. He opened, sucking her then biting her. Pain spiked to a sharp burn. She gasped, arched a little. Just when the discomfort became too much, he circled his tongue and soothed where his teeth had trapped her first knuckle.

Giving her ring finger over to his care, Heather tugged the hem of her skirt. She found her clit, as cool air rushed over her wet arousal. Jon gunned the engine and sucked deeply. More teeth, more tongue, while the car purred down the desert highway. Speed and sex made her work faster, building a steady, quick orgasm.

She retrieved her hand from his mouth and dipped inside her low-slung neckline. The lace of her bra gave way on a downward tug. Her

111

twisting pressure on the nipple ring was a steady counterpoint to the beat of her fingers. She dipped inside, scooping more of that slick wetness, soothing it over her engorged nerves. Breath labored, throat burning, she gasped.

"Let me hear you," he said, his voice carrying past the whip and rush. "No breathy sighs this time."

The wind made it easy. The speed made it easy. She leaned back into the leather, knees wide, cunt bared, and found the rhythm that reminded her of their slapping bodies. Fast. Steady. Utterly focused. The quiet sounds inside of her turned violent. She moaned, her hips grinding up, eager now for an aching hollow to be filled. That moan became louder—a hard scream bubbling, waiting to be freed.

She thrashed her head to the side, pinning her gaze to Jon's hard profile. His back teeth were pressed tight. A muscle bunched like a fist at the curve of his jaw.

"I'm coming. Oh, God, do you know what you do to me? Jon, I'm coming."

Fire jumped across her nerves. With a fierce shriek she snapped taut, chin lifted, bared breasts thrust out.

Jon downshifted, heavy on the brakes. The Aston angled to the shoulder until he brought it to a stop. Before the last of Heather's orgasm had faded, he threw it into park. Out of the car. Around the back.

He yanked the passenger-side door open, his hand clamped around her upper arm. All she could manage was to unbuckle the seat belt before he hauled her to her feet. He was all power, all violence, as if the ferocity of the sports car still pounded beneath his flesh.

Jon shoved her around the door and pressed her against the hood. Hot metal seared her back in a delicious burn. She hissed. Her muscles seized against that shock.

Dimly, beyond sensation and a dark buzzing in her ears, Heather heard his zipper.

"Condom," she managed to gasp.

"It's still there, Heather love. I'm so fucking hard." His mouth was at her throat. Teeth. A sucking, wrenching kiss. She hitched a heel up his back. Opened for him. "Ah, *Jesus.*"

He took her. Hard. That fabulous cock drove her back against the hood. Jon flattened his palms over her ass cheeks, forcing them apart. Sensation sizzled against that private skin. But she could no more escape him than she wanted him to stop.

Her body stayed exactly where he wanted, pinned beneath his rocking thrusts. The rushing wind had disappeared but none of the power or speed. His rhythmic grunts rumbled against her breastbone. He feasted on her breasts. The harder, sharper sound of their colliding hips fueled her arousal like gasoline on open flames.

Her other foot left the ground. She hooked her ankles behind his back. Jon took the opportunity to arch her even further, with one hand between her breasts until she lay fully across the hood. She fought that pressure, her hips working, but he pressed harder.

"You're not in charge here, Ms. Morris." Thrusts punctuated his rasped words. "You can tease me and tempt me, but I'm not letting you win every round."

A thrilling panic nipped at her mind. Jon had her. He wasn't stopping. Only the safe word would challenge his control now, but she didn't want to use it—didn't want the torment to end.

It was too much. She couldn't. The pounding. He was demanding too much.

"Can't. Jon, I can't."

His mouth found her nipple, but he didn't suck or tease—only whispered wet words against her skin. "No fear. Not now. Sink into it. Take it. Take *me*."

She eased along his voice as he flowed between English and French. Her body began to shake. She cried out. Again. Her hands found the back of his head then under his collar and down his back. Rough bunches of muscle tensed and flexed. His skin gave way beneath her nails. Sweat slicked her fingertips.

"I'm here, Heather love. I have you."

Her climax ripped a scream from her throat. She thrust her hips, overcome by long, wrenching gasps. Blood rushed in her ears. Jon's body pistoned, levering her pelvis higher as he continued to pound.

"Heather," he ground out. "I'm...holy *fuck*."

He tensed, his eyes rolling back, his parted lips frozen in exquisite bliss. A few shuddering pulses later he bowed over her stomach. His chest heaved. Heather lay against the hood as it cooled, her eyes on the stars, her hands caressing the back of his head.

"Happy birthday to me," she quietly cooed. A bubble of laughter wiggled up out of her gut. It turned into a full-blown laugh.

Grinning, Jon slid his hands to her waist, adding a tickle. She jerked away, her smile matching his. He pushed up. Strong arms bracketed her on either side. Rather than imagine being trapped, Heather felt protected. She remembered his gasping words, the words that had helped her let go.

I'm here, Heather love.

They froze. Face-to-face. Their bodies still joined.

Tentatively, as if for the first time, she touched his cheek. He pressed a kiss against the cup of her palm then nuzzled. She hooked her elbow behind his neck and drew him down for a long, slow, lingering kiss. This was cotton-candy sweetness. Decadent care. Tenderness that melted her spine.

Feeling languid and boneless, she accepted Jon's help in peeling away from the hood. His tie was loose and askew, with three buttons on his dress shirt popped. He looked as blasted as she felt.

He brought his hand away from the metal and flexed his fingers. "Christ, Heather, how's your back?"

"I'll find out tomorrow."

He only shook his head, his smile bewildered. She liked seeing him that way—slightly out of step with the man he pretended to be. She was getting used to feeling the same way about herself.

A shiver raced across her shoulders. Jon stripped off his suit coat. He draped it around her before she could protest. His heat held her as much as the wool. Fingers interlaced, he led her to the edge of the asphalt. They sat side by side, with the desert illuminated by only a slice of moon and the cab light of his Aston.

"Best birthday," she whispered.

"Hm?"

"My best birthday. This one."

He looked at her with something close to wariness, maybe suspicion. She knew because that was how she always looked at him. Nothing had prepared her for that realization.

"Thank you," she went on. "I... Your competition tonight was renting a movie."

"Maybe I didn't need to try so hard."

She smiled. The moment between them was so calm and close that she ducked into his arms, holding on tight. He petted a hand beneath the coat she wore, just where the tattoo colored her skin. Why was it so easy to be completely fearless with him, but difficult to simply...*be*?

"But after all, I deserve a bit of pampering."

"That you do," he said quietly.

Something warm and soft opened in her chest. This was dangerous, but she needed to do it. Needed to. The reward could be worth the risk, as it had been all along.

"Worst birthday was my seventeenth."

Jon stopped petting. He held his breath, as did the desert.

"It was the weekend of my dad's retirement. I was in selfish-bitch mode, thinking I owned the day. God, Jon, I was such a mess."

"A mess? I can't imagine it."

"Recall what you know about when I lost my virginity. Now picture that desperate girl three years later." She swallowed, biting back a hot rush of tears. "Dad was so proud that day. Mom only wanted me to behave. Just for the afternoon, and then I'd be free to party with my friends that evening."

"I don't think you made it." There was no teasing in his words, only a quiet understanding that scored her heart.

"I was drunk by four. I was in the backseat of a Ford Focus by the time night fell." She shuddered. "And the thing is? It wasn't even any good. Just...a thing to do. Not..."

Jon turned her body toward his, her face in his hands. She breathed his breath before they actually kissed. Lips softly met lips. His thumbs stroked the apples of her cheeks. "Not what?"

Heather closed her eyes. "Not like this. Jon, no matter what else happens..."

"You'll always have the happy memory of waking every gopher for a hundred miles."

She couldn't help but laugh. Every emotion was too raw, too close to the surface. So she indulged in the easy ones—the feel of his body, the surprising openness of his humor. Tension eased away on a shaky exhalation. "You can take me home now, Captain."

He arched one brow. "I fly at oh eight hundred."

God, that was sexy. Unbelievably so.

"Then you'll have to drive fast."

Chapter Eighteen

Jon had never particularly feared Darth Vader when he was a kid but dread curled through his stomach when the Imperial Death March droned from his phone. Served him right for assigning it as his parents' ringtone.

He sat down on his couch before answering and listened to the cell ring. Letting his parents twist was a bit of a hobby, so he might as well do it right.

Eventually he thumbed the phone. "Carlisle."

"I suppose we can thank heavens you haven't abandoned the family name." His mother's voice was cultured. Perfectly accented and smooth.

His shoulders tightened. He put his heels up on the low console table. A faint memory of a voice calling, "No shoes on the wood," echoed through his head, but it wasn't his mother's voice. That had been Constance, the housekeeper.

As far as Jon's mother was concerned, he could have tap-danced on the tables as long as he put up the appropriate front in public.

"So good to hear from you too, Mother," he drawled. "Did you and Father go to Europe this year?"

He'd rather thought they might have gone to the South of France for the summer. He hadn't heard from them for seven blissful weeks.

"Not for long. Only three weeks in Nice. Such a whirlwind trip, I barely had a chance to unwind. Not to mention the crown princess stopped by for four nights, and you know how much of a bother she is."

Jon's mother nattered on while he all but rolled his eyes. He would've, had she been able to see him, just to emphasize his disdain. For all her complaints, his mother absolutely lived to host royalty. It was the center and heart of her life.

He fished his computer tablet out from under a couch cushion.

Turning the volume down low, he played a game while letting his mother talk. And talk. And talk.

Eventually she ran out of steam. "Besides, darling. I called for you."

He glanced at the time. Thirty-seven minutes. "What about me?"

"I want to make sure you're going tonight."

Yes, that was exactly the way it worked. His mother went on at length about her life then concerned herself with Jon to issue autocratic orders. Their relationship couldn't continue like this—not if he wanted to stay sane—yet he had no idea how to fix them. Twelve years on from Sara's crash and...nothing.

"You know I hate those things."

"This is the biggest charity event in Las Vegas all year."

He put the computer down. Either that or end up tossing the thing when their conversation went down the road he expected. "It's a charity event to fund *golf courses*."

"Those courses sponsor lots of underprivileged youths! Every bit helps, Jon. You know I've made philanthropy my guiding principle."

Since Jon's sister died. Yeah. He knew. Except she and his father had a weird twist on real philanthropy. "The economy sucks right now, Mother. Golf courses are the best we can do?"

"Don't use such language in front of me."

"I'm doing fine, by the way. Contributing to the Air Force teaching policy letters. Top of my squadron."

A faint sniff came over the line. He pictured his mother's nose wrinkling. Even on a Saturday morning, she'd be perfectly attired in a tailored skirt and blouse, with her dark brown hair carefully styled. She didn't use dye though, claiming the silver that shot tastefully from her temples gave her "gravitas".

He let the silence drag out. No saving her. She sniffed again. "You know I don't like to think of you in danger."

If that were the problem, Jon would eat his flight suit with a knife and fork. "I'm not dropping Grandfather's hard-earned cash on golf courses. He'd turn over in his grave." At least Grandfather would've understood, even if no one else in his family did.

"I already paid for your tickets, including one for a guest."

He fisted his free hand. Almost forty-five minutes of being able to hold on and relax, but he'd had it. They'd made intrusions on his love life over the years. Background checks and gossip and instructions to come visit, all of which were suspiciously timed. The idea that they'd know anything about Heather was enough to make his skin crawl.

But at the same time, he'd love it. They wouldn't be able to say a single bad word about her. Elegance and class. Only he knew about the gorgeous tattoo under her clothing. Or the nipple ring. Or that she could fuck wildly on the hood of his car and come so loud he heard it over the screaming wind.

"Mother, I had other plans." Preferably making Heather gasp his name.

"You'll go, Jon." Her voice had turned ice cold. She'd perfected that tone over the years. It had been incredibly effective in shutting down a fourteen-year-old who missed his sister. "You'll go and you'll be on your best behavior."

"Or what?" He rolled to his feet. Too much anxiety riding his bones to remain seated. "Not like you can cut me off. You lost that weapon years ago."

The silence dragged out with weight. He could picture her pinched mouth, the way her eyes would've gone from pale brown to gold. "Fine. I hope you remember you've driven me to this."

"To what?"

"Our new housekeeper found boxes of Sara's books in storage in the west attic. If you go, I'll send them to you."

Something hard and cold clenched in his chest. "Is this what we've come to? For golf courses?"

"This is what you've forced us to, Jonathan. Don't abdicate your responsibility."

He'd go. Of course he'd go. No way could he pass up his sister's belongings. Yet again, his mother had twisted his arm. He'd do what she wanted because he missed Sara. Contemplating the woman she would've become, his lone port in the storm when they were children, was agonizing. Only the loss of his grandfather matched that old pain.

Maybe he could still redeem the evening. After signing off with his mother amid terse words, he paced through his living room. He'd call Heather. See if she wanted to go with him. They'd returned to The Palazzo twice since her birthday, and he'd swung by her house for an incredible hot quickie after work, but it would be fun to show her off in public again.

They'd make it more...exciting. One way or the other.

Jon hated country clubs. Not for any particular offense beyond reminding him of his youth. They were decorated with the same wood-paneled walls and similar schemes, as if museum-quality relics of the post-WWII era. Moneyed. Snooty.

Cold. Antiquated. Irrelevant.

At least with Heather at his side, he could keep his mind on more palatable activities. For his mother to use Sara's books as blackmail still pounded renewed spikes of disappointment into his heart. One would think he would've learned years ago that *emotionally unavailable* didn't change.

It still hurt.

The luscious dip of Heather's cleavage was a much preferred line of thought. She wore a dark purple dress with a heart-shaped neckline, over which he wanted to trail his fingertips. Creamy pale skin swelled and enticed.

She watched him from over a martini. "Your gaze drops rather often, flyboy."

He flashed a smile. She didn't deserve his foul mood, but it wasn't going anywhere. Best to hide it. "Do you blame me?"

"Considering this dress, I'd be disappointed if it didn't."

"It's not the dress so much as the lovely way you fill it out."

She took a slow sip of the martini. Before she could reply, a portly man approached with a blonde on his arm.

"Jon," he said in a friendly tone. "We weren't certain you'd be able to come."

Jon couldn't place the man until he recognized him as Alexander Maxwell, owner of a small casino. Off-Strip. Not one of the quietly luxurious ones. Second-tier society. That Jon was so programmed to callously assess the man within seconds added extra disdain toward how he was raised.

"It's very difficult to say no to my mother."

"You're such a good son. My daughters are so busy they can hardly be bothered to show up."

"Well. How lucky you are that their friends are more accommodating." He eyed the arm candy in the red miniskirt.

Two circles of bright red popped up on Maxwell's florid cheeks. He still didn't introduce the young woman. She hardly seemed to notice, flitting her gaze around the huge ballroom. She appeared awestruck and way too naïve.

Heather's eyes flicked between Jon and Maxwell. "Jon, perhaps you could introduce me?"

"Terribly sorry. Rudeness only affects certain people." He rested his hand along the sultry curve of her lower back. Under his fingertips was her tattoo. A wicked secret to keep him grounded and to put a lid on his goddamn funk. "Heather Morris, allow me to introduce you to Alex Maxwell. Alex, Heather is in internal audits at Hanover Financial Logistics. You ought to switch your business to her firm. If everyone else there is half as smart as she is, you'll be well served."

Another woman might have blushed or demurred. Heather only lifted her brows before holding her hand out. She looked at the primped blonde and extended the same greeting. "It's lovely to meet you too. I'm sorry, I didn't catch your name?"

"Courtney." She fluttered fake eyelashes.

"You seem like a sweet girl, Courtney," Jon said. His earnestness surprised him. Maybe there was *some* good to be done that night. "If you would, let me give you a word of advice: run. Before it's too late. Maxwell won't treat you well for long. Sin City tempts some men into thinking pretty girls are interchangeable."

The girl paled. Damn, she was young. A sheep among wolves. Her hold on her date's arm, however, didn't loosen. Maxwell puffed up his chest. His mouth slipped open, but he didn't say a thing.

Jon would've *liked* for Maxwell to gainsay him, to contradict him and stand up for himself. Hell, if he had, Jon would've written a check from his own accounts for double what his parents contributed. But Maxwell sidestepped Jon's comments, offering instead something about the "noble endeavors" the event was intended to promote.

All because inner-city kids needed golf. Sure. More like they needed safe homes and better education, but the same people who would congratulate themselves on a productive night would probably lobby to reduce teachers' union rights.

Ridiculous jackasses.

Of which he was part and parcel.

He sipped his scotch. Heather made small talk with both Maxwell and Courtney until they drifted off to find more friendly social opportunities.

Heather looked at Jon for a long moment. The weight of her blue stare burned through his skin. This thing they had was...interesting. Dirty with a shimmer of something more.

She wrapped her arm through his and led him to a relatively dark corner. A potted palm tree twinkled with tiny lights. Classy.

"You're in quite the snit this evening. Was it that man in particular?"

"No. Could've been any of them."

"Good to know. I'd hate to think I was making small talk with an arms dealer or a loan shark."

"Can't vouchsafe that. Skeletons in closets and all."

"Technically true." Heather smoothed the hair that draped across her shoulder. "Although I'm guessing this attitude is one hundred percent you. So give it up, flyboy. Why bring me here? I would've declined had I known my job was to run interference on your pissant mood."

"Does it really matter?"

She tilted her head, peering into him. "Why wouldn't it? Frankly, Jon, I'm surprised. I saw you spin Mr. La Rocca so fast that he wound up kissing your ass and thanking you for the privilege." She sipped her martini and caught a dribble with her tongue. "Tonight you'd rather burn the whole place down."

"Would look pretty."

"Nah. Not even four-alarm fires can compete with the Vegas skyline."

On a tight grin, he lifted the scotch to his mouth and let the cool liquid coat his lips. But he didn't drink. The show. The picture. The pretense needed to be enough because sometimes he felt like he was barely holding on. The man he wanted to be seemed a long, long way off.

Inside Bet

No more so than when Heather called him on his bullshit.

Maxwell hadn't said a word to contradict him, and his own mother ignored even the worst of Jon's sarcasm. Heather never did. If she could look at him on a night like this and see how far he'd sunk, she might have more to offer.

For a moment, he was ballsy. Truly ballsy—not that fake crap he threw around the squad room. "Would you like to come to my place once we leave?"

She flinched. Flat-out flinched. That unconscious, chilly response turned his blood to sludge. He'd asked out of some ridiculous hope that being blunt and perceptive made Heather different. Special. But Miss Dares-a-Lot was still the same locked-down woman who'd walked out of their hotel room.

Her flinch reinforced what he'd already known—stupid impulse aside. They would only go so far. Just sex. No more.

Hadn't he gotten off the phone with his mother only hours earlier? That should've been reminder enough.

Idiot.

Heather took a sip of her martini, this time in what looked like self-defense. Pale eyes flashed up at him, all but begging him to see it her way. "I was thinking we could go to my house. It's just...neater. Closer, even. Keeps it on the right...level."

He made a small noise of agreement. "Yeah. Fine." And he meant it, which came as a welcome relief. He knew the game—had practically invented the rules. Better to save ballsy for air combat maneuvers. "But if we're agreed on keeping it neat, Heather love, I don't owe you word one about my mood."

Chapter Nineteen

Heather kept her expression placid and friendly throughout the hour that followed. She knew how these games were played. Or, at least she'd learned them well enough to fake it.

Jon, however, was a master.

He was in a black, nasty temper that wouldn't let up, yet his façade never slipped again. He was glib when he wanted to be, smooth when he had to be. Names of children and cousins tripped off his tongue as if he stored a list of rich-folk contacts in his hard drive of a mind. His smile was bulletproof.

Heather alone seemed able to recognize his true mood. She saw deeper. Closer. So did he when he turned those fierce brown eyes on her. Had they been less wary people, they might have that in common. Instead, the tension between them grew.

Maybe all of their dares and unexpected intimacies had lured her into expecting more. She half-hoped he wouldn't pretend in front of her, but that would mean risking herself in ways that had nothing to do with sex. He'd opened the door. She'd closed it. Moping about it now was worse than useless. It was hypocritical.

"Another martini?" he asked.

"Not until you finish that scotch."

"I drove."

"Always your excuse."

He snickered and leaned his elbows back, turning away from the bar. Even in that crowded ballroom, he owned whatever space he wanted to claim. His innate arrogance was unfathomable. Yet Heather remained suspicious. He was still putting on a show.

"What do you drive, Heather love? Maybe we'll take yours next time and I can get blitzed."

"A six-year-old Camry. If I thought you'd actually get drunk, I'd be the designated driver in a heartbeat."

"Oh?"

She faced the bar. Their shoulders touched. Hers were bare. His were concealed, as always, in one of the most immaculate wool suits known to man. "It's for show." She turned to whisper against his tight jaw. "Drink like the rest of them but keep your head on straight. Do you ever lose control?"

Jon conjured one of his patented dirty smiles—first toward the hollow of her cleavage, then back to her face. "We both know the answer to that. But around these snots? Hell, no."

She pushed closer. As if by reflex, he angled his hand to caress her far shoulder. They were body to body now, facing the opposite direction. Perhaps that would always be a given.

"But...you're one of them." She took in the length of his exquisite suit, from the toes of his high-gloss dress shoes to his perfectly centered tie. "Is this self-loathing? Or some sort of high-end white guilt?"

"Watch it, Heather love. You don't want this aimed at you."

He was cranky, which made Heather bold. During their few hours together, he'd never behaved this way. Cool and calculated was different than simmering anger. Dark waves pulsed off him. The muscles pressed against hers, and those long, elegant fingers—as stiff as boards. He was revealing more now than he ever had. No matter her hypocrisy, she wanted to know more about the real Jon Carlisle.

That meant pushing.

It was a risk. A *huge* risk. Because now she knew how nasty he could play.

What the hell. Rising to his silent dares was more fun than wasting her time contemplating anything deeper.

"You bought the tickets. I know how much they cost. Why come here and then condescend the whole deal?"

The muscle at his jaw bulged. She kissed it again, this time touching the tip of her tongue against his smooth, hot skin.

"My parents paid for the tickets. I'm the Carlisle family representative."

Wow. Light bulb.

But to let him know how clearly those few words explained his disgust would shut him down.

"I suppose you support worthier causes than watering grass in Nevada."

The hand on her shoulder tightened almost painfully. He dragged her closer. She stood flush against him, face-to-face. The darkness in his eyes should've sent her packing. But heat and need and some sick curiosity coiled in her belly, then slid lower to heat her sensitive folds.

Surprisingly, he tossed back the last of his scotch in a single gulp. "Make all the guesses you like. Won't change how we've arranged this. No sense messing with a good thing."

Heather didn't have that impression at all. If she'd been able to open up, to trust... Even if that were possible, she couldn't risk it on a guy like Jon. He was too sharp. His words, his eyes, his perceptive mind—they'd slice right into her. How little would remain of her hard-earned control after she let that happen?

Not enough. Which is why it wouldn't.

"Of course." Nearly the same height when she wore heels, she nuzzled her upper lip against his lower. "We each have our defenses. Better to keep them that way."

His grin spread wider. At least she knew this one—not the disdain he held for others, but one of decadent intentions. "Six nights of sex doesn't mean we're going steady, Ms. Morris."

"Six? I only count five."

"Six. Or else why are we here? I'll give you a hint. It wasn't so you could remind me of my manners."

His hands rested lightly at her waist, but he moved them up, up, just slightly. The fabric of her dress followed that seductive lead, as if he might undress her right there at the bar.

"You play at this bad-boy shit." She was edging toward the limit of his patience. He'd lose his temper soon. She wanted to be on the receiving end of it—something real. "It's only putting off the inevitable. One day you'll leave the Air Force, marry some plastic Playboy Bunny, put on thirty pounds and blend right in."

Her dress hitched up four inches as Jon's eyes flared hot and angry. "Being a bitch doesn't suit you. Too sweet around the mouth. Try again."

"Your parents are a convenient excuse to behave like an asshole."

"Better. One more time so I won't regret what I'm going to do to you."

Heather's knees threatened to give out. Screw that. She wanted more. But she saw it on his face—the same locked-down ache she'd glimpsed when he described losing his sister. Whatever she said next would change things between them. End it. Or keep...whatever it was. The words were thick on her tongue as she weighed their worth.

Ultimately, she didn't want to add any more to his pain.

So she cupped his cheeks. His dimples were under there somewhere, as unlikely now as snow on the Strip. Stretching up on her toes, she kissed him. Lightly. Just a touch. He was too rigid to accept anything else, with his mouth set in that derisive smirk.

"You're better than this," she whispered.

He closed his eyes. Breathed out. Then the barest nod. "You see, *now* I feel properly chastised. Feel better?"

"Oh, no." She looped her fingers around his belt. Tugged. "Come out and play, flyboy."

He opened his eyes. They were clearer, friskier, and thankfully free of his chilling disdain. "I think I will. And I'm still going to do what I want to you." He took her hand. "This way."

Still dizzy from what felt like a heightened version of their games, Heather's anticipation gathered in a slow burn. He practically dragged her through the country-club ballroom. His profile was amazing. Aristocratic and bold, yet accentuated by his military buzz cut. The contrast always did hot things to her guts, melting her from the inside out.

"Perfect," he muttered.

He shoved her in ahead of him and closed the door to an abandoned coat-check room.

"What do you expect to do in here?"

"Jerk off while you stand naked against the wall."

She could only blink at his blunt statement. "Forget it."

"I'm serious, Heather love. Naked. Now."

"Jon—"

His shrug was almost enough to cut off the urge to ask him to back off, but his words killed it dead. "Don't tell me you're tired of our dares already."

"Here?"

"Right here. Strip. If anyone walks in, I want them to get a serious eyeful. Then I'll tell them to get the fuck out. Someone might get to look, Heather love, but you're mine tonight."

His expression was primal. Fierce and intent. He stood there as if they were discussing how annoying tourists could be. So casual, from his shoulders down to where his hands tucked in his trouser pockets. Not even fisted. If she could learn that artificial cool, she'd quit her job and forever earn a living in the casinos.

"And you?" she asked.

"Oh, I'm staying clothed. Just a wank, remember? No need to wrinkle my suit."

"I don't believe you. You won't be able to go through with it."

Amusement glittered in those rich brown depths. None of their tension dissipated, but their play had returned in full. She soaked it in. A relief. And a huge turn-on.

"I don't believe you will either, Ms. Morris."

There it was. God, resisting his dares was like resisting the urge to look over the precipice of a cliff. Or jump off.

She reached behind her back and tugged the long zipper. The dress parted down to the lace at the top of her thong. With a simple shrug, the purple satin fell into a pool at her feet.

"Bra."

His eyes and nostrils flared as she complied. One minute on, the next it fell to the floor. She shivered. But she would win this. All she needed to do was focus on his reactions. She was too turned on, too curious, to dwell on it now.

"Thong. But keep the high heels."

Heather lifted her brows. Then she was naked except for a pair of three-inch purple stilettos. She backed against the wall, hands behind her back. The pose deliberately shaped her hip into a slinky curve and thrust her breasts out for his admiration. And oh, did he admire. His lips parted.

Belt open. Fly open. Cock out.

She didn't believe him. No way. Not in a hundred years would he stand there and come without including her. But then, she hadn't believed him capable of shutting it down when he'd softly fucked her in the parking garage. When it came to just about anything, the man was as stubborn as he was clever and filthy-minded.

He was stroking now, flogging his long, beautiful prick.

"You won't." Her throat was dry as the Nevada sand. "You *won't.*"

"No telling." He'd gone breathless. His wrist jerked as he worked up and down that hard length. "Maybe I'll come so hard I stain that pretty dress of yours."

"Get off it, Jon. Come here."

"Nope." The tendons of his neck pushed against his collar. He looked up at the ceiling briefly, eyes rolling closed in obvious pleasure, before snapping back to her breasts—specifically her nipple ring. "Touch yourself, Heather love. Are you wet watching me?"

Every word was rough, so low and interspersed with his quick inhalations.

Hell, she might as well make herself come if he was intent on seeing this through. So slowly, she slid a hand between her thighs. The moan that surged from her throat was completely involuntary. No ruse for him. No tease. Just the pleasure of finding how keyed up her body was. He was capable of doing that to her with just his words, his stance, his goddamn dares.

"That lovely cock is about to blow. I think you're running out of time. Because if you come without me, I'm putting my dress back on and our night's over." She smiled and slipped two slick fingers into her mouth. "So fuck me or don't, flyboy."

One long stride brought him to her. His mouth slammed down over hers, their most brutal kiss yet. He pinned her hands above her head. Tongue deep in her mouth. Hard cock pressed against her naked belly. That he still wore his suit—that imbalance—always did such radical things to her self-control. She behaved as if she really wanted him to dominate her, even as she fought to control him in return. Each time, she craved the victory of yanking control out of his grasp.

He only released her long enough to roll on a condom. Heather sighed in his mouth. Yes. She would get what she wanted.

"You think you have the upper hand, don't you?" He sucked and bit the tops of her breasts. Eager hands twisted that sensitive flesh. Heather squirmed and fought back, but he shocked her to stillness with one swift plunge. He licked the skin he'd marred. "Damn," he groaned. "That's gonna bruise. And we still have to make it out of here.

All those eyes on my teeth marks on your tits."

The pace of his strokes amped until they matched what he'd done to himself. Sharp. Fast. Intent on a quick, hard come. Heather grabbed underneath his arms and curled herself into his lean strength. The gorgeous shock of being filled, then being fucked so well—Christ, she'd never get over it. He was simply that good.

Jon cupped her ass. "Feet up. Hold on. Don't scream, Heather love."

She did as he commanded, even finding the presence of mind to laugh against his cheek. "So that's your angle. Me being quiet?"

He kissed her, swift, smiling. "Dare you."

The weight of her head became too much to bear. She leaned back against the wall. Jon had her. His strong arms wrapped tighter under her ass and thighs. Again he ducked his mouth to her breasts. No slow, seductive tease. Animalistic. Just claiming what he could reach. His true energy was focused on each pulsing drive into her slick cunt.

"Knew you couldn't," she breathed against his ear.

"Fuck no, I couldn't."

After so many fake smiles, his harsh-edged admission sent Heather over the edge. She clung to him, ground her hips, buried her mouth against the shoulder of his suit coat. Tensed. Shrieked into warm wool that smelled of him.

"Head up. Let me see you."

Heather barely had the strength to comply as his thrusts drew out the pleasure. More gathered, threatening her again.

"You're going to come again, aren't you?"

She nodded weakly. So dazed. So damn good.

"Keep your head right there." He smacked and surged into her pussy. As relentless as a jackhammer. "Don't fucking move. I want to see it on your face."

Heather stared into his eyes. Her mouth opened on a silent scream as another orgasm set her body on fire. Jon grunted. Another three hard strokes and he shuddered on a long, low exhalation. His head thunked against the wall next to her neck.

"Just...fuck."

"Yes," she said on a smile. "Now let's get the hell out of here."

Jon lifted his face. He matched her smile. "I knew it from day one. You're wicked."

"Yay for you. Called it right."

But as she tugged at her dress—with Jon's assistance this time—she wondered just where this gamble would end. Power and seduction. Risk and reward. The unreal feeling that each encounter was digging a deeper tunnel, straight toward her heart.

Jon took her hand and led her out of the ballroom as if nothing had happened, as if their clothes weren't rumpled and his teeth marks didn't adorn the upper swells of her breasts. He led her out of the ballroom as if none of it mattered.

That was what scared her.

Chapter Twenty

Jon parked as close to the flight line as he could get, then powered down the top of his convertible. He propped his head on the windowsill, looking up. The sky had taken on the peculiar white of the desert before the sun revealed the full colors of sunset. Even that rich sight would be hard to compete with the view of Vegas on the other side of the flight line.

He considered ignoring the phone when it rang. "Hot for Teacher" meant Ryan, but Friday evening wasn't a guarantee of happy tidings. Ryan was just as likely to call with a question about next week's training exercise as an invitation to grab a beer.

Jon answered anyway. He owed his friend that much consideration. "I kind of thought having a girlfriend meant you'd actually spend weeknights doing fun shit."

Ryan's laugh was familiar. "Your jealousy is coming through loud and clear. Give me five minutes and I'll give you a million reasons why me and Cass are awesome."

"I've got all the time in the world. Throw 'em at me."

Jon could all but picture the man's serious look. Brow furrowed and mouth flat. "Why all the time?"

He almost lied, mostly because he knew what would happen. Sometimes a guy really did need some quiet. But he'd never lied to the people who mattered. Every time he tried, he heard his dad promising to be there for Jon's chess match. Or first solo flight. Or Air Force award ceremony. "I'm on the flight line."

"Gimme ten minutes."

Exactly what he'd expected. Like code talk, he and Ryan only had to admit they were sitting on the Nellis flight line for the other to come running.

He could always depend on his friends. Precisely what he needed that evening.

Sure enough, Ryan's giant truck pulled up just under ten minutes later. Jon slipped out of his DBS before the tire dust settled. Their manly heart-to-hearts didn't work in the low-slung sports car. Too much like lying down, and adding *talking* on top of it. Forget it.

Ryan met him at the back of his truck where they let down the tailgate and hopped up.

Jon squinted at the distant skyline. The sun was going. The lights never turned off in Vegas—the real city that never slept.

"So tell me, Fang. Doesn't Cass object to you jetting out on her?"

He shrugged those wide, corn-fed shoulders, even as his smile turned sheepish. "She's at the gallery."

"So *that's* why you can drop everything and come running."

"That and the way you light the dark parts in my soul."

Jon snickered. "Cass is going to be heartbroken when you leave her for me. Especially with Don't Ask, Don't Tell gone."

"Actually..." Ryan's grin turned megawatt. "Gotta say, I don't ever see leaving her. Things are damn good."

"Lucky man." Acid burned through Jon's guts. Jealousy? He'd never found that connection with any woman. The way things were going with Heather, he sure as fuck wasn't going to find it with her.

"What about your reason for being too busy to pick up Leah last month? Skipping this month's poker?" Ryan hitched an arm over the side of the truck bed and eyed Jon. "How are things with the mystery woman?"

"I don't know." He scrubbed the back of his neck. "I mean, the sex is amazing."

"Definitely a bonus."

Jon flipped Ryan off. Just a quick one, for good measure. "There was this shit with my parents, and an event I had to go to last weekend. I unloaded on her. Wasn't pretty."

"Did she stick around after?"

"More or less." Long enough for them to go at it hard and fast in that coat closet. So hell yes, she'd stuck around in the best kind of way. They'd even managed a meet-and-fuck on Wednesday. Same rules—her place in the dark—but great for taking off the edge after a hard day. But he hadn't asked to stay and she hadn't offered. Whatever. He didn't mind "closed off" from the chick he was banging.

Long-term didn't figure into any picture of their future.

He should be enjoying the fucking ride.

"Couldn't have been too bad, then."

"Not at all."

"You know, I once got a piece of excellent advice." Ryan looked toward the sky with a smug smile. "I was told I think too much, and that the cure to that was to fuck too much instead. I wonder who might have said that...?"

Jon's laughter felt good. Better laughter than other emotions. His mom had sent Sara's books. The deal was done. No point in wallowing. "Me, numb nuts. When I was being my most brilliant."

"I don't know about brilliant. Sometimes you're dumb as a rock. Only, on occasion, you accidentally say smart things."

"Good to know." Jon pushed off the end of the truck. "Want to go to a scotch bar?"

"You know, most men say 'get a beer'."

"Most men are Philistines. You're lucky to know me."

Ryan smacked him across the back. Hard. "If your existential crisis is over, I'm gonna ditch out. Pick up Cassandra at work. See if she'll set aside new exhibit plans long enough to have dinner with me."

"You're putting poon over bros. I see how it is." But he knew Ryan wouldn't take him seriously.

"If you're as smart as you think you are, you'll do the same thing."

Maybe he would. The time in the coat closet with Heather, the way she'd done exactly what he ordered—while challenging him in return... He was torn between knowing he could show her a better time and feeling faintly smug about how hard he'd made her come. Twice.

So, even as he watched Ryan's taillights fade into the distance, Jon pulled out his phone and dialed.

"Captain Carlisle," Heather answered, her voice full of spice. "I laid a bet with myself regarding whether I'd hear from you tonight."

"Did you win or lose?"

"Let's just say I enjoyed the surprise."

"Then meet me. If you thought the wine bar was remarkable, I've got the perfect place to show you. The Lux is new downtown. Three hundred different kinds of scotch and two levels of dance floors."

"That sounds like your type of joint, not mine," she said on another laugh. "Besides, I've got plans already."

"Do I know his name?"

"Aren't you amusing, flyboy. But no. *Her* name is Jenn. We're going to the movies, eat chocolate and popcorn, and talk about boys. Your name may or may not be mentioned."

He considered apologizing. Maybe not for their time in the coat closet, and certainly not for the hours after he'd taken her home. They'd stolen through her darkened house and headed straight for bed. But maybe he should apologize for earlier that evening. He'd let his mother's standoffishness ride him as if it were new, as if he were still a vulnerable fourteen-year-old kid.

He'd learned to create an impenetrable shield of attitude and insouciance, but he also knew what kind of frozen wasteland that left behind. No middle ground. He'd been a user for a long time.

It felt a lot like this. Only, at that moment, it didn't fit his skin.

"Hey, about the other night. You didn't deserve my shit."

A long pause faintly filled the line with static. "I'm not sure what to do with that."

"Neither do I."

"Well, then. Apology accepted. Don't you dare do it again." Her husky, teasing laugh unwound the tension he hadn't realized was so strong in his muscles. He especially enjoyed when her laughter was real, like right then. Warm. Inviting.

The more astounding realization was that he could apologize. Huh. Who knew?

He rubbed his head as the colorful Vegas lights brightened. Memories of every previous encounter colored his voice with a taste of excitement. "I'll make it worth your while some other time. Enjoy your night out."

"Two moments of generosity in a row, flyboy. Are you running a fever?"

"You keep teasing and I'll be as selfish as I threatened in that coat closet."

"You never could and you know it. Part of the fun. How about tomorrow night? Bring takeout."

He wasn't about to revisit *where* they hooked up. The fact he would have her again—have her in ways that remained unknown but promised exquisite pleasure—made him smile. "Tomorrow then."

With that, they signed off. But Jon's restlessness wouldn't abate.

He sank into the front seat of his car. If Heather wasn't going to play out, he'd find another option. It used to be easy. His buddies. Their haunts. She was beginning to dominate his thoughts and wants way too much. Time for a reminder that a relationship based on sex was just that. He wouldn't consider Heather a friend. An undeniable temptation, yes. After the recent reminders of his family, his old life, his youth—he needed the snarky ease of hanging out with his squad mates. Uncomplicated and mindless.

With a few quick phone calls, he scrounged up a decadent plan worthy of his tastes and reputation. High-end luxury wrapped around a smorgasbord of booze and music. A few hours later, he smiled as Leah, totally dolled up for clubbing, slipped into his DBS. She wore a skintight pair of jeans topped with a low-cut, dark pink halter-top.

After darting across the city, they rolled up to the valet stand at The Lux.

"Hey, there's Dash. Did you call him too? Cool!" Leah waved madly. "Dash!"

The woman had no restraint. Not like Heather, whose elegance was enough to believe she'd been raised among the elite and powerful. Sure he'd apologized—which was only right, after he'd behaved like such an ass—but perhaps her reserve reminded him too much of his world. She would never be an easy woman to open up to.

Now opening *her* up? That remained his prime directive in their relationship. She hid too many secrets for him to walk away. The challenge remained. The thrill of the hunt.

Liam "Dash" Christiansen strolled toward them, his hands in the pockets of slim-cut black trousers. He flashed his shark-wide smile. "I didn't dare brave approaching the entrance without you, Tin Tin. The line is as long as a runway, and the bouncer looks like The Hulk. Minus the green. I'm not above admitting this place is way out of my league. I'd need a personality transplant and a guest spot on *What Not to Wear* before making the attempt."

"Shit, you talk a lot," Leah said with a grin. "A personality transplant would be welcome."

Jon shook his head. "Besides, where the hell does a proper fighter pilot learn anything about *What Not to Wear?*"

"Sunny, dude. She loves that show."

Leah coughed around a word that sounded suspiciously like *whipped.*

Dash returned the coughed insults. Something like *ball-buster.*

She laughed. "You know it. But seriously. That line is intimidating as hell. I'd be waiting for hours."

"No way," Jon said. "Maybe Dash and his dorky loafers, but you'd be just fine. A bouncer would lose his job for keeping you out."

Dash looked down at shoes worthy of an aging high school economics teacher. "Come on, now. We know Princess would get in. She's bangable enough."

"You got that right," she piped up.

"But my shoes are just fine."

"They're not," Jon said shaking his head. "Honestly."

"JCPenney special."

"It's a damn good thing you're married, man."

Dash conjured one of his wide, wide grins—a deliberate jest. "They were *on sale,* even. Unbeatable deal."

Jon lifted an eyebrow. "What is this 'on sale' you speak of?"

"You dorks gonna stand here all day? If I have to listen to this crap all night, I'll need margaritas."

"You always need margaritas," Dash said.

Jon led them toward the club and gave his name to the concierge girl, who ushered them to the VIP area.

Massive crowds and sweaty bodies already crammed the club. Dim lights, of course, but the place was industrial chic. Iron gangways overhead were the best touch, where scantily clad girls did their best impressions of go-go dancers. As he strolled beneath their gyrating asses, Jon wondered if they were wearing panties. He couldn't catch a glimpse, which only made him more curious.

Damn if he wasn't addicted to mystery. Other than speed, it was his drug of choice.

His thoughts shot right back to Heather. What would she wear to a girls' night out? Didn't matter. He knew the secrets of her body, what she'd be hiding beneath the most demure ensemble. The thought made him smile, and he indulged in a surge of arousal. The sex in the air at The Lux only heightened his awareness of every female body, every gyrating hip, every pout—whether faked or genuine.

What sort of bullshit emotion had he been contemplating with Heather? She was the best time he'd had in years. Walking amidst that churning chaos of hormones, his impulses crystalized around the most relaxing thought he'd had in days. She was his for the taking. His for the pleasuring.

Fantastic.

When the petite hostess waved toward a round table encircled by a black-backed booth, he had no trouble picturing a much different end to his evening. He shot off a quick text. Let her try to ignore his invitation. For a moment he'd contemplated that maybe, just maybe, she was good for his ego. Knock him down a few pegs. Screw that. She *would* come to him. She had yet to refuse one of his dares, which was such a fucking turn-on.

He faced the hostess. "If a Ms. Heather Morris arrives, she's with me."

The woman nodded and made a note on her clipboard. Dash and Leah perked up, even as they slid into the booth. Leah waved down a waitress. The Princess of the 64th could always be counted on for a wild night.

"And who exactly is Ms. Heather Morris?" Dash asked. "A one-night stand or three-week stand?"

"I've stopped counting." Jon sat and hitched his arms over the back. "Let's just say she hasn't bored me yet."

"Miracle," Leah muttered, after ordering the first round.

"Don't get lippy, Princess. Shouldn't you be bumping and grinding by now?"

"In search of tasty beef? Definitely." Off she went, already shaking her ass in time to the pulsing rhythm.

Easing into the possibilities of the night, into that same rhythm of sex and temptation, Jon nursed a scotch. What really went to his head was anticipation. If Heather didn't come to him—a dare in itself—he'd make sure she knew that tomorrow wasn't soon enough. Bust down her door. Strip her bare. Take what they both wanted.

Chapter Twenty-One

Heather was just about to roll another hunk of hair around her curling iron when her cell rang. Not Jenn, thank God. Neither of them could stand another delay to their plans for a girls' night. And she was thankful it wasn't Jon. Only the trouble she and Jenn constantly had in aligning a night out had held off the temptation of saying yes to his invitation. The *yes, yes, yes* in her head had been loud, with her libido shooting into overdrive. God, he was good. A few slinky syllables and she was ready all over again. Nothing came close to the way they drove each other crazy.

His apology, however... She'd spoken the truth. What was she supposed to do with that? Ignoring it for now seemed the best answer. It had been polite and completely appropriate, considering his behavior at the country club. Mostly she'd been pissed that his anger continued to weave under her skin. Beneath his playboy exterior was a real person, a real man with real emotions. Dangerous stuff.

She thumbed the cell phone. "Hey, Dad," she said with a smile.

"Hiya, honey. How goes?"

Her father's welcome voice hadn't tensed a knot in her stomach for years. They were on fantastic terms now. So why the sudden unease?

High school. That weekend when she'd hopped on the back of a Harley and run away. She'd needed years to erase the damage she'd done, all because of the crazy chances she'd taken. Earning back their respect had propelled the ambition of her twenties. She still remembered the stony, hard-bitten silence of that car ride home from Jersey.

If her dad knew what risks she was taking with Jon...

And there it was. The answer to her tight gut. Her arrogant playboy added napalm to the fiery wildness she'd kept under wraps for years. A harsh reminder of what she'd inflicted on herself and her family.

"Honey?"

She put down the curling iron. "Sorry, Dad. Just sort of distracted. Getting ready to go out."

"Am I interrupting?"

"No way. How's Mom?"

"Good," he said, always so upbeat. Heather dragged that happiness into herself. "She's sitting by the campfire, reading."

"Where are you now?"

"Somewhere in the eastern half of Virginia. At a campground. You'd hate it. Total roughing it."

"Then I'll just say 'Gee, I'm glad you're enjoying it, Dad!'" She couldn't help but smile. Her parents had taken to the road on a grand RV adventure, as if their years of relocating from base to base had left them unable to settle. In the meantime, she took pride in being able to protect the assets they'd worked all their lives to scrimp and save. If she set aside a little more from her own salary to serve as an extra guarantee...

It was the least she could do.

"Warm here today," he said. "Really nice. But I suppose you're still sweltering?"

"AC's running full blast." She touched up her blush then found her killer black pumps. "I'll step outside and all the work I've put into looking nice will melt right off me."

"Hot date?"

At one time, so long ago, she would've taken those two words as quiet condemnation. She swallowed back the old reflex. She was thirty-two and she wasn't even seeing Jon that night.

An uncomfortable pinch of disappointment under her ribs made her movements edgy as she gathered purse and keys. "Nah, just a girls' night with Jenn. Cocktails and a movie, I think."

"Sounds great. I haven't been to a movie theater in... Wow, I can't remember."

"Too busy seeing real life. We cubicle types need Hollywood to live it for us."

"Don't sound so disappointed. At the moment, real life includes watching a squirrel taking a shit. I have to say, that's a first for me."

Inside Bet

Heather stopped in the doorway to her garage, holding on to the frame as she laughed. "You're gonna make my mascara run!"

"Seriously, Heather. I wouldn't have thought they'd have so much in them."

"You're gross!"

"Your mom tells me that at least daily. Normally I'm completely innocent."

"But not this time?" She gingerly wiped tears from her eyes.

"Nope. Pretty damn crass. But I'm keeping you from cocktails. Gotta be better than my nature-show narration. Have a good night, honey."

"Thanks, Dad. Say hi to Mom for me. Love you both."

"Love you too, Heather."

She switched off the phone and tucked it in her shiny metallic green clutch, a strong accent to her entirely black ensemble. For a moment, she stood in the garage doorway, her back against the wood. Had her father been any less forgiving and patient—odd considering what a hardass he'd been to his Army subordinates—they never would've made it. Relationship kaput for good. Her behavior back then had been bad enough to snap a saint in half.

Now he was the one person on the planet guaranteed to make her smile.

"Squirrel shit," she muttered to herself as she started up her Camry. "What a dork."

She was still grinning as she drove to a bar off the Strip. Called Inescapable Future, which was so pretentious as to add to her amusement, the place was decked out in sci-fi Japanese-style cute. Just cuteness *everywhere*, as if Hello Kitty had barfed up a cocktail lounge. Pink and iridescent polka-dot paint, strings of flashing lights in fuchsia and purple, and pictures of every cartoony cat and puppy and pony imaginable. Heather stood in the entryway with her mouth slightly agape. Only when she noticed a cutesy squirrel did she let loose another laugh.

"You're in a good mood," came Jenn's voice. "Good! Let's do this!"

Perfectly coiffed, perfectly put together, Jenn flew in the face of stereotypes about stay-at-home moms. She wore a low-cut fire-engine-red top and a dark, slim-cut pair of slacks. Only her flats gave away

141

the fact she didn't dress to the nines every day.

They settled onto very, very high barstools, the fluffy upholstery of which was pink-and-white leopard spots. Their round table was lacquered in black with itty-bitty seagulls flying in letters that spelled Inescapable Future.

Heather laughed again and smoothed her hair. "If this is the future, I'm pretty sure I want to die young."

"Damn skippy." Jenn flagged down the nearest waitress. The woman wore a uniform that included thigh-high metallic boots and a white sixties-style micro-dress. "Mojito," Jenn said. "A big one."

"I'll have one of those frou-frou martinis made with Godiva liqueur."

The waitress nodded, which barely shifted her black angle-cut bob wig. No telling her expression behind huge silver sunglasses and gold lipstick as thick as wax.

After chit-chat about work and Jenn's family, the cocktails arrived in massive glasses. "Ooh, I'm glad you drove!"

Heather grinned. "Suddenly the twenty-two-dollar price tag makes sense. You could measure these by the gallon."

"They're cheaper than La Rocca's would've been. You know, it's okay if you talk about the place. I promise my feelings won't get hurt since I got laid that night and you didn't."

It only took about two and a half seconds for Jenn's eyes to go wide. Heather wondered if she was really that easy to read, and hoped that ease was confined only to her closest friend.

"Did you meet someone?" Jenn leaned in. "You did! No wonder you sent those wine-tasting notes through your cell at, what, two in the morning? I noticed, you know."

"That doesn't mean anything. I could've been working late."

"You're a blushing liar. You've been having hot caveman sex and haven't told me!"

Heather took a sip of her chocolate martini, which was just *gorgeous*. Jenn moved in for the kill. "Don't think that old sip-and-look-away thing works on anybody but dudes."

"What, Rich not keeping it spicy enough for you?"

"He's not the problem. Midnight kid puke and a busted water heater can be wet blankets, though." She grinned in a way that proved married mothers in their thirties had filthier minds than society gave them credit for. "But we're here now, interruption free, and I need details. Our fate as friends depends on it."

"That serious, huh?"

"Spill."

After a deep breath, Heather started with the basics. Met at the wine tasting. Roulette. One-night stand.

Jenn raised her neat brows. "*You?* Rock it out."

"Yes, *me*," she found herself saying. Why? As if being seen as a stick-in-the-mud hadn't been her goal for more than a decade. "I'm not dead."

"Which is what I've been saying for three years now. Was he worth it?"

Heather answered with an uncontrolled giggle. She took another hasty sip, smiling without pretense. "You could say that."

"Caveman sex for the win!"

"Nah, that seems too...derogatory. Jenn, he's so damn upper class. Comes from old New England money."

"What does he do?"

"Air Force. Flies F-16s at Nellis."

"You're shitting me."

Heather shook her head. He sounded even more too good to be true when described aloud. "Nope. I thought he was teasing too, there at the wine tasting. But nope. Air Force ID and everything."

"Wow. And he's not an asshole?"

"Oh, no. He totally is. Perverted as hell. But..." She realized the weird, dreamy quality to her voice when Jenn's smile turned knowing.

"Keep it comin'. But what?"

"He's amazing. A gentleman. I've never met anyone like him. All cool culture on the outside. Swear to God, Jenn, he'd blend in at a White House Christmas party. He's funny. I just like him, attitude and all."

"Probably *because* of the attitude." Jenn sipped deeply of her mojito until only ice chunks remained. "I mean, who else do you have at work? That guy Grant? Please. Loaded fighter pilot sounds much more appealing."

As Heather filled in the details she'd gleaned about Jon's background, her respiration increased. Where was he? Who had he decided to spend the evening with? A flash of disloyalty to Jenn made her divulge more than she intended—or else she just needed to share.

"And he's a damn rock star in bed. Or in an abandoned coat closet."

Jenn laughed. "You whore!"

The waitress had returned, her eyebrows raised above the silver sunglasses. Jenn ordered another then leaned in to whisper, "A coat closet? Not, like, one in your house?"

"With all the crap I store in there? No way." Heat flushed up from her nape. Her whole face was bathed in the waves that danced off a bonfire. "At the Paulson Country Club ballroom."

"Double whore! Oh, I'm totally telling Rich on you."

"He won't believe you." The alcohol had gone to her head, just a little, or maybe it was the thrill of finally being able to tell her friend. "Wait, how does one become a double whore?"

"Doing it in a posh country club." Jenn shrugged. "Or two dudes at once."

Heather flinched, but perhaps they'd strayed even further beyond what Jenn believed her capable of having done—and well beyond what Heather would ever admit.

"So have you seen his plane? That would be hot."

"Not yet." So many times she'd meant to ask. Make a formal request, as opposed to how she'd placated him at her birthday dinner. She didn't like lying to her friend, but the alternative—admitting her cowardice—was not going to happen. "I can't just take off from work during the day."

Jenn waved a negligent hand. "I'm assuming you make time to hook up?"

"Yeah."

"I hear another 'but', don't I?"

Heather took a deep breath. The chocolate liqueur churned in her gut. Not so gorgeous anymore. "I want to know more about him. See where he works. Meet his friends. And yes, there's a but. Because all of that's scarier than getting caught doing..."

"The coat-closet sex."

"Yup."

Despite having dipped heavily into her second giant mojito, Jenn looked remarkably sober when she took Heather's hand. "It's been a while for you, hasn't it? The scary shit?"

Heather could only nod.

"Me too. I wouldn't know what to do with a new guy now. I'm glad those risks are long past and I get to go home to a man who loves me." She sighed a little. "But I also remember how it was at the start. The thrill. The obsession. Sometimes it's worth the risk."

"And when it's not?"

"Eh." Jenn's giggles were back. "Then you'll have played the field. No regrets when you do settle down."

Back to that word *regret*. Heather had plenty. It remained one of her life goals to create as few as possible. More and more, denying herself any chance to be with Jon, no matter how it worked out, felt like a future regret waiting to happen. She'd thought the same thing about her first night with him. Only now, it wasn't all about sex.

An hour later, when Jenn ducked into the bathroom, Heather checked her phone. A text from Jon. Her heart jumped.

The Lux. Come and get me.

He was so goddamn arrogant. She loved it. Her instant arousal had almost as much to do with his attitude as it did with their chemistry. One fueled the other, round and round.

Jenn had trouble walking back to the table, so they decided to call it a night. A movie wasn't in the cards. They'd moved on to other topics on the drive home. Not that Heather could concentrate very well. In her mind, she was already at the club. Already had Jon in her sights.

She parked in front of Jenn's adorable ranch house. The living room light was on. Rich was waiting up for her. Despite her anticipation of a fun night ahead, something like longing shivered over Heather's skin.

She walked Jenn safely to her front door, amid the woman's giggles and wobbly footsteps. "Go find him," Jenn whispered as they hugged. "I'm a pumpkin by eleven, but you're not. I bet he isn't either."

"Just what I had in mind."

"Oooh, bad girl. I love it."

Rich opened the door and led his wife inside, among a flurry of well wishes and good nights. Heather turned away. Her Camry looked like a smashed tin car compared to the monster that was Jon's DBS.

Heather shook her head. She opened her phone and read the text again, as if it would make the situation more real. Clear the confusion from her brain. Only one thought remained.

"No regrets."

Almost forty-five minutes later, just short of midnight, she arrived at The Lux. Clubs in Vegas shut down when the sun came up. The only problem now was the line of people waiting to get in. Dawn would reach her before she reached the door.

She couldn't imagine Jon standing in line. No way would he have chosen this place if he didn't have connections.

Heather unbuckled and stripped her lightweight Merino cardigan. The camisole underneath was also black, but nearly sheer. A tight black skirt and killer high heels. Her hair done up. Maybe this would work.

A valet took her car. She hid a cringe at the cost, then she strode toward the bouncer at the head of the red velvet line. She knew what it was to look a tough situation in the face.

"Is Jon Carlisle here? I'm Heather Morris. He's expecting me."

She waited a few tense seconds. Her pulse was pounding.

"Right this way, Ms. Morris." The bouncer led her indoors and handed her off to a scantily clad woman. Dancer? Waitress? No telling. "A guest for Mr. Carlisle."

The woman only nodded. Her hair was incredibly blonde. *Neon* blonde that glowed under a few scattered black lights. She led Heather upstairs and through a confusing maze of bars, dance floors and private rooms.

There he was.

So casual, he leaned with his arm stretched along the back of a thickly padded leather bench. A tall man and a fit, petite brunette sat across from him.

Heather tossed her hair and walked slowly forward, as if he were watching her. And soon enough, he was. His brows lifted. Dark eyes widened just a touch.

His reaction—slight, but pure interest—was enough to power Heather's slinkiest smile.

Game on.

"Good evening, Captain."

Chapter Twenty-Two

That low, sultry voice was *almost* too quiet to be heard. People chattered all around them, and a thumping bass beat never let up. Except there was no way Jon would miss it.

Heather.

She looked amazing. As usual. A black skirt clung to her hips and emphasized her sensual shape. While her camisole was also black, its deep V-neck displayed pale skin and plenty of cleavage.

Jon snapped his surprise back toward neutral and crossed one ankle over his knee as if he couldn't give a damn. "Good evening to you, Ms. Morris. Care to come sit on my lap?"

She barely twitched an eyebrow, but shared humor was obvious in her dark eyes. "The booth will do nicely. For now."

She slid in to sit beside him. Not close enough to touch but near enough to feel the warmth from her skin. "Nice that you could make it," he whispered. "My ego is much assured."

"Your ego is unbelievable."

"It works. Here you are."

He didn't want to examine how pleased he was that she'd arrived. Women were as thick as flies at The Lux, and plenty of them hot as fuck. He could've taken any one of them home. None were half so intriguing as the beauty beside him. Was that a benefit or a detriment? Any other woman would be easier to forget, but without Heather's innate challenge.

"Heather Morris, allow me to present a couple incorrigibles," he said, waving at the others. "Dash Christiansen and Princess Leah Girardi. My coworkers."

She lifted dark eyebrows. "That means fellow pilots, doesn't it? I'm surprised the three of you aren't holding court, basking in attention."

Dash laughed. "Some of us aren't on the market. Married eight years, since graduating from the Air Force Academy. She's in DC at the moment or I wouldn't be sitting here looking like a total loser."

"And as you can tell," Jon said, "Dash is not shy about divulging his life story to near-strangers."

Leah's eyes gleamed. She stuck out her hand to shake and shot Jon a look of approval. Good. He liked that. He wasn't above admitting how much he enjoyed impressing his friends with the women he introduced. "This calls for another round of drinks."

Dash sipped his beer. "As do Mondays and Tuesdays and completing a sentence. I'd have a six-day hangover if I tried to keep up with you. Probably not a good call for a dude who flies jets."

"You just wish you knew how to have as good a time as I do." The waitress deposited a margarita in front of Leah, who licked her fingers clean of dribbles of booze. She grinned at Heather. "Drink up, sweetie. There's dancing to be had, unless you're really sticking by this perv all night."

Jon trailed his fingers through the curling ends of Heather's hair. Dark silk seemed an inadequate description. He wanted to feel it skimming over his lower stomach. "Isn't that part of my indescribable appeal?"

Heather smiled as she picked up her own margarita. "I think she described it just fine."

Leah laughed. "Perv? Totally."

Jon offered a lazy salute. "No denying what we are. For example, you, Princess, are an adorable yet hardcore bitch."

She tossed her ponytail back over her shoulder, hard enough that a few locks came loose. "Have to be to whip male ass."

Dash laughed and affected a mock-sympathetic expression. "If that's what you want to believe, you go on with that. But really you're a sweet little kitten. We all know when the day is done, you sing sappy ballads using your hairbrush as a microphone. And bubble baths would definitely figure in."

"Let me tell you what I'd do with a hairbrush to a butt munch like you."

Leah and Dash got into it, turning trash talk into an art form. Normally Jon would be right up in the middle of it, but he found himself watching Heather.

More than that, he watched the way she examined the other two

149

yahoos. A tiny smile curved her lips as she slowly sipped her drink. She glanced at him. "Can I help you?"

An obvious tease.

"They're rather like monkeys in the zoo."

"I heard that," Leah snapped, flipping him off. She'd managed to find yet another shot of tequila. "You fling poop with the best of us."

"Nice, potty mouth," Dash said. "I never heard the real Princess Leia talk like that. Maybe you need a different hairdo, help adjust your attitude. Something with cinnamon buns?"

She rolled her eyes. "Oh, *Star Wars* references. How novel."

"I think it's remarkable." Heather finished the margarita Leah had ordered for her but refused another. "They just don't stop. How do you actually get any work done?"

He missed the feel of her skin, so he wiggled fingers beneath her flowing camisole. The hem of her skirt was next. "My extreme stores of patience."

"Sure," she drawled. "But it's fascinating too. You're all...a unit, for lack of a better word. There's no such thing as morale building. It's already there."

He liked her hair curled. The style gave her a softer look, made her more accessible. He pushed the dark strands off her shoulder and caressed her skin. "Accounting doesn't lend itself to cohesion?"

Her husky laugh went straight to his cock. "Not in the least."

Leah was all but dancing in her seat. The woman had a hard time holding still, which made it astonishing that she managed to drink so much. Two trips to the dance floor hadn't shaken all her wiggles out. "It's the war-zone thing. Does it every time."

Heather's pale eyes went large. She looked up at Jon from under her brows. "War zone?"

"Totally." Leah was blithely shaking salt on the web between her thumb and forefinger, then lining up a lime between ring and pinkie. She downed a shot of tequila like a pro. "Ask Jon about the time we launched out of Bagram on less than a half-hour prep."

Somebody was drinking herself a pair of loose lips. People who'd played in the desert together tossed around oh-shit stories when the booze flowed. Either they turned bad and someone ended up bawling in his beer, or they turned rowdy.

Jon rather liked nursing his slow-burn arousal. He stood, tugging Heather along with him. "We're going to dance."

She frowned slightly, as if chagrined by his demand. "I don't remember you asking."

Dash clapped, then tossed in a whistle for good measure. "You tell him, sweetheart. Make him work for it."

She grinned at Dash. "I'm not your sweetheart, handsome."

"I like your style," Leah said with a bounce.

Jon laced their fingers together and lifted the back of her hand to his mouth. "Ms. Morris, would you care to dance with me?"

"I'd love to, Captain."

Her smile was brilliant. Unforgettable.

The girl was bad for him.

The prospect of unraveling her mysteries would keep him interested for a good long time. But was that worth going deeper? Was she capable of letting anyone in? He'd learned the hard way that some people weren't built that way. Didn't mean they should be punished, but it did mean he should stick to those who'd proved worthy of his trust. Leah and Dash, Ryan and the rest of their friends.

Christ, that left the question of whether Jon was even ready for anything more. As interesting as Heather was, it wasn't as if he had a background of healthy relationships.

Better to watch her lead the way to the packed dance floor. His weakness wasn't her curvy ass, which certainly appealed. It was the look she threw over her shoulder. Mischief. Mirth. A hint of wickedness at the edges, as if they were already alone and naked. He'd never get enough of that challenge, that promise.

On the parquet floor, he grabbed her hips and tucked his pelvis against the lush ass he'd just been admiring. One hand followed the natural curve of her hip into the shallow of her waist. His thumb played in the hint of her navel, under her shirt, as they moved to the music.

He tucked his chin along her neck, took a sip from her skin. She smelled sweet. He wanted bigger and bigger bites. "How about me? Can I call you sweetheart?"

"I like it better when you speak French."

"You mean when I talk dirty in French."

She wrapped an arm back around his neck. "I've become too obvious. You'll be done with me soon."

That seemed incredibly unlikely, although part of him almost wished it were true. He'd shake off the weird mood that always took over when he wasn't in control.

The playlist was eclectic, everything from house to rock to rap. The only connection was the sub-mental bass beat that whipped packed bodies into a frenzy.

That she danced well was no surprise. Every movement was erotically charged. She didn't seem to notice how men's eyes tracked her, how they followed every pulse and dip. Jon noticed—both the men and her body. She caught fire with the music.

Mostly guys left them alone. After dancing for a good thirty minutes, the only person who approached was a tall, slender blonde. The woman danced nearer, edging closer. Jon lifted his brows at Heather. She gave him one of those secret smiles and turned away.

The finger she crooked at the blonde was packed with attitude.

Then, whoa damn, was it on. Heather and the woman didn't bother to speak. None of that. Just hips pumping and asses shaking. The blonde's petite chest pressed against Heather's back before they switched.

If Jon were a lesser man, he might have overloaded. No chance. This was one of the highlights of a lifetime. He made the most of gorgeous, grinding eye candy. Watching Heather twine around the slender woman dragged his mind toward thousands of possibilities. He considered his time with Heather exclusive, as he did with every sexual relationship—one mystery at a time, rather than any forced morality. His natural inclinations toward novelty, however, jacked his arousal to new heights. Nothing wrong with a powerful imagination.

Except Dash tapped him on the shoulder. "We've got a situation, Tin Tin."

Jon sighed. He gave Heather the option of staying to dance, but she waved goodbye to the blonde. Dread took a walk down Jon's spine as they made their way back to the VIP area. Leah was a master of getting into the deep shit.

Though really, dancing on a tabletop didn't top the list. Could have been worse. She'd stripped off her pink shirt. The bra underneath covered most of her goods, but that didn't matter. The waitress stood next to the table. Her expression was less than pleased, mouth pinched and eyes narrowed. "She threw a glass."

"Hit anyone?"

"No. We run a better place than this."

Jon peeled off a small stack of bills from his wallet and shoved them in her hand. "I'll get her out of here."

"Make sure she doesn't come back."

Leah had stripped the band from her ponytail. A dark mass of hair spread over her shoulders. "Hi, Jon." She beamed. "Hear that song? This is *my* damn song. I think they played it for me."

"Why don't you come off there?"

"Don't wanna."

Heather laughed. "Come down or I'll tell Jon he can spank your ass."

"Crap. Can't have that." Even as Leah slurred the words, she scrambled down.

Dash took the shirt from the waitress and held it out to Leah. "Time to cover up. Save all the pretty for Han Solo."

"God I wanna smack you tonight."

"Don't talk dirty to me. Sunny would have your head."

Leah stuck out her tongue and flipped the shirt over her shoulder. She led the parade out of the joint. At least she was mobile this time.

She frowned when they made it to the valet. "I need a cab."

"No, you don't," Jon said. "I'll drive you home."

"C'mon, in the Aston?" Dash shoved his hands in his pockets and laughed. "You're out of your mind. She's gonna puke all over your upholstery. Do you know how much it takes to get a car detailed? No wait, don't answer that. Far too practical for a platinum-card guy."

Leah wandered off, chatting up a knot of guys. One of them put a hand on her bare waist. Was that a *cigarette* in her hand?

"Whatever happens, it needs to be quick," Jon said. "I've done it before. Besides, putting her in your little zipper of an Evo isn't any better."

"My car has four doors."

"And an engine that belongs in a Ferrari. You take one turn too fast, and she'll toss her cookies all over *your* upholstery. Explain that to Sunny."

"Too true. Night, all."

Heather angled closer to Jon. Most of the curl had dropped out of her hair. Damp tendrils stuck to her forehead. She looked gorgeous, as if freshly fucked. "I brought my car. Four-door sedan. No scary fast engine. Just give me her address and I'll drop her off."

Jon watched her for a moment, then helped secure Leah into the passenger seat. Only after discharging that duty did he catch Heather's wrist and pull her close. "You know our night's not over."

"I'd be disappointed if it were."

"Can't have that. I'll lead."

"Driving, or with something else in mind?"

"Try me, Heather love." He strode back to his Aston, once again riding high on anticipation.

Chapter Twenty-Three

As she drove, Heather kept glancing at Leah. The woman was hot. Shorter, fitter, with an effervescence that probably explained why her male friends put up with her antics. But then, Heather could relate too. She saw her old self in Leah's behavior, so much so that she almost didn't want to get involved. Almost. The stricken look on Jon's face had convinced her. She'd never imagined he could look helpless.

The urge to take that burden from his shoulders had overpowered her fears about looking her past in the face. Only Leah's face was elfin. Her baby-doll eyes listed to half-mast just before she popped the window and hugged it with the devotion of a lover.

"Oh, crap. Worse off than I thought."

Heather nodded. "Always is."

"You don't seem the type."

"Everyone says that. But everyone has a past too."

Leah swept damp hair from her eyes and tossed a half-grin over her shoulder. "Ain't that the truth. Only mine seems to be happening now."

"Future regrets?"

"Something like that." The woman covered her mouth with the back of her hand, swallowed a few times and closed her eyes.

Heather stopped at a red light, with Jon's panther of a car right in front of her. She could imagine his anxiety from even that distance.

What was it about him that compelled such loyalty? And what would it be like to be on the receiving end of that same loyalty? Almost too bright to look at fully. She might want it too much when their relationship meant it was way out of reach.

She remembered what Jenn had said about taking the risk. Not yet. She just couldn't. The thrill hadn't worn off. Jon still scared the shit out of her. She couldn't possibly open herself to a man that powerful. The hurt it caused when it fell through was something she never wanted to endure again.

"You two having fun?" Leah asked. "And don't play dumb. Last thing you are is dumb."

"Yes, we're having fun."

"He's kinda known for that, but choosey with his chicks. You seem different, though."

"Why's that?"

"He hasn't moved on yet. Makes sense to me. You're a cool character."

"Um...thanks?"

"Yup, meant as a compliment." A giggle came out of nowhere, then disappeared on a flash of puke face. She hugged the open window once again.

"You need me to pull over?"

Several deep breaths later, Leah mumbled a negative. She slumped back in her seat. "He's a good guy under all the bullshit. Would lie down in front of a truck for his friends." She waved a hand toward her disheveled appearance. "As you might have noticed."

"Any clue why?" God, she hated pumping an insensate woman for information, but it was a lot safer than playing head games with Jon to get the same answers. Ugh. She hadn't thought herself quite that much a shrinking violet.

"His sister, I think. His parents. When folks leave, it's hard not to cling hard to the ones who stay." She seemed to warm to the topic, mostly sitting up. A relatively cool breeze added white noise to the inside of Heather's Camry. It seemed almost private, as if that was the perfect place to divulge secrets—even if it still edged uncomfortably close to prying. "He comes across all playboy and shit, but he's a fucking genius and a softy to boot."

"A softy? That I don't get."

"You know what he does with his salary? The whole thing? Sixty-some grand a year goes straight to Operation Homefront. Supports hard-luck military families."

Heather blinked. She could see it. Know it. When had that become possible? The suave stranger at the wine tasting didn't give to home-front charities. But Jon Carlisle did.

"Did he actually tell you that?"

"Nah. Saw the envelope on his desk during one of our poker games with Ryan. We grilled him until he fessed up. Stubborn butthole." Leah groaned and held her stomach. "Not much farther, by the way. Up here on the left."

"Thank God."

"Bitch," she said with a grin. "I don't tease him about it much 'cause he gets so damn prickly. Trash talking is easier, you know? He likes to keep it quiet. Not show off."

Heather kept her eyes on the DBS's lights just ahead. "That's a switch."

"You know fronting, right? You seem the type." She grinned again. "One bitch to another."

"Sure." Heather kept her voice even. Noncommittal.

"Yeah, that's him. Two years, and it's a fucking miracle I know this much. You strong enough to dig past?"

Heather kept her attention trained carefully on the apartment numbers, away from answering the question. "Here we are, yes?"

Leah waggled her finger. "I saw that."

"You're awful insightful for being so drunk."

"It's a gift."

Heather turned into the parking lot of a halfway-decent apartment complex. The stucco could use touching up, and the roof had seen better days, but the lot was amply lit and the walkways had recently been redone.

Maybe it was the sudden shift from forward motion to park that sparked Leah's renewed nausea. She popped the passenger door open and swung her head outside. Heather didn't need to look to know what came next. Listening was way plenty.

Jon gracefully unfurled from his sports car. He appeared to stroll as casually as always, hands stuffed in the pockets of his slacks, but he wore a tension across his shoulders that was easier to identify now.

"So you made it, Princess Leah."

Heather shut her door and came around to the passenger side in time to see Leah's thumbs-up. "No problem, Rin Tin Tin. Got it covered."

"Well, your *shoes* are covered."

"Dammit. I like these heels. But leather washes off as easy as rubber sheets, right?"

"Wouldn't know," he said. "I'm a Garnier-Thiebaut man myself."

"I've never heard of it. Means freaking expensive, yeah?"

"You could say that." He held Heather's hand and spoke near enough for privacy. "Well worth checking out, Ms. Morris. Decadent stuff."

Was the look he slid Heather another dare? She knew he wanted her to see his place. Again came that shiver of intimacy she feared. Jerks didn't want girls to come by and take a look at the ranch. Maybe playboy trust-fund boys did—showing off what they could offer beyond a slammin' good time.

That just didn't seem to be Jon anymore, especially after Leah's slurred revelations left Heather more confused than ever.

Fielding his silent expectations was freaking her out. The urge to call it off battled right alongside the need to grab on and not let go.

He was too *good* to let go. So why were her hands shaking at the thought? Why did she want to jump in her car and run right back to her safe, placid, well-earned life?

She smacked into that word *coward* again.

Leah wiped her mouth with her wrist. "Ugh."

"Classy, Princess. Up you go." He used those strong, lean arms to haul the increasingly dazed woman to her feet. "Where are your keys?"

"Ass pocket."

"Then you fish them out."

"Aw, Dimples, don't want your girlfriend to watch you feel me up?"

Jon scowled. "First off, you smell like a tequila factory with a side of vomit. Second, I'm pretty sure feeling up a fellow officer is frowned upon." He put her arm around his neck. "Hold on, dumbass. I'm not carrying you again."

Heather grabbed both purses and locked up, following the pair toward a first-level apartment. Leah managed to fish her key out from skintight jeans, but Jon unlocked the door. Lights on. In they went.

To say Leah's apartment was a shock would've been an understatement. Everything was tidy. Spotless. Not a book or throw pillow or piece of hanging copper cookware out of place. The contrast was astonishing, considering her current state.

"Couch, bed or bathroom?" Jon asked.

"Bathroom, bed."

"A fair improvement from last time. Kitchen floor wasn't your best choice."

"Neither was red wine with Jack and Coke."

"Wine before whiskey, mighty risky."

"How terribly folksy, rich boy."

Jon snorted. "At least I took it to heart...about ten years ago. Get with it, Princess."

That last line was sharp enough to jerk Heather's attention away from an alphabetized Blu-ray rack. Although he continued his snide jokes, Jon revealed his fatigue in tight lines around his eyes and in the way his mouth never quirked. The rapport held the same bitter twinge as when he'd leveled country-club prigs with quietly sarcastic comments.

"Anything I can do?" she asked.

Jon looked back over his shoulder. His expression was nearly apologetic. "Take what you want from the kitchen. This'll only take a minute."

"Always with the chatter like I'm not here," Leah said on a laugh. She surged out of Jon's arms and flew toward what must've been the bathroom.

Jon's shoulders slumped. Drawn to him, Heather crossed Leah's immaculately vacuumed carpet—the lines from each pass still made a sunburst pattern in the pile. She exhaled then draped herself along his back, arms around his tense middle.

"You okay?"

Only a shrug, but eventually he relaxed. It took time, as if he was certain she'd pull away, that the comfort she offered was only temporary. He smelled good. A combination of light aftershave and sweat from when they'd danced in the club. Sex standing up. The thrill of when he'd watched her dance with that pretty blonde seemed very long ago.

"Let me get her into bed and we'll get out of here," he said. "She'll sleep it off just fine."

"No problem."

He turned, his expression coming to life. "How was your girls' night?"

"Fun. Really nice, actually. Jenn got bombed too."

A ghost of a grin tipped one corner of his mouth. He rested his hands at her waist. No passion there, just what felt like a man holding on, needing something steady. Heather only wished she could offer that.

"So we've both been tending lushes all night?"

"Seems like."

He kissed her forehead. "Glad you showed up. They were boring-ass company tonight."

"Can't have that."

A steady, salacious look down her V-cut top tempted her playful Jon back to life.

Her Jon?

Get it together.

"I do like this one." He skimmed his hands up her body until he cupped her breasts. One thumb toyed with her nipple ring through the sheer black fabric. "But then, you're wearing it. Adds an undeniable appeal."

"Flirt."

"Unapologetically so."

So, she couldn't offer to see his place. Not yet. But maybe there was a safer middle ground to take that possibility off the table. A distraction.

She curled her fingers under his lapels. They stood nearly eye-to-eye. "On my birthday, I mentioned seeing your plane someday. Is that still a possibility?"

His brows lifted. "On your birthday, hm? Was that before or after you'd awoken every innocent creature in the desert?"

"Before." She toyed with the lapels of his suit then began unbuttoning his coat. "I've heard you're a fighter pilot. Need to see it for myself."

"Because fighter pilots are fucking studs."

The vest beneath was hot with the pulse of his body. "Oh, yes."

"A week from Thursday." It wasn't a question, which she liked more than she could understand. Her idea, but his commitment to it. "Maintenance day. Boring-as-hell classes, but no flights. We'll have pretty easy access after, say, four."

Heather did a mental check of her calendar and nodded. "I'll clear what I need to."

Frank satisfaction shaped his mouth. A flash of dimples. "Cool."

"Oh, God, no making out in my living room."

They turned to find Leah in the doorway to her bedroom. She'd wet and combed her hair and put on a pair of yoga pants and a camisole.

Jon only flashed his asshole smile. "Keeping ourselves occupied while you proved perfectly capable of taking care of yourself. Well done."

Leah flipped him off, but dark circles already hugged beneath her rich brown eyes. She stumbled back into the bedroom.

"Right back," Jon said with a soft kiss.

He found a bottle of aspirin in the hall closet, poured a glass of water from a pitcher in the fridge and grabbed a stainless-steel bowl out of a cabinet. The actions were unerring. How often had this scene been repeated?

Heather stood in the bedroom doorway and watched as Jon forced his friend to drink all the water. "In the bowl, this time. Clean-up will be a bitch and you know it."

"Ugh. Yes. Now go. I fucked up your date enough already."

Jon said nothing, only shut off the nightstand light. "Sleep, Princess."

Heather backed away as he left the bedroom then took his hand. She couldn't say anything about what she'd witnessed. It was too close, too personal. She needed time to sort through what that evening had done to her heart. Wrapped it in barbed wire, maybe. Growing tighter every day.

But she needed it too. She was beginning to need him.

"Come on," she whispered. "Time for your reward."

He cocked an eyebrow. "Reward?"

"Oh, yeah."

"I don't know anyone who'd turn down a reward from you."

They locked Leah's apartment, with Heather still leading him by the hand. To her Camry. She thumbed the key fob but didn't get into the driver's seat. The backseat instead.

Jon loomed over her, framed by the door and a parking lot light five spaces away. "Do you live for this stuff, Heather love?"

"I haven't." *Not for a long time*, she added silently.

He shed his suit coat and vest, dropped his suspenders—right there in full view. "So I bring it out in you?"

"You do."

"You should know I like the sound of that."

She tipped him a saucy smile and leaned back onto the seat, stretching as much as possible. "Thought you might."

Although a tight fit, Jon climbed in and shut the door. Locked it. They pressed together in the dark, their bodies still scented with sweat from the club. She liked that. Primal and real.

Jon flipped her onto her stomach and unfastened her skirt. "Otherwise we'll have to take them all the way off, and frankly, that doesn't seem possible."

Her cheek pressed against the seat's upholstery. "Better than in your DBS."

"You're not by chance double-jointed?"

"Nope."

"Then you're right." The sound of his zipper sent a pulse of want straight to her pussy. Then the condom. Then his prick right against her slick opening. "Now hold on, Heather love. I'm ready to claim my reward."

Chapter Twenty-Four

Three hours into a class on avionics, Jon was two hours past frustrated. Pissed, maybe. He sat at the back of the briefing room, popping his pencil up and down on a notebook. Annoyance ate up his spine and twisted his muscles. He crossed an ankle over his knee. But boredom wasn't even the problem.

Captain Eric "Kisser" Donaghue sat in the front row. He talked so much that he might as well have been teaching—except he didn't understand half the trajectories he was bullshitting.

Jon couldn't keep his mouth shut anymore. He leaned forward, elbows on his desk. "Kisser, run the route you're describing, and plant your nose in the dirt. The numbers don't support it."

Capt. Donaghue twisted in his seat and sneered. "Flying isn't all about the numbers, Tin Tin."

"Planes don't stay in the air because they *want* to. You have to do your part."

Ryan stepped out from behind his podium, hands lifted. "Gentlemen. We're in the middle of something here."

The class wasn't going to do Donaghue much good if he refused to listen or get his head out of his ass. Jon had seen the other man fly, been at his wingtip. Same as everyone else in the room. Apparently only Jon saw what a danger the man was.

The problem originated with sharp edges. Every time Kisser got in his plane, he pushed his yaw too hard. All jerky moves and lost opportunities.

The beastly F-16s were designed to work within specific parameters. The relaxed static stability meant enhanced maneuverability, but the engine couldn't be pushed the way Donaghue fucked around.

One day he would go too far. Jon just hoped those he cared about were well out of the way.

By the time class dismissed and he made his way to the office he shared with Leah, Jon let his head wrap into the numbers—a predictable place where everything made sense. If any pilot flew so hard and low, the way Donaghue advocated, the drag on the aerodynamics would catch hold and pull him down even farther. The speed required to overcome that difference would be too significant.

After dropping into his desk chair, he scratched out the numbers on a piece of scrap paper. He punched them into a calculator, just to make sure he was right. He always was.

Tossing the pencil down, he sighed and pushed his palms against his closed eyes. The slight burn didn't help.

Christ only knew why he was trying to make Kisser's flight plan work. The man had all the charm of an orangutan, and he and Jon had never gotten along.

The door to the office opened to reveal Leah, looking as clean and put together as she always did in uniform. She grinned at him and sat without grace. "How they hangin', Tin Tin?"

He leaned back and laced his fingers over his utilitarian flight suit. "You always recover so well. As if nothing even happened."

She shrugged. "The benefits of healthy living."

"Uncountable margaritas and half a dozen shots of tequila is healthy living?"

"Nope. But my five-mile run this morning?" She pumped her fists as if she were running before folding her hands behind her head. Elbows out. Legs stretched to full length. She looked as chill and relaxed as possible. "That set me up right and tight."

He shook his head while he laughed, then shuffled papers around on his desk. This right here. This was why he couldn't help but see if Eric's numbers worked. These people were his family, and it was in his nature to try. Try and try, even when people like Leah seemed more like solid concrete. Or the fact that Jon knew he'd always give Donaghue another shot. If the opportunity came up, he'd sit the man down and have a chat about the limitations of their planes.

Leah's mouth quirked. "Spit it."

"*You.* You drive me nuts, you know that?"

"You're just jealous of my recovery time."

"You're wasting your potential, do you know that?" he echoed, this time with deliberate harshness. Maybe something would sink in for once.

Darkness filtered across Leah's features. "Bullshit. I fly fighter jets for a living. I'm about as awesome as they come."

"Right. That's why you don't remember how you got home on Saturday night."

"Your girlfriend. Her car." She winked. "Besides, we had fun up until then. You've got to admit that."

Jon's mouth opened, but before he could answer, his phone chirruped. He dug it out of his pocket and swiped the screen. It was an email, which was normally no big deal. Except the sender was Heather.

He wished he were actually as laidback as he made people believe. Mr. Cool's heart jumped into a heavier, faster beat. He should've been more worried that he was a sap, but his head filled with images of their round in the back of her car. The way they twisted and grappled. The way they'd fogged the windows until she gasped his name.

"Now there's a look I could have done without." Leah made a show of holding up one hand and putting the other over her eyes. "Just *wrong*."

"I don't know what you're talking about." He glanced up even while he held the phone. He should wait. He shouldn't open the email yet.

He clicked.

"Dirty thoughts. You were thinking dirty thoughts." She paused. A little frown pinched her mouth. "I didn't... I don't remember everything I said that night."

He stacked his hands over his phone. "Look, you were fine."

She shifted in her seat, picked up a flight manual, tapped it on her knees. "It's one thing if I wreck myself. But I wouldn't ever want to put you in a bad place. Or say the wrong thing to your girl."

His girl.

Maybe she was. Maybe she wasn't. The email was the first time she'd initiated contact.

His issues with Heather were secondary for the moment. Jon targeted Leah in his sights. "Wreck yourself?"

"I don't mean anything by it. Just if I get myself in trouble, it's no big deal. I'm my own responsibility."

165

"That's where you're wrong. We're friends. Changes everything."

She laughed, although it sounded strained. "Your Tin Tin is showing."

"Whatever." He sat back again. "I can tell when you're not in the mood."

"You just make sure it's Heather's moods you pay attention to." Leah all but launched out of her seat. She shoved a notebook and her running shoes into a black workout bag.

He ran his thumb along the cool metal edge of his phone. "Her moods are my business, thank you very much."

She kept him on his toes, even more so than his friends—Leah and Ryan and the rest. Things worked out with them because they gave him the same support in return.

It remained to be seen whether Heather would prove to be that real.

Leah stopped in the doorway. "We should go out this weekend."

He couldn't help his chagrin. "I'm not up for another vomit fest."

"I get it. You don't think I do, but I do. Maybe rock climbing or something?"

"Yeah. I'll give you a call."

A minute later, she was gone. He hated to attach the word *finally* to a friend, but there it was, hovering in his head. He flipped his phone, woke it up and scrolled down to Heather's message.

The first line was in carefully researched French, but he thought by the formal conjunction that it might have been translated by a website. He didn't care. The content made him smile. An invitation to dinner at a place Jon recognized as a dive joint with awesome malts. She'd attached a caveat—she would be there exactly at six and she wasn't waiting.

A glance up at the military-issue wall clock showed he'd be cutting it close. No time to scramble to his condo and get changed. He had a spare T-shirt and pair of jeans in his office. Locking the door, he stripped out of his flight suit and changed in the tiny, windowless room. At the last second, he grabbed his flight jacket. Plenty of dry warmth lingered in late summer, but once the sun went down, cold would kiss the air.

At one minute before six, he pulled into the diner's small asphalt lot. He battled the impulse to wait in his car, simply to make the point of a precise entrance. Or maybe it was the realization that he hadn't been on a date with Heather when not dressed to the nines.

He shook it off. Not exactly worth worrying about.

Pushing through the plate-glass doors, he found a square room with little depth. At the far end was a pick-up counter and a window into the kitchen where an army of cooks swarmed. The booths were small and laminated, with black-cushioned seats. The walls were covered with a mural that must've been painted by a cadre of eight-year-old girls obsessed with neon colors and fantasy animals. People gobbled fries and burgers out of red baskets.

He stood in the doorway until he spotted Heather. She was seated in the far corner, fiddling with a white straw and a Styrofoam cup, as if she was nervous. He liked that possibility too much.

She looked up. Her expression didn't change for a long moment. Jon's chest contracted when she smiled—slow, drawn out. That smile promised all the things she'd like to do to him later.

Or maybe those were *his* thoughts.

As he approached, he couldn't help but admire how good she looked. The blouse was ivory against her pale skin, with a hint of lace at the buttoned-up collar. Technically her breasts were covered, but the slick satin gave him a visceral reaction. His hands wanted to take and touch, to let tits settle in his palms.

He followed pure instinct without second-guessing. Once he reached the table, he leaned down and took her mouth, fast and swift. Their kisses spiked so quickly—wet heat under his tongue and the scrape of teeth over lips.

He only pulled away once their breathing roughened. "Hello."

Heather rubbed the corner of his mouth with her thumb. "You certainly do know how to greet a girl."

"You looked so neat and proper. I wanted to mess you up a little."

She tugged the hem of his T-shirt. "Funny, I could say the opposite about you."

He helped her up and led her to the ordering window. "That doesn't sound like a complaint."

"It's not, flyboy." She slanted him one of those gorgeous, challenging gazes. "Not in the least."

Chapter Twenty-Five

"Number eighty-five. Order up."

Heather looked toward the window where a large man in an even larger greasy white apron slid two red baskets under a string of heat lamps. Beneath the table, she snuggled high heels between Jon's boots. His jeans rubbed against her bare calves.

She took a long sip of her drink. "What do you think? Eighty-five hours at the gym to work it off?"

"Hmm." He rubbed his chin as if in deep thought. "Perhaps eighty-five health-code violations?"

"Eighty-five drips of sweat in the hamburger meat."

Jon leaned his elbows against the white Formica table, which was, thankfully, squeaky clean despite the dive's grungy atmosphere. He grinned. That full-on devastating grin. Complete with dimples. The one made of pure fun, with only a few glimmers of sexual intent. She saw it so rarely that Heather could only sit still, taking in the sight.

He cocked that one amazingly expressive eyebrow. "Eighty-five former employees who've been convicted of felonies."

"Eighty-five barrels of fry oil used every week."

"Eighty-five...nope. Shit. I'm out."

Heather leaned back in her seat on a laugh. "Eighty-five reasons why I'm way cooler than Jon Carlisle."

"Oh, come on." His mouth twisted ruefully. "If I want trash talking, I have Leah for that."

"How is she, by the way?"

A shrug did nothing to ease the tension that shaped his posture. "Same as always," he said. "A Tasmanian devil by night. A squared-away captain by day."

She'd enjoyed the teasing so much that she regretted having asked. But the things Leah had revealed about Jon were unforgettable.

He was so much more than he seemed. No, that didn't sound right. He was *less* than he seemed. Dressed in a black T-shirt and jeans, he looked his age. Young. Relaxed. Less intimidating. Less like a well-groomed cat on the prowl. Less in control of the world and his place in it.

This version of Jon was a little closer to real, and a hell of a lot scarier. But Heather was getting tired. The walls were hard to prop up, especially when he seemed intent on breaking them down. She'd only wanted to assert her authority, to see if he would jump when she called.

Control. She wanted some semblance of control in this increasingly hypnotic affair.

Her ultimatum had actually worked against her. She knew his suits and his suave bearing. She had no idea how to handle him being ordinary. His version of ordinary was *magical.* Same sharp jaw, sarcastic mouth and dark, dark eyes. The glare from the light above their table added silver tips to the ends of his buzzed hair. Shoulders and arms, all shown to perfection by that simple T-shirt.

And the flight jacket. Holy Christ, she hadn't been prepared for that at all. Aside from the war stories Leah and Dash had told at the club, she had proceeded with Jon's military service as mere background knowledge. He was so different from the servicemen she'd known growing up—her dad's men, or the guys she'd eventually made her hobby. No way was her pretty flyboy of that same ilk, ready to fight and die for his country.

But he was.

Stories about Jon had chipped through that artificial barrier. Seeing him in his flight jacket when he'd walked into the diner—that had crumbled them altogether. She glanced at where he'd hung it across the back of the booth. The man in the three-piece suit was the slick nighttime version of this genuine fighter pilot.

"You're a good friend to her," Heather said quietly. "She's lucky to have you."

"Tiring." He muttered that single word on an exhalation. Then he seemed to check himself. A shadow of his usual insouciance covered his features before he just sighed again. "Hell, it's not worth the effort to say otherwise. You saw how she was. Ryan and I have been trading off for going on a year. She keeps getting worse."

Heather swallowed. She couldn't stop herself from digging deeper, revealing more. What the hell had he done to her? It was more than the flight jacket. Keeping everything elegant and proscribed had been safer. She felt as if her ribs were being pried apart. Maybe because she so desperately wanted to breathe.

Her voice shook when she said, "I knew a girl like that in high school."

"Oh?" Tilting his head to the side, Jon took her hands. Their fingers twined in the middle of the white tabletop. "What happened to her?"

"Got scared straight."

"Must've been difficult."

"She...struggled."

"Did she make it through?"

Her nod felt like balancing the weight of the world on her neck. "Took years, but yes."

Deep brown eyes, so perceptive, looked right into her. Right down into the dark. "You'll have to tell me more about her sometime. She sounds like a strong chick."

God, he was even sexier when he meant it. No games and no dares.

"Order up," called the man in the apron. "Number eighty-nine."

"Eighty-nine frogs used to spice up the hamburger," she said with a forced smile.

But Jon's grin was sudden and genuine. Damn, those dimples were insane. "Nah, you don't want that. Believe me." He tapped a finger against her order ticket. "Get 'er done, eighty-nine."

"That *so* doesn't sound right coming from you, Richie Rich."

"Doesn't change the fact you've cursed yourself with a fresh, juicy frog burger." He made a shooing motion, until the cook called his number too. "Well, shit. Here we go."

They returned to the booth with red baskets in hand. Heather had ordered a shake, but it was still too cold to drink. She tried anyway, slipping Jon a coy look as she hollowed her cheeks.

He stopped mid-motion. A fry drooped from his fingertips. "You're doing that on purpose."

After popping back from the straw, she nodded at his fry. "I'd have to suck that hard to get your limp prick up."

Expression still fixed, entirely deadpan, he tilted it up to a more eager angle. "All yours, Ms. Morris."

She grabbed his wrist and brought the fry to her lips. One quick lick with the tip of her tongue. Then she bit it in half. "Mmm...nice and salty."

Jon's deadpan slipped. He laughed, ducking, shaking his head a little. Heather wanted to curl her hand around the back of his neck and stroke, pet, hear him purr under the attention.

"How's your frog burger?"

"Shouldn't you be asking me that in French?"

"Oh, so witty tonight." But he hadn't stopped smiling.

"What do you think," she said, glancing toward a woman at the takeaway counter. "Aspiring, current or former call girl?"

Still as cool as if he'd been wearing a three-piece suit, he eased against the booth and managed to look without looking. She'd witnessed that same skill practiced at the country club. Here, the need for such subterfuge was absolutely nil, but all the more enjoyable because of it. Compared to his behavior at the charity event, Jon was stripped down to bare bones.

Oh, but she did enjoy that idea. And not just emotionally. She'd never entertained the idea that filled her brain. Jon. Open. Vulnerable. Hers to command.

Now it would just be a matter of seducing him around to it.

"Current," he said at last. "She looks tired. And she's only getting a half portion of fries. Watching her weight. But her shoes are new."

"Damn, you're good."

"Gotta have a hobby, right?"

She picked off a sesame seed, tried to keep eye contact but couldn't. "Makes me wonder how quickly you sized me up at the wine tasting."

"You really want to know?"

"Do I?"

His grin had taken on a sly edge. "I think so. Even if only to satisfy your curiosity now that you've asked."

171

"Go for it."

"Beautiful. Great rack, of course."

"Of course." She went back to nursing her shake to keep him slightly off kilter.

"But to be honest, I wondered if you'd live up to the hype. Seemed...tame. Predictable."

"A forlorn woman alone at the table."

"Conservative in her blazer."

"And you, so unprepared for how wrong you were."

Jon finished the last of his cheeseburger and licked each finger in turn. *Then* he used a napkin anyway. She was tempted to ask how he'd managed so well without utensils and a placemat but she was too busy admiring his response to her provocation. His eyes had gone sleepy, perched between intense sexual awareness and the same playful vibe they'd been riding all night.

"I was unprepared. Yes. But I returned the favor."

"Yes. You did." Heather rested her chin on her folded hands. "Would you answer something for me, Jon?"

"Well, now." He pushed the empty basket away and settled back. The posture said relaxation. The sudden tension around his mouth said *bring it*. "Jon, is it? This sounds serious."

"It is. Very. You really want to know?" she asked, echoing him on purpose.

"Oh, hell yes. Ask away."

"What *haven't* you done?"

"Go back to sucking while I mull it over."

Heather lowered her mouth to the straw. This time she was rewarded with chocolate malt. She licked her lower lip. "I'm waiting."

"I've never been snowboarding. It's tacky."

"Fascinating."

"I've never been to Central America."

"Also tacky?"

"No, just not so many excuses to fly jets down there. Well, not since the eighties."

Although she loved flirting with him this way, almost sweetly, she had a definite angle now, ever since imagining him stripped and vulnerable. She could imagine Jon Carlisle doing almost anything sexual—except willingly giving up control.

"Have you ever played football?" she asked innocently.

"Pick-up games, sure. For some reason, the NFL never returned my calls."

"Have you ever been in love?"

Jon froze. Heather's heart skipped. She had wanted his body stripped, not his heart. Maybe she could blame the rush of questions. She'd asked. He'd answered. Some deep part of her wanted to know.

"Have *you?*" He leaned in, elbows braced on the table. "Come on now, Ms. Morris. Fair's fair."

"I'll answer if you do. Truthfully."

"Nope. Never been."

"Me neither."

The world tilted at the edges as they stared each other down. Heather couldn't breathe. She might as well have been under a dozen spotlights for how little she could hide. The scariest part was that he wasn't holding back either. For a few seconds over red baskets of cold fries, they told the truth.

She'd never been more scared or more thrilled.

Which meant their quick snap back toward the status quo was as inevitable as it was confusing. Just what the hell did she want? Jon grinned, so filthy and ready to play again. Heather laughed under her breath and smoothed her hair. Like retreating to corners.

"Have you ever...?" She swallowed chocolate malt.

"Go for it. The last one didn't detonate the building."

She exhaled, shoving questions about love aside for ones about sex. Blatant, hard, uncompromising sex.

"Have you ever been on the receiving end of an anal plug?"

Jon lifted one eyebrow in a high arch. "Well, well."

With her voice intentionally breathless with excitement, she asked, "Oooh, did I get you again?"

"You did. What brings this up?"

Heather shrugged as casually as she could manage. The interest in his eyes was chipping away at their earlier calm. She wanted this now. How kinky was he willing to play?

"Just a question, flyboy. Like all the others."

"No," he said at last, the word drawn out.

"Intriguing. So, does some deep, dark, unexplored part of your perverted psyche want to be explored?"

Jon patted the bench next to him. "Come here and ask me what you really want."

Standing felt...liberating. They were going to blow each other's minds. Again. This time it was her idea. Why was that even more important than what they eventually did?

She slid easily into the booth, then crossed her legs so that her thigh draped over his. Again, jeans rubbed against bare skin. Her wispy crepe skirt rode up. Jon wasted no time in giving it another shove. His fingers, hiding beneath the pale fabric, traced the lace of her panties.

Heather nuzzled until her lips grazed his jaw. A beautiful tension hummed from his body. She touched him behind the neck as she'd imagined. Bristling hair gave her a thrill. All this and more to come.

"I want to know if you've ever participated in a sexual encounter where you knew going in that you weren't in control." She lowered her voice. "Have you ever been dominated, flyboy?"

His fingertips dug into her ass. "No."

"Not so coy now." She nibbled his earlobe. "Because I would enjoy trying. I've never had that power before. Girls tend to be the ones with their arms tied, bent over a chair."

"Oh, but you looked so pretty."

"Tell me, Jon," she whispered. "The safe word still applies. And you can dictate terms. But the question remains. Will you give me your body tonight? To do with as I please?"

Chapter Twenty-Six

Since they'd both arrived separately at the diner, they met back at Heather's house. Jon could have beaten her there. Easily. Not only did he have the faster car, he was driven by a ridiculous amount of curiosity. And nerves. He could admit to some nerves. He'd never willingly put himself at the mercy of someone else's sexual whim.

He wasn't sure if he had it in himself to just...lie there. Seemed unlikely.

But he kept his foot chill on the gas pedal and didn't zoom past her tin can. He even managed to keep himself in check as she opened her front door.

He thought they might chat first, maybe hang out. Have a drink. But Heather skipped right past her tidy living room and small kitchen, heading directly toward the bedroom.

He'd seen it before, but generally when it was dark and Heather had worked her hand down his pants. They hadn't bothered with trivialities such as light switches.

The bedroom was fairly big considering her small bungalow. The furniture was all pale oak, and the bed was covered with a lace-trimmed afghan. The lack of frou-frou pillows or cutesy accessories struck a balance between feminine and comfortable.

She walked to her vanity, though she didn't sit. A mirror with a lacquer frame reflected how she watched him while she unhooked long silver earrings. "Nervous, Captain?"

He crossed his arms and leaned against the doorjamb. "More like wondering how you plan to do this, considering your bed has no posts."

"Hmm. A one-piece headboard too." Her hair was pinned at her nape. She drew long hairpins out one by one. The tiny plink of metal dropping into a glass dish was the only sound in the room. A dark fall of silk spilled over her shoulders. "You don't think you can hold still?"

"Probably not."

She turned and focused her gaze on him, like a pale blue laser. Her steps were slow. Luscious hips swung in a grind that reminded him of sex. Naturally. She meant it to.

On a deep breath, she grazed his T-shirt with her breasts. Her mouth hovered near his, even as she dipped her chin to look at him through her lashes. "Are you sure, Jon? If I asked you to? Without bindings or restraints. Just...wait. For me. And what I do to you."

She certainly made him want to try. His hands reached for her hips as if on their own. He needed her flesh, needed her heat. Soft material slinked under his touch. He dragged it up a few inches, the better to see her lush thighs.

"Maybe."

"Do it," she said, low and certain.

So much challenge. She seemed to expect him to balk. To quit. "You can be more specific than that."

Her brows lifted and that sharp chin came back up. Her mouth tweaked into a tiny smile. "Jon Carlisle, take off every scrap of your clothing, including boots and socks."

"I'd never leave my socks on. That would be a travesty."

She managed to get her smile under control behind a tiny cough. "Do it slowly. Then lie down on the bed, on your back, with your hands laced behind your head."

"But how will I touch you?"

"God, you're mouthy."

"I'm pretty sure it's in my breeding."

"Lots of things are in your breeding." She backed up until she stood in the middle of the floor. He might have believed she was taking well to this idea, except her toes curled into the weave of a thick rug. Practically twitching. But her voice was still steady. "Do it."

"You're not even going to dim the lights for my modesty?"

"Nope."

Flight jacket first, shucked down his shoulders and tossed over the back of her vanity chair. He kept his movements slow as he pulled the T-shirt over his head, but he didn't add any silly bump or grind. That would be beneath them both. More, it might scatter the slow heat that had built since leaving the diner.

He toed off his boots and socks while he folded the shirt and set it down on the seat of the vanity chair. He found her smirking.

"You fold T-shirts?"

"You don't?"

She twirled her fingers for him to get on with it, but her gaze went to his stomach first then skipped over his shoulders. His arms. She was eating him up with every inch of skin revealed.

Maybe this wouldn't be so bad after all.

The jeans went next—and yes, he folded those too, lifting his brows at her in challenge. But she didn't say a word. She was smoothing her own hips, so obviously restless. When Jon pulled down his boxer briefs, her breath hitched.

The sheets were cool under his ass, his back.

It was harder than he'd expected to stack his hands behind his head. His muscles protested. His respiration jacked. He bit the tip of his tongue.

Most of the time, control didn't seem like such a big thing. Untouchable and ephemeral. He'd never made any bones about how much he liked it. There was something to be said for a woman who'd challenge him. That had been Heather from the start.

He had no idea where they were headed. Maybe nowhere. Tonight at the diner had almost been enough to spark impossible thoughts, but then she'd corralled him back into her bedroom. All in a neat line. She liked order. He liked it himself.

Contemplating more was no good for either of them. Just this. Just this fierce, explosive moment of potential.

So he waited, but he didn't do so comfortably. He figured the odds were fifty-fifty whether he broke and tumbled her over. He'd wind up fucking her rather than the other way around. She'd need to break out some restraints to have it any other way.

When Heather opened a drawer and pulled out a silk scarf, he thought she might have figured that out. Her lips parted. Her gorgeous chest rose and fell on deep breaths. Apparently she liked what she saw.

Score one for his ego, at least.

But as she came closer, she narrowed the scarf into a slender strip. "Lift your head."

"Hang on now," he found himself saying.

Her smile turned wicked. "Don't tell me the great Jon Carlisle is going to safe word because of a simple blindfold. Are you afraid of the dark?"

"Mostly afraid I won't get to see your body."

"You've seen my body before."

"I happen to like it." He took one hand from under his neck and slid it inside her thigh. The side of his palm grazed her panties. Hot already. Damp. He got such a rush off that simple tell.

Anything was worth it if Heather got off.

She tilted her head. Another dare. He expected nothing less from her. She stripped efficiently, though she didn't fold her clothes. Rather, she let them puddle on the floor.

Jesus, he loved her curves. The neat sweep of her waist. Hips designed to be held. The weight of her breasts and her rounded shoulders. All gentle. Made for fucking and bearing a man's weight. She left on her satin thong and bra, which cupped those parts he most wanted to touch.

The dark descended when she wrapped the makeshift blindfold over his eyes. The scarf was light purple silk, but it blocked out everything.

He was left in blackness.

His other senses roared to life. Smell brought him Heather's sultry scent. His hearing caught the rush of his jerky pulse. And Heather too, every rustle of clothing and a tiny whimper.

"Are you touching yourself, Heather love?"

The mattress dipped along his side as she edged onto the bed. "Wouldn't you like to know?"

"Fuck yes, I would." He bared his teeth. Couldn't help it.

He shifted. The sheets were warming, sliding against his back and ass. His left his legs flat on the mattress. All hers. Playground. He had to keep himself calm but he was rapidly losing control of his cock, which lifted from his stomach. Wanting Heather.

Her touch came from out of nowhere. She skimmed two fingertips along his bottom lip. He jerked. He licked and instantly recognized her taste. Slightly salty. A little bit of sweetness. He followed her fingers. His tongue curled around her, took her into his mouth. More of that taste.

"Ride my face," he growled.

"I'm in charge here."

He unfurled one of his best smiles, ignoring the fact he was starkers and splayed out for her whims. "Are you really going to try to convince me that it wasn't what you wanted?"

"Maybe."

He shut his mouth. Had to let her make up her own mind. But when the bed shifted and her knees rested above his shoulders, hard and fast triumph rocked down his body. Even better than flying.

Cool hands found purchase on his chest as she turned away from his face. Her fingers splayed wide and left a wash of sensation across his skin. She didn't lower her body to his mouth. Not yet. She was close. He could tell by the weight to the air, the strength of her aroma.

He couldn't help but fill his palms with her thighs.

She pinched his nipples, fast and mean. "I didn't tell you to move."

He skimmed his fingers up, higher, to the bottom curve of her ass. He liked exploring her by touch alone. She was a miracle of curves and hollows. The satin skin between her cheeks welcomed the tips of his thumbs. "You're not telling me to stop, either."

He tugged her down. Gently, but inexorably, he tilted her hips for better access.

He opened his mouth over her pussy and licked. She tasted almost too good. Went right to his head. A few more flicks and he delved between her damp lips. A flood of moisture was his reward. Sucking her skin left her shaking under his grip. There was nothing better.

Her moan drove him crazy. He lifted his face closer. He needed all of her, every bit, until she melted. Until she spread her knees and ground her pussy against his mouth.

He kept his mouth firm and added a slight edge of teeth—a kiss of hurt to balance all the softness.

More. Closer. He could feel when she was almost there, another wash of her taste across his tongue. So good. He followed every bit, every drop. Took it all into himself.

He flattened his tongue over her clit and stroked. Relentless. Her shakes told him she was on the verge of coming. So soon. He nudged her along with a couple fingers stroking deep into her sheath. All slow. The upward angle made it awkward, but Jesus, so worth it.

Especially when she broke apart in orgasm. Quiet, breathy moans filled the air. She curled over his body, scratching his torso. All but lost. Her hot breath practically burned him.

On the laugh that rose from his depths, he realized he was actually giddy. They did this to each other.

Heather curled along his side, but he could tell from the beat thrumming through her lax body that they weren't done. Not yet. Her hands started roaming.

Thank God, because if he didn't come soon...

That unexpected rush of happiness might start him thinking about things best left alone.

Chapter Twenty-Seven

"Do toys insult your manhood?"

"Toys are for play and having fun," Jon said with a smile. "Are you having fun, Heather love?"

"Oh, yes." She leaned in and licked his jaw, his mouth, his cheeks. He was stubbly and tasted of her. The groan that rumbled through his chest spoke of both arousal and satisfaction. She adored how much pride he took in ensuring she was satisfied—almost as if his pleasure would always be secondary. No matter how much he took, he always held back. He made sure she writhed and gasped before demanding his turn.

Only now, he was in no position to demand anything. Technically.

She traced a finger between his pecs, through the line of hair below his navel. He took in a sharp breath when she stopped just short of the base of his cock. "You're not really good at this submission thing, are you?"

"No."

"At least you're not coy about it."

"Never lie, remember?"

"Then tell me what you want. Right now."

Twin dimples peeked out. "To flip you on your back and fuck you. I wouldn't care if you came now. You've had your chance. Would take me about...oh, twelve strokes."

"I'm nearly tempted to let you, just to check your math."

Restless male hands kept touching what he couldn't see. "I'm good with numbers."

"So I've heard. But no." She flicked her tongue into the hollow at the base of his throat. The reward, each time, was his surprised response—a jerk or a quiet hiss. "That's not what will happen. Back to toys."

"Toys are fine."

"Pain?"

He hesitated. Swallowed. Oh, she *fucking* loved that.

"Sure. But what if I said the lack of control was actually killing my good time?"

Heather laughed, gratified when he joined in. His chest heaved on it, and his whole face shaped around a smile. Combined with his beautifully muscled body, the purple silk blindfold and his fresh-from-juvie buzz cut, he was an exotic amusement park. All hers.

She finally took hold of his prick. His lean hips bucked softly between her hands. "I'd say you were a lying bastard."

"Oh, come now. My parents are unpleasant, but I *was* born legitimately."

"Do I really give a shit right now, Captain Carlisle?"

Another smile. "No, ma'am. Proceed, ma'am." She gave the tip of his penis a hard pinch. "Ow! Fuck off!"

"Mind your manners," she said, bending over to lick it better. He reached out to hold the back of her head, but she pushed his arms away. "Remember who's in charge and you'll come in spectacular fashion."

"So full of yourself, Ms. Morris."

"And you thought me, what was it? Tame? Predictable?"

"Have you always had such a good memory, or have I been in willful denial?"

"Shut up so I can suck your cock in peace."

She took his hard, swollen head between her lips and sucked, just as she had when teasing him with the straw in the diner. Roughly. She'd swallow him like a milkshake.

After popping off his head and giving it another lingering, appreciative lick, she said, "And if you touch me, *anywhere*, I stop. Got it? So hands up, flyboy."

Again, that hesitation. Slowly, so slowly, he exhaled. Even his face relaxed. He lifted his arms above his head and wrapped them around a pillow. The pose stretched his lithe muscles and showed off the pure masculinity of his lats, his ribs, the way the muscles of his arms folded against his shoulders. He turned his face toward the pillow, which

Inside Bet

accentuated the tendons along his throat. He swallowed thickly. A small nod.

God, she was taming a wild mustang. She was getting wet all over again.

Heather returned to his prick, which surged beneath the first touch of her tongue. She ringed both hands at its thick base and pressed hard. He grunted. She wanted to hold off the promised orgasm for as long as possible. She'd heard of edging a man. It had always struck her as...cruel? Why would she want to draw it out so long?

Now the answer was fabulously obvious: to make him suffer in the best possible way.

By turns aggressive and soft, she fucked him with her mouth. It wasn't making love, or teasing, or playtime. It was full-on fucking. Fast, then slow and torturous. She flicked her tongue, sucked hard, stroked him without mercy, then trailed her hair from chest to knees. Jon twitched and made the most delicious noises with every switch. She looked up at the way he fought his body's impulses. His hands clenched and released the pillow sham. Ropes of muscles popped on his forearms and frustrated fists.

"You're enjoying this," he rasped.

"Yes. Are you?" She suckled his head and flicked her tongue along the sensitive ridge just beneath. "No lies, remember?"

A long exhalation. "*Yes.*"

Win. Win. *Win.*

She barely contained the bubbles in her blood. Knees clamped together, she stroked him as if in reward for his honesty. Then she backed off. Again and again, she took him to the edge and kept him from flying over. After exquisite minutes of watching him writhe beneath her deliberate torture, she put the full force of her mouth and hands into making him come.

But not really.

When he bucked his powerful hips off the bed, really fucking her clasped hands—that's when she pulled away. His solid prick thumped onto his flat belly and arrowed toward his navel. His hips jerked to a stop.

Jon actually yanked down the scarf. In his eyes blazed a decadent combination of arousal, surprise and a tiny snap of anger. "What the hell, Heather?"

"Shut up and turn on your side."

"Bullshit."

She lifted her brows. "Really? I thought you were up for more than this. I can climb on and get it over with if you want. Pandas are very pretty, after all. We could talk about them." With the haughtiest expression she could muster, she stared him down. The anger was gone. So was the surprise. A battle remained, some fight between his curiosity and his need for control. "But if you decide to keep going, don't stop again."

"Ah, fuck it," he said at last. He slumped back against the bed. Another full-bodied laugh. Heather's heart flipped over. "Might as well. Make it good, Heather love."

"Spectacular. I promise."

He tucked the scarf back over his eyes. "Bring it."

"Mmm, I love the sound of that. Now hold still. I'll be right back."

"Heather?"

"Toys, remember? Relax. You're a little tense."

That big, beautiful grin. His eyebrows were so animated that they poked out above the blindfold. "Can you blame me?"

Heather opened a drawer in her nightstand and grabbed what she was after. "Nope. I seem to remember having my arms tied behind my back, pressed against a hotel-room window."

"That was quite a sight."

"Consider yourself lucky I'm not telling you to do that."

"Hah. Wouldn't happen."

She grinned, leaned over, kissed his stomach. Muscles flinched under her lips. "So you think. Now, on your side."

Jon turned away from her. She stopped to admire the long line of his spine and the bunched muscles of his upper back. His ass was a work of art. Taut. Pure power. No wonder his hips were so amazing when he fucked her.

She nudged his top leg forward, half pushing him toward the bed. Her prize was the way his ass cheeks parted. Heather trailed her nails up the inside of his lower thigh, again, again. Then she used a small black comb and repeated the gesture. Each pass harder, until red streaks colored his skin and Jon shuddered on a long, low moan. She gave his ass a slap, which was louder than it was powerful.

"Again," he gasped.

Instead of chastising him for the slipup, she did exactly as they both wanted. It wasn't inflicting pain. And for Jon, it probably wasn't receiving it. No, the thrill was in the power. Giving and taking. That flow passed between them without choreography, but always with the results they both sought.

Soon her hand stung and Jon's ass was covered with a wash of pink. Sweat slicked them both. Heather shed her bra. She stretched along his back and pressed her damp breasts against him. He breathed as hard as she did.

"Good," she whispered.

"Yes."

"That wasn't a question, flyboy. It was praise."

"Fuck, you're cruel."

"Not yet." She reached behind her on the bed and grabbed her bottle of lube. Two fingers. The slightest touch of chilly and slick. "Hold still."

"That was the deal, right?"

She smiled against his spine and licked his sweat. "Yes, it was." Then she touched her fingers between his ass cheeks. Slid. Massaged. Teased. She had no idea what she was doing, but her pussy didn't seem to care. Absolutely drenched.

When that lean, tense body relaxed against hers, Heather started the real test. She nudged the tip of a bullet vibe right against his anus. He flinched. His ass clenched tight.

"Nope. Relax."

"Heather..." Her name was a deep growl.

"Call panda and I win. I know you won't."

"Then do it."

The vibe slid in more easily than she'd anticipated. He was enjoying this a hell of a lot more than he might admit. So ready for that slight invasion. Heather turned the toy's cap until vibration buzzed between them.

Jon groaned and pushed his forehead into the pillow. "Ah. Shit."

"Good? And that *was* a question."

"Good," he gasped as she pushed deeper.

Soon she had a rhythm going. Gentle. Slow. She added more lube, then deepened each push. The vibe was small, only about three inches. But it must've felt huge inside him—a man who'd never submitted to anything of the kind.

"Normally I keep this in my purse," she whispered against his nape. Just enough space between their lower bodies to permit room to play. "I use it in the private bathroom at work when the day's been too crazy. When I need a release." He grunted an unintelligible curse. "More, flyboy?"

"More."

"Talk to me in French."

He complied instantly. Hell, she didn't know what it meant, but she could guess by the hard-edged growl in his voice that it was mean, filthy, even threatening. She shifted her thighs against a sudden rush. Yes, he would get back at her for this. She wanted it. Each word softened her muscles into aroused lassitude. All except for her right arm. She turned the vibe on high and kept up a strengthening pace. He was thrusting back now, meeting her each time.

She paused only a moment to press a condom in his hand. "On."

Smiling, she'd never seen him so graceless. His fingers shook as he rolled the latex over his rock-hard prick. Christ, he was *huge*. Throbbing. She ground her palm against the flared base of the vibe, seating it there nice and tight.

"Uh," he moaned.

"Not so articulate now." She sat up. "It's the magic recipe for silencing Jon Carlisle's clever tongue."

"You're gonna get yours, Ms. Morris."

"Clinging to that thought, aren't you?"

"Hell, yes."

"I'm glad we're still on the same page. Now. Come fuck me."

Jon had her on her back so fast the room spun. He pushed into her without finesse. Just hard power. Blindfold stripped, his face was a mass of contradictions. Pretty-boy features. Determination and fierce passion. He hooked his forearm beneath her knee, opening her wide. He was brutal. Each slam shot through her body until her eyes rolled back.

"What happened," she gasped, "to twelve strokes?"

"Gonna make you scream. Need more than twelve."

"This was for me, remember?"

"Enough of that shit."

"No way. I want one more thing from you. Then you can spend the rest of the night paying me back." She arched forward and pushed the vibe, making sure it still worked inside him. "Take me. One hundred percent greedy fucking. You've got this fabulous tickle buzzing your asshole. You've got my cunt and my tits right here beneath you. *Take*, Jon. Just take."

His mouth parted on a dirty smile—then it was gone. The last semblance of Jon. He grabbed her arms and tossed them above her head, catching both wrists in one hand. Oh, holy damn. He held nothing back. Every pulse and thrust showed on his face as pure, furious greed.

"Mine," he rasped against her neck. "Fucking *hell*."

So close. And now *she* was so close. Heather met each thrust. She fought his hold, but he was a beast unleashed. "Wait." Her voice was a dry whisper. "Jon, God. No. Wait for me."

But it was too late.

He came. Exploded, really. Fierce. Gorgeous. A shudder climbed up and down his spine, with one last slow grind and a string of French curses.

Just as Heather had wanted, he pulled back before she found her release. She cried out at the sudden loss of his cock. Curling onto her side, she couldn't help a shiver of frustration that traipsed between pain and pleasure.

Vibe removed, condom gone, he knelt above where she lay stretched, sweaty and practically moaning for her release.

"You told me to be greedy." His chest still heaved. No sense of balance or calm had returned to his eyes. A man possessed. Blasted and liberated. "I complied to the letter."

"You loved it."

"I did. As good as you promised." He slid his fingers between her pussy lips and flicked her clit. She cried out. So sensitive. So close.

"Jon, please."

"Oh, yes, Heather love. One spectacular orgasm, coming up."

Chapter Twenty-Eight

Two Thursdays later, Jon lounged against the wall of the visitor's center at the front gate of Nellis. The thick material of his flight suit protected his back—and the scratches Heather had inflicted—from the rough stucco, but only intensified the afternoon's sweltering heat. Sweat dripped down his neck. Sunglasses shaded his eyes from the glaring sunlight.

It didn't help his mood that he'd been up since four. He'd planned on a no-stress day of maintenance and classes. That itinerary had been postponed in favor of more hours in the air with a visiting squadron of Marines. As an extra special bonus, he'd had the pleasure of another run-in with Donaghue.

The dickweed who was supposed to be on Jon's side.

Residual tension from that encounter turned his neck into a bar of steel. He checked his watch, bothered more than he'd like to admit that she was late. Only by a few minutes, but the delay made him want to bounce on the balls of his feet, as if he were the sort to give in to overeager displays.

Instead he crossed his arms.

By the time Heather pulled into the lot, he was chomping at the bit.

None of it made sense. So, she wanted to see his plane. No big deal. She wasn't the only woman he'd been with who got off on the fact that he was a fighter pilot. He'd learned early that most women did.

She looked incredible as he signed her into base. Her blouse was a rich peach silk with a mandarin collar. Jon couldn't look at it without remembering she'd worn it the Monday after he strangle-fucked her. Spike-heeled shoes brought her to his height. A demure tailored skirt clung to her full hips.

"Hey," she said shyly.

"Hey, yourself."

She kept up a light stream of chatter as he ran her through security and then drove her over to the 64th Squadron's headquarters—observations about the base, mentions of a project at work. Jon wanted to be able to match her, but he had nothing other than nerves. He could almost feel the defensive reflex as he dropped into his persona of cool.

"It's almost the same as my dad's posts," she said, looking out the window of the car. "Except for the planes."

"Some things never change."

She laughed as he pulled into the parking lot. He helped her out of the low-slung Aston. The black business skirt flashed a nice length of thigh as she swiveled and stood. Since the parking lot was half-empty, with most people gone early as repayment for having come in at o'dark thirty, he risked a fast, hard kiss.

If he could change one thing about their quasi-relationship, he'd take down a few more of their strangely walled-off borders. With sex, it wasn't a problem. These quieter moments...

But the words had come from his own mouth: some things never change.

Ignoring the cranked-up feeling that climbed his spine, he laced his fingers through hers. No one lingered to get on him about public displays of affection. That Princess Leah had popped smoke and left early was no surprise, but even Major Fang, normally the last one out, had headed home to Cass.

Part of Jon wanted to show Heather off—again, as he had at the club. He'd known she would look slick and put together. Class personified. But it was probably for the best that she didn't see those two knuckleheads after a long day. Ryan, of all people, would take one look at him and know he was losing his footing, that Heather tied him in knots.

They walked across the street and around the back of a huge hangar to where the ranks of jets lined up like soldiers. Mean, angry-looking soldiers painted in gray and desert brown camo.

Heather drew to a halt. "Wow," she breathed.

"Are you finally impressed?"

She laughed. It made her blue eyes shine. "Yes. I'm impressed. Are you happy now?"

He wrapped an arm around her waist and brushed kisses over her neck, tipped his tongue into the soft divot behind her ear.

"So sorry," drawled a voice laced with attitude. "Didn't mean to interrupt."

Heather practically flew out of his arms. Bright pink flushed her cheeks. Jon snapped ramrod straight. He knew that voice—that brassy, crass jerkwad had been his bane since showing up in the unit. Hearing it after briefings made him want to hurl sharp things against walls.

"Captain Donaghue," he said, pivoting on his heel. "What are you doing here? Everyone's done for the day, and we both know it's not like you to put in extra time brushing up."

Even though he spoke to Jon, the pilot aimed his smarmy smile straight at Heather. "I was just looking for Major Haverty. Wanted to ask him something."

"He left." Jon's reply was clipped and formal.

Confusion turned down Heather's mouth. Jon had never let her see him so overtly irritated. Even at the country club he'd maintained a certain disdainful cool. This was stronger. More potent. Kisser didn't deserve manners beyond what the military dictated.

Donaghue had pushed the limits of his fuel supply during sorties that morning. He'd flown too fucking long—all to get in just another hit. He'd crash someday, or get a buddy shot down—one who was only trying to stay on his wing. That sort of asshat behavior was deplorable, especially when it put the members of the 64th at risk. They were a *teaching* squadron, for fuck's sake.

"That's fine," Donaghue said. "I'll find him in the morning." He thought he was hot shit, in and out of the cockpit. Incredibly tacky. Crass. Trying too hard to hide the chip on his shoulder. He eyed Heather again. "Like I said, ma'am, sorry to interrupt."

Her smile made the skin slither along Jon's nape. "Please don't trouble yourself," she said. "It was no big deal."

It was no big deal.

She'd vaulted out of his arms, but it was no big deal.

The further Jon pushed, the more she withdrew. He could give her orgasms that rocked her world and let her push his boundaries just as much as he pushed her.

Goddamn. That ought to be enough.

After Donaghue left, Jon tried to regroup. "Where were we?"

She wiggled away from his hands and stepped toward the lines of planes. "You were going to show me which of these is yours."

He led her to the one stenciled with *Capt. Jon Carlisle* below the cockpit's seam. "This one."

She folded her hands behind the sweet swell of her ass. "I like it. It looks...cold. Cruel. Exactly how it's meant to, I'm sure."

He stepped up behind her, cupping her upper arms. "That's a good way to put it. Do you want to look inside?"

"No way. How much does it cost?"

"Almost thirty million."

"There's no way I'm touching it. Not at all."

He couldn't help but laugh. "Heather, it's a war machine. It goes Mach two point five if pushed hard enough. I doubt you could hurt it."

She curled her hands back around his thighs. "Doesn't matter. I'm not risking it."

"Then why did you want to see it at all?"

"So I could picture you in it." Her voice had dropped to a husky murmur. The look she slanted him was pure sex. "When I play with myself, alone in my bed."

He dropped his forehead to her nape. Her soft hair brushed his cheek. The way she intentionally turned him inside out was nothing short of evil. "We're getting out of here. Now."

"Lead the way, flyboy."

He wanted nothing more than to speed right out of there. But he had to grab a flight manual from the office he shared with Leah. He needed to brush up on two sections before morning. Check his stats against the original schematics. Bad data meant bad results, and he wasn't going to be responsible for either.

He left Heather in the main entrance to the squadron's headquarters building.

"I'll be right back," he said, brushing a kiss over her delicate temple.

"Don't be too long."

He wasn't. In and out in a second, with the paper printout of the manual in one hand. Heather had already found the corkboard plastered over with regulations, safety office posters and a few PowerPoint printouts. The one she focused on was printed on lemon-yellow paper with tacky clip art on every corner.

"What's this?" she asked.

Jon scratched the top of his head. His trim was getting fuzzy. He'd need to have it shaved soon. "The Nellis-Creech Air Force Ball. It's an annual event."

"Are you going?"

"Yeah. I have to make an appearance. One of the duties of being an officer: putting up with protocol."

"You didn't mention it."

"I didn't think you'd be interested. It's a lot of speeches, overcooked chicken and a DJ who's usually half in the bag by the time he starts the music. Last year we had a ventriloquist. Pure joy."

She stepped near enough that the peach silk of her blouse brushed his olive drab flight suit—an arousing contrast. Looking up at him, she plumped her mouth into a pout. It was obviously feigned but no less effective.

"I've never been to a ball."

"I didn't know that." Really, he was enjoying watching her squirm. It was petty as hell, and he particularly liked it after seeing her smile at Donaghue.

She trailed a finger down the front placket of his uniform. "Might be interesting. Just for a lark. Is that Captain Donaghue going to be there?"

Fucking hell, no. Just *no*.

Blood froze in Jon's veins. He locked down his expression. A sharp bite of anger clawed at his neck. The thought of Heather even talking to that asshole, much less dancing with him or sharing a drink, pissed him off beyond belief.

"Hey," Heather said, her voice soft. She curled a hand around the nape of his neck, rubbing her thumb over the granite muscle in his jaw. "It was a joke. A bad one."

He forced a smile. That she wrapped her arms around his middle slid tension out through his boots. "Donaghue and I have been having a problem lately. He's...dangerous. In the sky, I mean."

"Then I'm sorry I teased you about him." Her lashes dropped, shielding her pale gaze. "I mean it."

"It's all right." No one would miss the off-kilter tone of his voice. He took a breath as slowly as he could without making his anxiety ridiculously obvious. "Would you like to go with me? To the ball? It's a formal event."

"Does that mean I'd get to see you in your dress uniform?"

A laugh amped from his chest. He'd worn finely tailored suits almost every time he'd seen her, and she'd appreciated them. Avidly. But it was the prospect of his dress uniform that put a girly giggle in her voice.

"Of course."

Stretching up on her toes, she brushed a kiss across his cheek. She slid her hand from his nape to his crown, her fingers spread wide. "Then I'd love to go."

Chapter Twenty-Nine

"Heather, you have to let me see," Jenn called through the dressing-room door. "I'm not here *just* to feed the kids mall food and watch them play hide-and-seek in the clothes racks."

Lips tightly pressed, Heather forced herself to look in the mirror. Simply a woman struggling into a formal gown. Nothing wrong there.

Then why did it take such an effort?

Oh, but she knew the answer. Her shudder had nothing to do with the A/C blasting down from a ceiling vent. The last time she'd gone shopping for formalwear had been with her mom. They'd found just the right dress—sexy enough for Heather's seventeen-year-old taste and classic enough for her mother. The perfect gown for the prom.

The prom she hadn't attended.

Why had she niggled Jon about going to the ball? They could've booked a Bellagio suite without forcing the night to mean something. Of late, *everything* they did had taken on that added weight.

With a huff she opened the dressing-room door. "I need help with the laces."

Jenn sat on the waiting-room bench amid a stack of packages, bags and two kids' backpacks. They'd picked Ethan and Polly up from preschool before heading out to the mall—the only way Jenn could swing a quick shopping trip. Heather didn't care. She needed a second opinion. She no longer trusted her own.

"Well, I can already tell the color's gorgeous." Nimbly, Jenn stepped over the clutter and tied up the silken cords that cinched the bodice. "All set. Give me a spin."

Heather stepped away and turned. She swung the full skirt into place.

"Oh, wow. Like, a damn sort of wow."

"You don't think it's too poofy?"

Jenn shook her head. "Just the right amount of poof. He could feel you up at the table and no one would know."

A blush singed Heather's cheeks—not because she wouldn't consider such a thing, but because it had been her first idea upon spotting the dress. "Be serious," she managed.

"I am. You look fantastic."

Heather found her reflection in the waiting-room mirror. The corseted bodice hugged her rib cage, and the heart-shaped neckline showed off just enough skin. Blood-red taffeta flared out from her waist, with a hint of crinoline underneath to give it shape. She looked like a grown-up vixen version of a fairy princess.

"I'm thinking finger waves," she said.

"Oh, yeah. Very peekaboo glam." Jenn had opened Ethan's Clone Wars lunch bag and was munching leftover Goldfish, but her eyes remained on Heather. "I never knew you had a tattoo. It's very cool."

A jolt of panic was quickly followed by disappointment. The cut of the gown's back revealed her tattoo, where that flowering vine peeked out from the taffeta and curled over her shoulder blade. Only about four inches showed, but it was four inches more than she ever displayed in public.

Damn. And the dress had been so *right*.

"Maybe I'll try on another," Heather said.

Jenn shoved the empty sandwich baggie into a jacket pocket. "Don't you dare. A, that one's perfect. B, the kids are about to strip a mannequin. Get dressed and I'll treat you to the untold luxury of Chuck E. Cheese."

"Jenn, I can't—"

The confusion on Jenn's face asked a plain question. *Why not?*

"Forget it. I'll go get changed."

"Be quick." Jenn's head whipped toward the waiting-room's doorway. "Ethan Douglas Kimble!"

Knees shaking, Heather left her friend to avert catastrophe and locked the dressing-room door. She eyed the tattoo one more time. She didn't regret it—far from it. But she had always intended it to be private.

Jon would probably make it into a big deal, and why shouldn't he? She had. She'd teased him with it and made the eventual reveal into a sexual game. The symbols and the sentiments she'd chosen for herself were altered now. Memories of his fingers and lips tracing that lone vine up her body would be with her as long as the tattoo.

He was changing her. Changing them.

She pulled the silk laces until Jenn's bow unraveled. The bodice eased away from her torso. As she climbed back into her jeans and twin set, Heather made a decision. Jon could sexualize the hell out of her tattoo. *Go right ahead, flyboy.* It was far easier to deal with his desire than the way he'd been so possessive at the airbase.

"Heather, come on!"

She left the other dresses on a rack and hurried to make her purchase—before she changed her mind.

Jon called when he was five minutes from her house.

Almost unbearably nervous, Heather smoothed a hand down the waves in her hair.

Stop it.

She grabbed her beaded black silk clutch then wiggled her toes into patent high heels that barely poked out from beneath the full skirt. The throaty purr of Jon's Aston sent a hot shiver down to her belly. The only sexier sound was when he whispered in French.

After locking the front door, she turned. And stopped.

Captain Jonathan Carlisle stood at near-attention beside his outrageous sports car. His gaze devoured her as Heather absorbed every detail of his formal uniform. A fitted blue jacket like that of a tuxedo layered over a white dress shirt, accented by a satin bow tie and cummerbund in matching Air Force blue. Everywhere gleamed silver accents: button, cufflinks, the epaulets perched on his shoulders, and the braid circling his sleeve cuffs.

Unfamiliar medals and ribbons adorned the left breast of his jacket, but the pilots' wings were unmistakable.

Walking down the two porch steps required steady patience. Balance and grace had deserted her. His eyes still intense, his expression taut, he met her at the passenger door. He placed a lingering kiss on her bare shoulder. *"Tu es parfait,"* he whispered. "Perfection, Heather love."

She sucked in a slow breath. The bodice hugged her breasts, her rib cage, her waist, denying the air she needed. "You're not so bad yourself, Captain. Very snappy."

Jon lifted his head. He'd been to the barber, his dark hair buzzed with expert precision. "My Uncle Sam told me what to wear. It's mess dress, for black-tie functions."

"What does this one mean?" she asked, touching one of the medals pinned to his jacket.

"Iraqi Campaign."

"And this one?"

"Are you going to ask about all of them?"

She nodded, and he pointed to several in turn. "Afghanistan, Air Medal, Distinguished Flying Cross."

Soft pride filled Heather's chest, like trying to breathe past wads of warm cotton. More than that, the reality of his dangerous life squeezed down on her shoulders. Why was she getting into his car? Welcoming him into her body, time and again? He wasn't calm or safe or stable. Nothing about Jon Carlisle was what she'd imagined for a partner.

But there they were, going to a ball.

"So you're not just a pretty face, flyboy?"

"Pretty? I was hoping for dashing." He arched a brow then gestured to her waiting chariot. "Shall we?"

Heather made the trip to the Bellagio in a daze. As he'd been in the habit of doing lately, Jon put on music—this time "Mr. Brightside" by The Killers. She thought he did it on purpose, to fill the air with sound. They never said much in the car. Nerves and sex and tension got the better of them.

After handing his black beast over to the valet, Jon extended his arm. All so formal. All so cleanly practiced. But underneath the uniform she knew his body, his passions. That intimacy left her dizzy and in need of solid footing.

"You won't be looking so wonder-struck when speech number eight gets rolling," he said.

"By then I'll be playing with myself under the table."

His startled intake of breath lit a fire at the apex of her thighs. "You're kidding, right?"

Inside Bet

"Kidding. Sure."

With his hand locked around her wrist, Jon tugged her beyond the flow of foot traffic. "I'm not messing around here, Heather. This is my job."

She shouldn't have been surprised by his intensity. Likely she'd have had the same reaction if he proposed sex play among her colleagues. But something had switched over. This seriousness was not why she'd first climbed into his DBS. Deflecting blunt comments about her body was far easier than reconciling the startling, intense pride so plainly written on his youthful features.

She wanted the walls back. The competition.

"Make it worth my while," she said. "I don't know how long I'll be able to hold out with you dressed this way."

He held her arms out to each side, with the backs of her wrists flush with the wall. "What's it going to take to keep your hands out from between those gorgeous thighs, Ms. Morris?"

"A promise for tonight. Anything I want. Sexually."

"Again?"

"I'm a greedy girl."

"No argument here."

"Do we have a deal, flyboy?"

"You drive a hard bargain, Ms. Morris."

"Not true. You just want to have it all—a perfectly respectable evening *and* a guaranteed good time." She peeked up at him. "So, besides protecting your job, do you have any conditions?"

"You've already done your damnedest to unhinge me. It's your turn to be undone, but you choose the method."

"Hmmm. Agreed. Anything else?"

"Other than condoms and respecting the safe word? None."

She'd said the same to him while standing at the roulette table, weeks ago. Smiling, she whispered, "Let me think about it."

"Hey, Tin Tin. There you are."

Jon surreptitiously released her hands. Smoothly he turned her away from the wall to greet a tall, handsome officer and his date. The man was G.I. Joe personified, all sturdy good looks, but he wore the mess uniform with surprising grace.

"Fang," Jon said, "I'm gonna bitch-slap you for wearing that. I told you I had dibs."

Blue-blood suave layered every move as he shook hands with the officer and kissed the woman on the cheek. Heather couldn't help but be impressed by his slick recovery.

"Heather, this is my boss, Major Ryan Haverty. His lovely lady is Cass Whitman, who was just promoted at the Hungerford Art Gallery. How was Italy?"

"Gorgeous. Wonderful." The woman was almost petite, with silky red hair and a cutely turned-up nose. She wore a form-fitting black crepe dress that flared playfully just above her ankles. "But you probably already knew that."

Jon only shrugged, his smile gently teasing.

"Right," came a woman's upbeat voice. "So where's the party?"

"You don't have a built-in GPS for that, Princess?" Ryan's expression was mock innocent. She tossed him an "eat me" look.

"And you remember Leah," Jon added. "Always doing her best to make the rest of us look like schmucks."

The woman shrugged. "It's not hard."

With his thumb grazing her tattoo, Jon said, "Ryan, Cass, this is Heather Morris."

Heather smiled her way through the introductions, a little lost amid the dizzying flurry of insults, in-jokes and nicknames. The three officers were tight; that much was obvious. Cass held her own too, but as they walked deeper into the Bellagio, she hung back a bit.

"They can spin your head when they launch into full trash-talk mode," she said to Heather. "I still have to ask what most of the acronyms mean."

"My dad was in the Army for ages, but each branch is so different."

"God, I'm nervous."

Heather cast a quick glance toward the shorter woman. "Really? You don't look it."

"Petrified. Ryan and I have only been together since April. This is the first big Air Force thingy we've attended. I don't want to screw up. So how do you know Tin Tin?"

"Who?"

"Jon. Captain Jon 'Tin Tin' Carlisle." She nudged her chin toward where he walked ahead. His fellow officers flanked him as closely as prison guards. "That's his call sign. Ryan's is Fang. And then there's Princess Leah."

Heather couldn't help a chuckle.

"Yeah, don't let her hear you laugh," Cass said. "So, what were you saying? About meeting Jon?"

Smiling indulgently, Heather knew she hadn't yet been saying anything...and Cass knew it too. The woman's mischievous air was hard to resist. "We, ah...we met at a wine bar in late July."

"They're pumping him for information, just so you know."

"Were you sent to try another angle?"

Cass grinned. "Nothing so devious. If I'm curious about you, I'll ask you myself."

"Thanks."

Jon dropped back as they entered a massive ballroom. "Excuse us, Cass."

"No problem. Ryan darling, don't lose me. I'll never find you in all these blue penguin suits." Only as she walked away did Heather notice how Cass's hem nearly obscured a fantastic pair of Cuban-heel seamed stockings.

The ballroom was a tidal wave of noise—conversations, clinking glasses, laughter. Heather estimated about a thousand people. Air Force blue was everywhere. She reflexively gripped Jon's arm.

"Can you give me a hint?" he asked, his voice silken.

"Hint?"

"Of what we're playing for? I thought the application of some sexual creativity might take the edge off your panic."

"I'm not panicking."

"Of course not."

She wove around to join the others at their designated table. Another round of introductions. She kept hold of Jon's hand, even as they sat.

"Why Tin Tin?" she asked quietly. With the example of Princess Leah to draw from, she assumed it must be derogatory. Something for poking fun at one's fighting brothers and sisters. "Is it like Rin Tin Tin, the dog?"

"That's right." Jon kept his eyes averted, his tone casual, but he appeared surprisingly uncomfortable. "For my unerring loyalty."

Heather laughed. At first. His seriousness didn't relent, nor did the strange feeling that she'd caught him doing something wrong.

No, not wrong. Just...out of character. He'd have loved a nickname like "Playboy"—grinning and licking his lower lip, enjoying the compliment. But friendship? Loyalty? That made him squirm. His call sign was a daily reminder that he wasn't all he pretended to be.

That her observation rang true scared her just as much as one simple realization. She wanted him now more than ever.

Chapter Thirty

Jon shifted, running his thumb along his empty bread plate as he endured Heather's scrutiny. Amusement had slid off her face, replaced by a look of confusion? Surprise?

The collar of his dress shirt was uncomfortably tight. He tilted his neck to the side, looking away from her.

He could believe loyalty wasn't easy for Heather to imagine of him. He played the role of the dirty fuck, and she was content to leave it at that. Except it...unsettled him. Jon didn't appreciate being unsettled. An off taste gathered in the back of his mouth, one that cheap wine wouldn't be able to wash away.

"So how did that happen? Why did Tin Tin stick?"

He leaned back, determined to keep this discussion casual. "The very first morning I was supposed to report to my very first duty station, I was late."

"I bet you were in some seriously hot water."

"Absolutely. The commander spent a good twenty minutes dressing me down, until a friend knocked on the office door." People still milled around their tables, chatting and hunting down the bars at each side of the ballroom. "Billy told the CO I was late because I'd been at his house until two in the morning. I'd been coaching him through a sticky situation with his ex-wife."

Pale blue eyes glimmered with compassion. But she shook it off almost intentionally.

Leah plunked down in her seat at Heather's far side. "Score." She displayed a bright yellow band around her wrist.

"It doesn't match the uniform, Princess," he said.

She pulled a face. "It's the drink band. Forty bucks up front and it's practically an open bar."

Jon and Ryan exchanged a look over Cass's head. Hopefully Leah would keep her shit together, but it wasn't likely. The woman seemed bored with life. Alcohol was her fastest route to not-as-bored.

And shit, it was Jon's turn to bail her out. By far. Dash was seated two tables over with his wife, Sunny—and with Eric Donaghue. So Dash was out too. Ryan had covered the last two midnight phone calls since Jon had been too wrapped up in Heather.

She was still doing it, turning him inside out. The temptation of her side bet had him on pins and needles. He knew she was perfectly capable of fingering herself under the table. The question was whether she actually would. Anticipation was a keen, welcome distraction.

Jon had never particularly liked military balls. They reminded him too much of the formal events his parents often held in the guise of charity financing. None had been more painful than the event they'd hosted only seven weeks after Sara's car wreck. Rubbing elbows to keep the beaches of Hyannis pristine. He'd still held out hope that their family would huddle together, grieving in private.

It hadn't happened. Instead, he'd sat at the back of the ballroom with his grandfather, watching the spectacle with matching disdain.

Having a keyed-up, obviously excited Heather sitting next to him made the night entirely different. No simpler. A split second after the waiter removed the salad plates, she brushed her lips over his ear. One fingertip circled the sensitive divot at the base of his skull.

"Do you remember my birthday?"

Her husky voice was going to have him doing something stupid. Damn soon.

He schooled his face into a subtle, smiling leer as he eyed the shadowy valley of her cleavage. Things ran more smoothly between them when he was being overtly sexual. Safer for him, as well.

"Clearly."

"Then you have a good idea of what I'm not wearing under this gown."

"Very little?"

She nuzzled the crook of his neck. "You're a brilliant man."

Jon glanced around the table to see who'd noticed. Absolutely no one, thank God. After all the shit Ryan had taken, particularly when he first hooked up with Cass, he would revel in the chance to turn it around on Jon.

Heather's bare toes wiggled under the hem of his slacks,

emphasizing her lack of undergarments. As if he'd needed any further images in his head. The sultry way the deep red dress clung to her curves was already enough.

He traced the top inches of her tattoo, exposed by a dip of scarlet fabric. Usually she dressed so conservatively that he'd only seen her ink bared during sex. Eroticism charged every line and flower. The ends of her silky hair barely grazed the top-most bud.

"You're a very bad girl," he said quietly.

"We seem to be learning that."

Somewhere around the third speech, Jon was ridiculously wound up. Heather kept up their game. Every few minutes she'd whisper something raunchy in his ear. Something wickedly dirty. He'd harden all over again, despite trying to keep his attention on the other people at the table. Following the stream of conversation took every ounce of ingrained training.

Heather scooped some of the chocolate pudding that was supposed to be mousse, then dipped it into her mouth. The spoon slid out between her lips as she watched him.

She licked at her lower lip. "I think I've decided what I want. As my reward for behaving."

He brushed the heavy drape of hair back from her face. Her features were classically beautiful, such a nerve-racking contrast to her decadent thoughts. "And what's that, Ms. Morris?"

"Playing with your ass that time got me thinking. In fact, I haven't been able to stop imagining switching places." She lowered her lashes. "I want anal sex."

Jon choked. On absolutely nothing. Air turned to oil in his lungs. His cock reared up under his dress trousers, ready to obey. Instantly.

Wearing a lovely smirk, Heather patted him on the back as he reached for his water glass.

Two seats down, Ryan quirked his brows. "Problem, Tin Tin?"

Jon coughed another time or two. He wanted nothing more than to haul Heather out of there. Now. Do not pass go.

"No problem," he answered tightly.

"Really? Because for a second there, it looked like I was going to have to whip out the Heimlich." He widened his eyes and rested his chin on folded hands. "But wait. You weren't eating anything. Care to explain?"

"Would you please shut the hell up?" he hissed, quietly enough that only his friends could hear. At least Leah was off at the bar, *again*, or she'd likely blow it to the rest of the table.

Cass giggled. "Gee, that sounds awfully familiar."

Jon didn't want to glare at Cass. She was too damn nice. So he aimed his ire back at Ryan.

"What's wrong, flyboy?" Heather whispered. "The idea of stroking your cock in my ass gets you that hot?"

Under the long tablecloth, he gripped her thigh. Satin slid beneath his palm. "I don't think I'd be the only one," he said with every last dredge of silky charisma. Cultivated smoothness was all he had left.

The dangerous Ms. Morris wanted to play up-the-ante. Bring it. He could meet her every move. It'd be a hell of a lot more fun than trying to make sense of them. They didn't need to make sense when their bodies took charge.

Jon edged up her thigh until her skirt bunched around his wrist. He brushed her mound, just enough to hear the small hitch in her breathing.

He bent so that his mouth grazed ruby earrings that matched the dress. "When I've got you on your hands and knees, face pressed into the pillow? And you screaming loud enough to wake the neighbors? And my cock pounding your sweet, tight ass? Then we'll see who's hot and bothered."

Red lips parted on a silent gasp, even as the rest of the table stood to applaud the keynote speaker. With a hand around Heather's elbow, Jon levered her to stand. He joined the applause as if nothing else occupied his mind. She followed suit, her eyes gratifyingly hazy.

When the music started, he held out his hand. "May I have this dance?"

Her long, graceful throat worked over a swallow. "Since you actually asked this time."

On the parquet floor, Heather melted into his arms. He pressed his cheek against the dark, silken fall of her hair and breathed deeply. He fought to keep the mood light, but sex and tenderness made that nearly impossible.

She pressed her mouth against his neck then licked the hollow

Inside Bet

behind his jaw. He only restrained a shiver by locking his arms across her back.

"We need to leave," he growled.

She shook her head, but he felt her smile blossom against his skin. She was enjoying herself. So much. Truth be told, so was he.

"I want to dance for a little while."

"You mean you want to torture me."

She snuggled in closer. Her breasts pushed across his dress shirt. "That too."

Jon ran his fingers down the visible section of her tattoo, then continued down her back and across her waist. He knew its path by heart. "There's a corridor approximately two hundred feet away, at the other end of the ballroom. If you don't agree to leave right now, I'm hauling you in there and fucking you up against the wall. And you won't get my cock in your ass like you want."

"I don't believe you."

"No?"

Her tongue slicked across her bottom lip. "No. You enjoy novelty too much. That scenario sounds entirely too much like our evening at the country club."

"Fuck," he said on a grin. "You're right. Now behave."

He nodded to where Ryan and Cass swayed alongside them.

"Princess is up to no good." Ryan's normally open features were drawn tight with worry. "Behind you, ten o'clock."

"Fucking Christ," Jon spat. "Isn't that Mr. Preston?"

Leah wasn't quite sitting in the man's lap, but goddamn she was close. She'd tucked her chair directly next to his. Their heads tipped together as if no one else occupied the cavernous ballroom. A glass of something frothy and blue dangled from her fingers. Her bun had come loose at the edges, with a strand of brown hair curling around her jaw.

"Sure is," Ryan said. "We have to get her out of here."

Cass tightened her hold on Ryan's biceps. "I don't understand."

"Me either," Heather added. "He looks like a perfectly nice guy."

Ryan shook his head. "He's married to the executive officer of 505th Operations Group. This is a hot mess waiting to happen. Two minutes more and she'll sure as shit catch wind of this."

"I've got her," Jon said automatically. "I'll take her home."

Cass's mouth fell open. "Don't be ridiculous. We'll take her. More room in Ryan's truck, anyway."

They didn't have time to go rounds over who'd take her home. Immediate extraction was necessary. He agreed.

He and Ryan cut in on Leah with a minimum of fuss while Heather and Cass waited at the edge of the ballroom. Leah went willingly enough. She only twiddled a finger wave to Mr. Preston.

In the corridor, Heather and Cass fell into step behind them. When Leah stumbled, Ryan and Jon each took an arm.

Jon was pissed. Flat-out pissed at his friend. More than a year of covering for her stripped the last of his civility. "What the hell was that? You're a *captain*. A goddamn fighter pilot. You ready to flush that down the shitter?"

"I do my job," she protested weakly.

Ryan's thundercloud expression said he'd reached his snapping point too. "Doesn't count for much when you act like a terminal screwup every night. I'm done, Leah."

"Fine, fine." She tried to wave a hand, which only added to her unsteadiness.

Jon tightened his grip on her upper arm. "Why the fuck do you pull this crap?"

Her eyes were glassy, but she wasn't insensible. Not yet. Nearly too quiet to hear, she whispered, "I don't know."

They'd finally done it, he and Fang. They'd chewed her out the way she deserved. Not that it stood much chance of doing any good, and Jon felt no better for having unloaded on her. As Ryan's truck pulled away with all three inside, he shoved his hands in his pockets. That Leah teetered so close to ruin was easy to point out. What to do about it became murkier.

Her call. Her life to ruin.

Jon couldn't do a damn thing more. That turned his guts to ice.

Heather curled against his side. "You okay?"

He nodded. Filling his hands with the skin bared by her gown helped. More than a little.

For a moment, he'd almost thought she would offer to talk about it. He would've taken her up on the offer. Idiot.

Instead she trailed a finger down his lapel. "Do you think going upstairs might make you feel better?"

Chapter Thirty-One

Don't think. Just feel.

Those four words had been pounding in Heather's brain since sitting beside Jon for dinner.

Don't think. Just feel.

That was harder to do, so much harder when he made her feel more than the physical.

They'd been lovers for nearly two months—such a long time to hold back the momentum of her fascination. She'd found no disappointments. None. On her end, she was practically ready to take it to the next level. Fear kept her silent. It wasn't so much about her reputation anymore and how hard she'd worked to cultivate a squeaky-clean image. No, it was because her recklessness remained. Jon tempted her to it, urged her to indulge. She'd succumbed to that temptation before when she was young and stupid. Fourteen years should've put enough distance between naïve kid and competent woman.

Yet the longer she stayed with Jon, the more she became convinced some breaking point was coming. Soon. Once again she would wind up feeling like the girl who'd missed prom because of a fast-talking corporal and his motorcycle. Or worse, she'd tell Jon she was falling in love and have that raw emotion shoved back in her face. Laughed at. It had happened before—far more humiliating than what her first love and his buddies had done to her for the rest of the weekend.

She'd trusted the wrong man with her heart. She hadn't been that trusting since.

She led Jon into the elevator at the Bellagio. Her smile was painful. He leaned against the interior paneling and toyed with their room keycard. What she'd proposed layered between them, building strength. Her anticipation far outweighed her fear. She knew without doubt that he would do as he always had.

Drive her crazy. Make her come. Keep her safe.

The difficulty was that she had never wanted this with anyone else, or could never imagine wanting it with anyone else. Jon was taking up far too many exclusive places. Every time she tried to prove he was just a crazy good time, he did his job—and by that fact proved he was someone special.

"Second thoughts?"

Don't think. Just feel.

"Not at all," she said smoothly. "I was thinking that you have a lot of whispered promises to keep."

"Liar."

"Hm?"

"That's not what you were thinking."

Heather smothered her surprise in a pout. "Trying to change the subject, Captain?"

He shoved off from the elevator wall. Stalked closer. Pushed her back. "Why are you doing this?"

"Doing what?"

"You know what? Forget I said anything." He tongued his bottom lip, his gaze on hers. "You want to play bad girl with my cock? By all means. Ready, willing and able."

Occasionally she'd believed him easy to read, when the playboy act stretched too thin. Not right then. He was either being sarcastic, or he was covering something very close to disappointment. Heather was so tangled up and inside out that she had no perspective. All she knew was that he looked breathtaking in his uniform, and that under Jon's blatant scrutiny, she felt sexy and desired.

Maybe this would be enough.

Maybe then she could stop.

"Glad to hear that." She stroked Jon's satin cummerbund. "I'd hate to think I've restrained myself with no reward to show for it."

"Perish the thought."

The elevator door opened. Jon held her hand, almost as if they were lovers bound by genuine caring, not by a series of escalating provocations. Heather sauntered through the door to their suite, which was only slightly less ostentatious than the one they'd shared at The

Palazzo.

Jon unraveled the ties of her gown's bodice almost as soon as the door clicked shut. A slight sting of disappointment needled her skin. Why should it matter if he didn't play and toy and take his time? His tenderness was harder to bear than the steady, even pace of his fingers loosening the laces.

Don't think. Just feel.

So she did. Heather sank into the rush of being undressed. The gown released her rib cage. She took her first deep inhalation of the evening, only to catch a breath of Jon's cologne. He stood behind her and slid his fingers from her hips, up, until he palmed her breasts.

"Do that again," he whispered against her nape. "Deep breath." She complied, arching slightly. The movement pushed her body into his hands. "Again. Breathe, Heather love."

Air rushed to her brain. A fresh burst of oxygen fueled her anticipation. Her skin prickled as the rest of her dress dropped over her hips.

Jon offered his arm. "Step."

Knowing how she must appear, she stepped out of the puddle of her gown. All she wore were her earrings, her black high heels, and the nipple ring he flicked with his tongue.

Oh, it was easier now. No worries. This was Jon. She'd trusted her body to him in singular ways. His decadent smile warmed every inch of her skin.

"You are a filthy, beautiful woman."

She purred against his throat. "I'm going to go wait on that chaise. And I'm going to start touching myself, like I've wanted to do all night."

"We have much in common, Ms. Morris. Because I'll enjoy watching that."

"I want you naked too."

"And here I thought you were a real lady," he said, unfurling his bow tie.

His words, spoken harshly, tightened her vertebrae, but she shoved away the reflex. Just an act. Just the game. If it wasn't, why should she care? This was what she wanted from him—a hard, sexy time, well beyond the safe life she'd made.

She repeated that to herself as she found her evening bag and retrieved a bottle of lube. Making him wait for her request had been another game. She'd known all along what she wanted from their evening.

Like throwing down a gauntlet, she placed it in the palm of his hand.

Then she draped across the sleek leather chaise. "At your pleasure, flyboy."

"If we do this at my pleasure, you won't enjoy it very much."

"Don't make assumptions. You know how satisfying I find it when you lose control."

Jon stopped in the process of laying his dress jacket over the back of a chair. Cruelly handsome black suspenders hugged his chest. "With regard to this particular intimacy, that wouldn't be a good idea."

A flutter of nerves kicked up in her stomach.

Damn, why was she doing this? Why was she pushing him? She'd lost track of so many conflicting motives: hiding from how much she enjoyed his company, loving that she surprised him, wanting to keep his attention.

Forever.

A cold shiver made her rub her upper arms.

"I thought you were going to torment me." Jon slid down the suspenders, ditched the bow tie and cummerbund, and began unbuttoning his shirt. "*Touchez votre chagatte, mon amour.*" He grinned at her slight moan. "I said, touch yourself."

Heather obeyed. Her body was well ahead of her conflicted mind. Nerves jumped at the first touch of her fingers. Jon's soft chuckle flamed her skin. He was running this show, and damn if she wasn't thankful. She'd lost control the moment she stepped out of that dress.

He shed his clothes until they trailed behind him, a dotted line on the carpet. No tidy piles tonight. Lean, ripped muscle flexed with each deliberate step. Her attention caught on the details. The layered scoops of his ribs, the sharp V-line at his hips, the bottle of lube still in his hand. His erection angled toward his navel, long and ready for her. Heather's cunt tightened, wet and waiting, but that wasn't her destination. She stroked faster—half pleasure, half restive suspense.

His every motion leashed, Jon knelt on the chaise. He spread her knees and took hold of her high-heeled foot. Her ankle hooked over his shoulder. The lights were still bright. She was utterly exposed, her skin feverish now.

Jon held the outside of her calf. His thumb gently stroked the tense muscle underneath. Dark hair dusted his forearms and the backs of his wrists. He slid her a fierce look. "Hug your breasts. Hold them up for me."

If she took her hand out from between her legs, she would remove that last barrier. He would have complete access. She licked her lips, once, twice, then cupped her forearms under her breasts. Jon's irises deepened, nearly black now. He breathed tightly through his nose.

He flipped open the bottle of lube. Drizzled a few drops on his fingers. Smiled.

"So many things I could do to you from here. I could stroke my cock between those lovely tits. Maybe I wouldn't even last." He shrugged. "I don't think I'd regret it."

Heather tweaked her nipples. "You have your orders, Captain."

Swirling his thumb and fingers together, he spread the lube over his skin. "Indeed I do."

Jon placed his palm, fingers down, against her pussy. His middle finger curled, nudged, pushed, until that slick tip nestled against her tight opening. Heather tensed, then forced a long exhalation.

He released her ankle so that her legs spread wide, one high heel on either side of the chaise. Dipping at the waist, he feathered kisses from her navel on down. A quiver began at her belly and radiated out in wide circles. She watched, transfixed.

His taut tongue found her clit. All the while his middle finger waited against her anus. The pressure grew more insistent. Jon rasped rough French phrases against her pussy. His breath heated and cooled at the same time. Every vibration rumbled against her thin, sensitive skin.

The tip of his middle finger pushed inside.

Heather gasped, then groaned softly. "So good," she whispered.

"And we've only just started."

He sucked her clit and caught that tight bundle between gentle teeth. His finger pushed deeper. Slow, slow pulses created a lulling rhythm. Heather pinched her nipples out of frustration as each stroke

Inside Bet

relaxed her, eased her toward pleasure—the anxiety long gone.

More lube. Another sleek finger.

Jon's skin shone with a light sheen of sweat. He lifted from between her legs, his expression wrapped in an artificial calm. The muscles of his forearm and biceps bunched as he pulsed. Only after those two fingers worked steadily, in and out, the pace faster, did he stop to grab a condom.

Heather couldn't hear over the hard pulse in her ears. Desire drummed away her fear. She was eager now, curious, waiting for the next step.

Again he hooked her ankle over his shoulder. The spiked highheel still clung to her foot. Long, elegant fingers positioned the sheathed head of his cock against her pussy. His hips did the rest. One plunge, two, and they were fucking on that leather chaise.

The buildup had been so steady, slow, hot that Heather nearly let go. Only Jon's low laughter brought her back to the moment. "Don't come, Ms. Morris. If you do, your clenching pussy might finish me off."

Gasping his name, she arched toward the jarring smack of his hips. He bent over her. One hand propped against the chaise's curved back. The other found her hair, tangled, pulled. Her scalp flushed with sweet pain.

"I said, don't come," he whispered against her throat.

Heather groaned, spread wide for him. The position was too much, the pleasure too much. A quick orgasm shuddered over her. Her cunt flooded with hot release.

Jon hissed. Pulled out. His chest heaved and his back teeth clenched tight. "God*damn*, Heather."

Her mind still hazy with that flash of pleasure, she found him tugging her legs, shifting, flipping her on the chaise. He smeared her arousal between her ass cheeks. A dose of the chillier lube made her shiver.

Floating, relaxing, she let him in.

Slowly at first. The tip of his head pushed past a tight barrier that barely resisted his entry. Heather groaned long and low. His hands shook as he squeezed her hips. Squeezed *hard*. She felt every ounce of his restraint in those tense fingertips.

She took more of him, more still. Such a dangerous indulgence.

She drifted to a place where pain and pleasure walked together.

His hips pushed flush with her ass. That was their limit, as deep as he could go. Totally filled. She'd never been so aware of her body's limits—how far she could widen to accommodate Jon's iron-hard prick. Every nerve screamed. She wanted him to take it slow. She wanted him to pound her so hard that her mind shut down.

Each successive stroke drew out more sensation. Facedown on the chaise, she scored her nails into the leather, imagining it was Jon's chest. His strokes were smooth. Slick. He pumped her asshole with the steady throb of his cock. She was so open now. Her body offered no resistance. He may as well have been fucking her drenched pussy. Each deep thrust rocked her, filled her, stretched her. She blinked back tears, just her moans and gasps became an unstoppable outlet for the sweetest, darkest agony.

Jon bent low over her back. Reaching around, he found her clit and matched their rhythm with flicking circles. His tongue licked up her spine, until he laid his cheek in the valley between her shoulder blades. Their hot, sticky bodies arched in tandem.

Heather thrashed her head, but his relentless thrusts didn't stop, didn't even slow. His hips smacked her ass. He drove deeper, worked his finger faster. Harder.

Her release, when it came, was unlike any she'd ever experienced. Her world centered where he invaded the slick pucker of her anus. Sensation pounded her from all sides. Feverish. Vital. Filthy.

The dark behind her eyes went bright white. She screamed and kept screaming.

"Ah, Christ," he gasped. His pelvis jerked. He grunted and blew out a long exhalation that matched her withering moan.

They huddled on the chaise, both panting heavily. Jon slipped free then soothed her with slow caresses along her slick cleft. His breath petted up her spine.

"Just amazing," she whispered against the leather. "Just...thank you, Jon."

"That's what I'm here for."

Coldness slinked over her skin, raising goose bumps. In the last few minutes, he could have done anything—*anything*—to hurt her. Instead he'd given her an exquisite initiation, an intimate treasure unlike any in her life.

Only at the last did he do her injury. No matter how much Heather wanted their affair to remain simple, his words left her hurting.

Chapter Thirty-Two

Jon loved very little in the world more than flying. Maybe nothing. The desperate grab the earth made to keep him grounded. The thrill of takeoff. The rush of speed. His fellow pilots off his wingtips and the steady hum of the radio worked in concert to take down their assigned target.

The whole enterprise was a mastery of human initiative over a wickedly difficult puzzle. Princess darted ahead of him, her jet skipping gracefully. To his right side was Fang and his dogged determination. Being part of the Red Force meant balance: putting pieces together and taking them apart, all to make other pilots better. Everything they did helped save lives.

Fucking beautiful.

More proof that he'd made the right call in bailing on Heather for their date.

Even as Jon drew off a heat-seeking missile with a flare—that orange pop trailed by white smoke—the more complicated puzzle of Heather kept him preoccupied. Would she realize the basket of chocolate and strawberries he'd sent to her office was his way of disengaging? As much as he relished fucking her, and as much as he still wanted to figure out what made her tick, he was tired of being used as a hot cock. Not when she was so unwilling to let any real part of herself open up.

He never would've thought it possible, but the dares had worn thin.

A German Tornado swept up fast from the south, searching low. For the enemy. For him.

Jon pushed Heather out of his mind. His job was to focus.

He skimmed over the top of the rocks and hugged the terrain for cover. His plane, an extension of every calculated choice, responded perfectly through the slope of the canyon. He saw the way it would move even before he shifted the throttle. No mystery in an F-16. Just power and deadly elegance. He visualized the numbers and made it happen, each and every time. Straightforward.

Nothing left to chance.

He hadn't planned on running into Donaghue again that day. But the single BX on base meant sometimes shit happened.

Jon turned down an aisle with a Gatorade in hand, only to draw up short. He'd spent too long paging through Sara's books the night before, indulging in maudlin sentiments. Combined with two hard flights, his reserves were shot.

Donaghue stood before a display of cheap electronics. He held two packs of whatever, seemingly debating between the two. Should've been easy to avoid notice. Jon turned away.

The Aggressors were a small, elite crew. If Ryan and the rest of the chain of command thought Kisser deserved a spot on the team, it wasn't Jon's business to say anything else. Keeping his distance was safest, especially when repeated attempts to make the stubborn bastard see sense had all failed.

But the blunt accent of an inner-city thug called him back. "Good flight today, Tin Tin."

Jon faced him. "For whom?"

Donaghue grinned. "Me, of course. You went down twice. Lucky Red Force pilots can regenerate or your day would've ended real quick."

Pain spiked behind Jon's ears as he ground his back teeth. Hard. "I went down the second time because you deviated from your flight path. You almost took out the air command."

Fluorescent lights flashed over plastic as Donaghue tossed down both pieces of crap. "I didn't though. Those Germans learned their place. All's well that ends with winning."

"Bullshit." Jon stalked forward. The other pilot was roughly Jon's height, but he was a solid wall of muscle. Didn't matter. Jon was so pissed that Kisser retreated a half step.

He kept his voice to a low hiss. This was between him and Donaghue. Alone. "All's well that ends with your fellow pilots alive and safe. You'd do well to remember that. Those are your buddies. Your friends. I hope you don't find out what it's like to get one of them killed because you made another dick-first choice. Or plow your own fucking face into the ground. Guys who fly like you don't come home."

Kisser's rough features pinched tight. "It's just training."

"If you think that, you need to bail. Immediately."

Tossing the Gatorade onto a random shelf, Jon strode out of the BX before he could do anything stupider. Like slam his fist into that huge cocksucker's jaw.

His Aston was aimed at Heather's house before he could actually think about his destination.

Fuck, he had it bad.

Even as he knocked on her front door, he realized he wasn't going to get what he needed. Catharsis. Someone to talk to about his fellow pilot's foolish decisions. A tight, hungry fear crawled up his spine and drew his shoulder blades together—one he hadn't experienced in years.

The fear of rejection.

Heather would want Jon to make her come. Hopefully her dares would be enough. He couldn't seem to get anything else out of her.

He shouldn't even *want* anything else. He'd learned the hard way that sometimes a man didn't get what he needed, that he had to take people as they were. Some people weren't capable of opening up.

Heather was one of them.

That didn't stop him from knocking again. The door swung open slowly.

"You look like shit," he blurted.

She did. Her dark hair was skinned back into a messy ponytail. Faint purple shadows clung under her pale eyes. A cotton camisole and bare feet under flannel pajama bottoms were the last touches.

"Way to make a girl feel good."

Jon curled his hand around the sun-warmed wood of the doorjamb. "I always tell the truth, remember? What's wrong?"

She crossed her arms under her breasts in an obvious *don't touch me* signal. "I didn't think you were coming over."

"Change of plans." He couldn't explain it himself. No point in poking at something like that.

"Look, I'm not feeling well." Her mouth pulled down. She rubbed her stomach. "I know you don't want to stick around for this. So I'll just call you tomorrow, okay?"

He brushed his knuckles over her cheekbones. At least she wasn't running a fever. "Tell me what's wrong?"

"The usual icky—" She broke off. Her eyes flared. She spun and ran off down the short hallway. The bottoms of her feet flashed.

Jon followed, slamming the front door behind him. Heather had already disappeared. He followed to where the bed sheets were a tumbled, snarled mess.

But she'd shut the bathroom door. Even locked it.

"Come on, Heather." He knocked on the white wood. "Let me in."

"Don't be—" Retching noises punctuated her words, along with a cough or two. "Don't be ridiculous."

Jon bowed his head as he took a deep breath. If Heather was sick, he wasn't going to be put off by some nastiness. The Air Force trusted him to keep his shit together in the face of death and destruction. Vomit was nothing.

"Open up, Heather. Let me help you."

The silence stretched until it became tangible. His words took on an extra weight as he listened for her reply.

All she said was, "Gimme a second."

The toilet flushed, followed by running water. She opened the door. Water gleamed on her dark lashes, turning them spiky. Her skin was streaked pink.

Jon couldn't help but frame her face in his hands, although it went against her silent rules. He kissed her damp forehead. "Let me tuck you in bed."

She looked up at him. Something intangible washed over her wan features. Then she found a listless smile. "You going to play knight in shining armor?"

He laughed as he led her to bed. "Leah's given me enough practice."

Heather snuggled into bed and curled on her side. Her cheek pressed into an overstuffed pillow. He tugged the sheets and her comforter over her shoulders, then went about neatly tucking in the end of the bed.

"Did you just make hospital corners on my bed?"

"What?" He glanced down to what he'd done. The sheets were inspection perfect. A flush crawled up the back of his neck. "If I say yes, are you going to kick them right out again?"

"Maybe."

He eased nearer and brushed dark, damp hair back from her temples. "What happened?"

"I got sick."

"Duh." He tugged on her ponytail—softly though, because she really was a mess. "I mean what's wrong?"

"I'm not sure. It's either food poisoning or the flu."

"Have you had anything to drink?"

She almost turned green. "No way. Nothing's going in my mouth. Nuh-uh."

"You have to keep your fluids up." He stroked her shoulder. "You don't want to get dehydrated."

"Thanks, Dr. Carlisle," she said dryly.

He chuckled. "Stay here."

"It's not like I'm going anywhere."

Her kitchen was practically stripped bare. The stainless-steel fridge was a barren wasteland populated by single-serve cups of yogurt, a few boxes of takeout Chinese and Diet Coke. No way was he pouring caffeine down her throat.

He put in a call to his favorite delivery service and placed an order for crackers and liquids with plenty of electrolytes. He accepted the rush delivery fee, paying by credit card. "If I don't answer, just leave it on the porch," he told the clerk.

Resolved to waiting, he poured a glass of water from the filter pitcher on the slate counter.

Heather was no longer in the bedroom. The covers had been tossed back and the bathroom door was closed. "Heather love?"

Two minutes passed before she reemerged. "I'm going to have to buy a new toothbrush after this."

"That's it," he gritted. "We're taking you to a walk-in clinic."

"I'm not going anywhere."

She tried to crawl back into bed, but Jon wrapped his arms around her waist. "Come on. Doctor. Now."

"I don't wanna."

"I didn't figure you for quite so stubborn."

"No? Have you not met me?"

"Good point." Her head tucked neatly under his chin. The strokes he smoothed down her back, over the cotton of her camisole, were long and calm, intended to soothe.

"I make a really shitty patient."

"I'm beginning to see that. Come on, on your feet."

He hauled her off the bed and found a pair of slippers tossed at the end of her bed. The way she cuddled against his side was surprisingly gratifying.

So...great. She was willing to let him in under two conditions: when he dangled an orgasm as a reward, or when she was completely worn out.

Ignoring how that grated, Jon snagged her purse from the table by the front door.

She dragged to a stop at the edge of her driveway. "Are you seriously going to put me in your car when I'm liable to puke?"

Even sick as she was, nothing hid the graceful lines of her cheekbones or the complicated thoughts lurking in her pale eyes.

"Why wouldn't I?"

"How much did that thing cost?"

He stifled a sigh. "Enough."

She nibbled her bottom lip, studying him. Then she stretched up to brush a feather-soft kiss on his chin. All she said was, "Thank you."

It was more than he'd expected.

Chapter Thirty-Three

Heather contained her inappropriate giggles for most of the ride home from the walk-in clinic. The feat wasn't too difficult considering the knot of pain in her gut.

But then they arrived at her house. The scene of the crime against her stomach was still laid out on the kitchen counter.

One look at the delivery of chocolate and strawberries was the end of her. She laughed so hard that she needed to sit down. A barstool at her kitchen's island took her weight.

Jon stood in the doorway, tense arms folded over his chest. His glare was downright impressive for a man with such pretty features. She covered her mouth, but the giggles wouldn't quiet.

Salmonella, the doctor had said. The sweet red culprits had been easy to identify. Twelve hours at work had made it too crazy to stop for lunch. She hadn't eaten anything all day—except for Jon's strawberries.

"It's not funny," he said for the tenth time.

"It is. Come on. A little." She was gasping for breath, still grinning. "Besides, shouldn't I get final say? I'm the one who's sick."

He prowled over to the counter. Chocolate, strawberries and the delivery tray hit the trash with a bold thud. Only then did he permit a chagrined smile. "Next time I'll send edible underwear."

"No fun without you here."

The quip came automatically. He'd been so good to her in the clinic—her advocate when her stomach hurt too much to do paperwork. The four-hour ordeal left her exhausted and certain his stores of patience were quickly depleting. To learn his gift had been the cause of the ordeal should've been the last straw.

God, she must look a mess. Any minute now he'd find a reason to scram.

Jon crossed the kitchen. His legs nudged between her knees. He

Inside Bet

placed a kiss on her crown. "I'm sorry."

He hadn't said *that* ten times. The quietness and sincerity messed with her emotional compass.

"It wasn't your fault." She stroked one of his forearms where his dark hair emerged from beneath rolled cuffs. "It was, by far, the nicest brush-off present I've ever received."

His flinch confirmed her guess. "I had to work."

"Then tell me you have work." She waved a hand toward the strawberries' trashcan grave. "Don't smarm your way out of it. I know better."

The skin between his brows furrowed. Soothing hands dropped away from her shoulders. Only then did she find the strength to let him off the hook.

"Jon, you don't have to stay."

A little roughly, he hauled her off the barstool. "Come on, let's get you in bed."

Her exhaustion made it easy to let him lead. She tripped after him, back to her bedroom and the sheets he'd straightened with unconscious efficiency. Heather slumped onto the mattress. The hot ache in her stomach remained, but at least the nausea had dimmed.

Once he'd tucked her in, Jon sat on the edge of the bed. "Your choice, Heather. I can stay or go."

His expression was a marvel of composure. Not quite blank. Not quite present either. The curve of his top lip seemed almost sarcastic, but his gaze bored into hers. He expected something from her.

What could he expect? That she'd ask her lover to stay and play nursemaid? The doctor had said the food poisoning could take a day or two to run its course. Heather hadn't wanted to disturb Jenn, not with Rich just back from Tampa. Their time together as a family was so fleeting.

Yet facing the whole weekend on her own left her cold and already lonely.

Would Jon really stick around to look after her? That idea was scary. Scary and...wonderful.

"Stay," she whispered.

She didn't want to take it back. Something like relief brightened his face before he hid it away. "Done. I'll get your Gatorade."

Oh, she was sunk. Torpedoes and direct hits. *Sunk.*

She'd seen him in her home before, but always as partners intent on sharing one another in the bedroom—not sharing a living space. She'd also known him to be meticulous in how he dressed and cared for his clothing. His car was never short of immaculate. Although she feared getting so close, she couldn't help but wonder what his condo would look like. Orderly, sure, but how would he fill his place of refuge?

He'd only asked once. The lurch in her stomach had nothing to do with food poisoning. More to do with her total lack of a spine.

The reality of watching him bustle around her bedroom gave her a secret smile. She peeked out from where she'd half-buried her face in her pillow. He brought a bowl and a towel from the kitchen, as well as a foul electrolyte concoction.

But Heather drew the line when he asked for cleaning supplies. "Why?"

"The bathroom counter."

Surprise and embarrassment fought for control. "Sit down, Jon. Please. You're making me tired from here."

"That's a step up. At least you're not laughing." His wry expression took the sting out of his words. "Will you puke again if I order a pizza? Yogurt doesn't do it for me and I'm starving."

"You're the man who practically volunteered to clean my bathroom. Order whatever you want."

Forty minutes later he sat beside her on the bed, propped up on the headboard. Heather ate crackers, finally able to keep them down. Jon had turned on a rerun of *The Daily Show*. Laughing with him felt good, no matter the acrobatics in her stomach. She snuggled against his chest. The steady beat of his heart pinched longing around hers.

She hadn't felt so cared for in a long, long time.

She must have dozed because her next blinks were in darkness. Jon had shut out the lights. Only the streetlamp outside her house illuminated the room through lace bedroom curtains. His eyes were closed, his face relaxed, but she didn't think he was sleeping.

"Why did you come over?" she asked quietly.

"It doesn't matter now."

Heather swallowed a sliver of dread. She couldn't think of a joke or an innuendo. Too tired. Nothing came to mind except the truth. "It does matter. Did you come by for sex?"

"No." His voice was a low rumble. "I had another run-in with Donaghue, the captain you met. Wanted to talk about it."

Warmth prickled her skin. She'd assumed he was there for an unplanned quickie, which was their obvious MO. That he had stopped by for another reason, and such a personal one, sped her shallow respiration. When had that mattered? When had she secretly wanted him to see her as something other than a fun time?

Maybe when she'd opened her front door in her pajamas. When she'd needed him.

No, that was the easy answer. These moments and this...*wanting* had been gathering for weeks.

"Talk about it now," she said.

"No, I don't think so."

"Why not?"

He angled on the headboard to look down at her. The top two buttons of his soft blue cambric shirt revealed the notch at the base of his throat. "Because it goes both ways, Heather love. I can't do this on my own."

She wanted to disavow any knowledge of what "this" meant, but she owed him more than playing dumb. A shiver made her dive back into his embrace.

She was tired. Blasted. Exhausted. Holding up the wall between them had become impossible.

"Do you know why I got you to ask me to the ball?" she asked.

"I'd rather not guess if you can tell me."

"Because I never went to my senior prom."

He huffed a quiet laugh. "Neither did I."

"No?"

"I was at an ROTC welcome mixer."

Of course he was. Nothing about him was typical, she'd learned. He constantly made her look twice, to the point of pinching herself. Words like "too good to be true" were always followed by doubts.

Why me?

"But your reason?" he asked.

Heather shut her eyes. She was glad for the dark and glad for their closeness. She wouldn't have to see his expressions. "I was on the back of a motorcycle on my way to Jersey."

"You ran away?"

"With a twenty-five-year-old corporal named Sam." She shivered. Something old and dark and scary lifted the hairs across her nape. Jon's hand tightened around her upper arm. "We'd met just after my dad's retirement—that fabulous seventeenth birthday of mine. Things weren't so great at home after how I'd behaved, and then there was Sam. He was...he was everything wild and crazy. Smooth-talking. Cute. Hot bike. I was a senior with a grown-up boyfriend. I snuck out all the time. Drove my parents nuts and made my friends crazy jealous. *Such a rush.* I loved the attention and the thrill." Her cheeks flashed hot. "I did anything he wanted me to."

That time Jon's reaction was unmistakable. He sighed and tucked inside himself. She could sympathize. She wanted nothing more than to hide. But she was doing this for him as a show of faith. Maybe she was doing it for both of them.

"When we ran away together at prom...I told him I loved him." She swallowed. "Not well received, I'm afraid. A year on and off with a teenaged girl didn't mean love to him. It meant a good time, every time. I honestly hadn't seen the difference. So that weekend, he had other things in mind for us. Some friends of his came over—two buddies from his platoon. We got high. We..." She swallowed convulsively. "I woke up alone a few days later."

"Fucking hell," he whispered.

"I called my dad. He had to come pick me up from some shitty little beach motel." Shame rolled over her in hot waves. The terror of waking up naked, with no sober memories of the weekend, had rattled the foundation of her life. "I swear to God, the strongest thing he's ever done was not going after Sam. Dad could have had him kicked out of the Army on statutory charges. We drove home in silence. I was almost too high to give a damn, but his silence got through to me."

Heather forced herself to sit up. Her hair was a sticky disaster. Her guts ached. Maybe it hadn't been such a good idea to revisit that horror show when vomiting remained a possibility. Recalling those days was absolutely nauseating.

"My medical tests all came back negative. I was... Jesus, I was lucky." She shrugged, not brave enough yet to look Jon in the face. "I clamped down after that. Hardcore. I worked all summer and took summer courses. Nothing mattered but getting clean and proving myself. Dad... It took awhile, but we managed. I don't think I was ever happier than when I saw him wipe his eyes at my college graduation."

Tears filled her eyes too. She pushed at them with the heels of her hands as fatigue and a long-ago grief pushed back.

Jon's fingers rested beneath her hair, caressing her nape. "When did you get your tattoo?"

"That week when I graduated." She was feeling stronger now, as if emerging from a dark tunnel. "I'd been accepted to my first-choice MBA program and already had an internship lined up for that summer, but it was in Florida. I was afraid."

"Of a challenge? That doesn't sound like you."

She shook her head. "I was afraid of slipping up."

"Being her again. What's done is done."

"Yes."

Jon gathered her in his arms, kissing her forehead. "I chewed out Donaghue at the BX for being a reckless dickhead. Shouldn't have. It wasn't my place. But better than that, I kept from hitting him." She heard a smile in his voice. "I wanted a cheering section to tell me I'd done good."

Amazed, Heather drew in a sweet breath. He hadn't offered pity or trite condolences. He hadn't judged her. Instead he'd given her an out—one she grabbed with both hands.

"You did good, Jon. Really." She frowned slightly. "But why not seek out Ryan or Leah to talk about it?"

"Too personal with them."

"I don't follow."

"I got pissed at Donaghue because guys like that put my friends at risk. I couldn't explain that to them without coming across like a goddamn putz."

Heather smiled. "Tin Tin strikes again?"

"Oh, don't you start too." He rolled halfway on top of her. "I'm a callous, cold, unfeeling playboy. Don't you forget it."

"That's the first lie I've ever heard from you."

"I prefer to call it an evasive maneuver. You're pretty good at them too."

"Not when I'm this tired."

He looked her in the eyes, hand at her waist. "Is it a little better? At least?"

"Still feeling bad about it?"

"Sure."

"I'm better. Honest."

"Good."

Jon slipped off the bed. A streetlight cast him in silhouette. "Should I sleep here or on the couch? I'm good with either."

"Here." The word slipped free so quickly. Honest and sure. "But no funny business. I'm liable to puke on you."

"That could possibly establish an outer limit to my kink, Ms. Morris."

He stripped off his button-down and shucked his jeans. Soon his body nestled against hers. Despite feeling as if she'd been run over by a semi, Heather hadn't breathed so easily in years.

For the first time since their meeting in that wine bar, she let herself hope they had a chance. Something more. A future.

Chapter Thirty-Four

Despite having never awoken there, Jon knew before he opened his eyes that he was in Heather's bed. Her curvy body wrapped around him. Silky hair spilled over his chest. Their legs pretzeled together. Most curious of all, Heather had a death grip on his waist. At least in sleep she'd let down a few of those close barriers.

That wasn't exactly fair. In the dark of night, she'd laid at least one secret bare. Despite the years that separated her from her mistakes, and despite having created an entirely new version of herself, her voice had sounded frightened. Of what she'd done. Of the choices she'd made. Of what she remained capable of losing.

Jon wanted to hunt down that long-gone corporal and cut his balls off. Slowly. Using dull nail clippers.

Extricating himself from her grip was difficult considering he didn't even want to. But certain things needed to be taken care of first thing in the morning.

At least it was Saturday. He had nowhere else to be.

After padding back from the bathroom, he stood over her and admired a singular view. Bright yellow sunlight spilled over the bed, which added a glow to feminine features already softened by sleep. Heather's camisole had twisted around her ribs to reveal smooth skin and a few inches of her tattoo. He slid back into bed as quietly as he could manage.

But she shifted sleepily then rubbed her eyes. Blinked a few times. Her mouth tipped into a small smile. "Hey, you."

A tight, wadded place behind his chest unfurled. Apparently he'd been worried that she would close off again. The absence of her usual wariness set him at ease. An unfamiliar sensation.

"*Bonjour,* Heather, *mon amour.*"

"It is way too early for you to play dirty like that." She groaned as she pushed her torso up.

Jon laced his fingers behind his head and grinned. "You think I play dirty?"

"I don't just think it, I know it." The look she shot him was indulgent. "See? You're doing it even now."

"Feel free to tell me more."

"You're the one wearing only a pair of boxer shorts, lounging in my bed. You know what you're doing."

Laughing, he scratched idly across his chest. "I guess you're feeling better."

She rubbed her stomach as she seemed to take inventory. "You know, I think I am. I could probably even eat."

"But you won't," he said firmly. "Nothing more than toast at first."

"Yes, Dr. Carlisle."

Dragging his slacks from where he'd tossed them, Jon pulled them on. A rumpled mess. When he caught Heather staring at his ass, he realized he didn't care. What were wrinkled clothes when they shared a smile that was half-fun, half-curious hello? He padded toward the kitchen.

Dry toast and an electrolyte drink in hand, he returned to find Heather still in bed. But she'd changed her pajamas, her face was pink from washing, and she'd brushed her hair into a loose ponytail. She frowned at the glass of bright orange liquid.

"Is that more Gatorade? I need some caffeine."

"No way. Not until we see how this stays down."

"I'm fine, I'm sure of it." She accepted the plate and glass.

Jon lay down on the bed and laced his fingers behind his neck. He stared up at the plain white ceiling. The only sound was the crunch of toast and an occasional clink of ice against the side of the glass.

"Do you want to come out with me and my friends on Wednesday night?"

Goddamn it. He hadn't exactly meant to go there. Not yet. But the words had popped out of his mouth. They'd only just hauled one another back from the brink of a kiss-off that would've ended the whole affair. He should take it slow if he wanted more. Which he did.

Inviting her out was different now. She'd already met everyone. But this request held so much importance. It would mean risking even more.

"If you're feeling up to it," he added.

She set her cup on the bedside table. "Where are you guys going?"

"Karaoke."

"You sing karaoke?"

He laughed to cover his awkwardness. "Yeah. And I'm damn good at it."

She set the plate aside as well. Then she folded her hands over his chest and leaned her chin on them. Her body stretched fully along his. Only when she smiled, another mix of shy and playful, did Jon get a clue as to her answer.

"I wouldn't miss that for the world."

Jon hadn't been able to see Heather after leaving her bungalow on Sunday afternoon. She'd stayed home from work a day and a half, so he didn't press for a renewed invitation to stop over. By Wednesday she swore she was well enough for a simple night out.

Everyone arrived at Paulie's, the tiny bar just off post. The place was truly dive-bar-esque, its walls lined with certificates and plaques from various Nellis units. But they had one hell of a karaoke setup, including a stage and lights.

Ryan and Cass sat along one side of their usual table. The major looped his arm around her seat as his fingers trailed down her arm. Leah sat at the head of the table where she said she had the best view of the stage. Jon figured it was more about ease of access to the bar.

Leah was the driving force behind their frequent trips to Paulie's, the one off-duty place where she stayed relatively sober. She claimed boozing it up impaired her ability to remember lyrics, although she usually still had a beer or three.

Wonder of wonders, she'd ordered a Dr. Pepper.

Upon catching sight of Jon's raised eyebrow, she scowled. "So help me, Tin Tin, if you say a word, my first priority tomorrow morning will be shooting you out of the sky."

He held up his hands in mock surrender, though inside he felt genuine relief. *Maybe.* Maybe she could do it.

The night only got better as he discovered a surprising bonus. Heather wasn't only game to sing, she did it well.

Onstage the cool white light clung to her features, just as Jon had imagined. She'd chosen a Billie Holiday song, which perfectly suited her husky voice. Hearing her sing a lament about not having a ghost of a chance with a man sent chills down his back.

Cass scooted into the seat next to him. "She's lovely, you know."

"She's beautiful, yeah."

Leaning her chin on a fist, she skewered him with a reproachful glance. "Don't be dense."

He'd known what she meant. After the surprising way Heather had opened up about her past, he'd discovered a spot inside him that was still too raw to probe, much less talk about. He'd never been one to trust happiness.

Cass snagged her glass of lemonade. "You should see the way she watches you."

At that he had to laugh. "I know *exactly* how she watches me."

"No, it's more than that." Her expression turned contemplative, with her mouth twisted at one side. Jon caught the direction of her glance—across the table, where Ryan and Leah were laughing. "It's like she's not sure if she can risk it."

Jon coughed and faced the stage. The conversation verged on territory best kept between her and Ryan. He focused instead on Heather, who looked sexy as hell in a slim, hip-hugging pair of jeans and a dark red blouse.

"I'm no risk," he said. "I wouldn't hurt her."

Had he ever been able to say that about any lover—and mean it in every sense? No. He sipped his scotch, heart lurching.

Cass patted his hand. "Sometimes the risk doesn't have anything to do with you." She grinned. "And believe me, it sucks fish fins to wait for the stupid to wear off."

With that she crossed behind empty chairs and reclaimed her place on Ryan's lap. The pixie and the All-American. Jon shook his head, took another sip and returned his attention to Heather.

She finished her song to a healthy smattering of applause. She seemed to wake from a daze. A pink blush stained her high cheekbones, but then she gave a laughing bow.

Everyone at the table cheered as she made her way back. "Thank you, thank you," she said. "No autographs, please."

Jon laced his fingers through hers when she returned to her chair. "Not bad for a newbie."

"In elementary school I was in the church choir."

Not for high school, though. He finally knew what she'd spent those teenage years doing. But she wasn't poor, lost Heather anymore. She'd recreated herself into someone completely independent. Why couldn't she see that?

"Hey, Tin Tin," Leah called. "Don't think we've missed that it's your turn."

"Really." Heather's smile was a teasing curve. "It's not fair to make me go when I haven't watched you."

He leaned close enough to whisper in her ear. Silky hair brushed his cheek. "What are you willing to do for me if I do?"

She drew back. They looked one another in the eye. "This time?" Her throat worked over a swallow. "Nothing."

He traced the delicate skin of her jaw. No dares? He hardly knew what to make of that. Was she finally inviting him in?

"No kissy-face," Leah said with a groan. "You guys promised. If I came out as the fifth wheel, there would be no kissy-face allowed."

The half-kidding, half-serious quip was enough to dissolve the thick tension between him and Heather. He leaned away from Heather, hooking his elbow over the back of his chair. "I know for a damned fact that I did not say kissy-face. I can't remember those words coming out of my mouth. Ever."

"You just did, Dimples." Ryan tucked his chin over Cass's shoulder. "I heard it."

Jon mock saluted with his tumbler. "I'll remember that one, Fang. Don't think I won't."

Leah knocked on the table. "I call this meeting of the flying jackass society to order. First order of business is Tin Tin singing."

"I second the motion." Heather's pale eyes glittered with mirth.

Gathering a semblance of dignity, Leah nodded solemnly. "First motion passes. Second is his song."

"Hey, now," Jon said. "No one voted."

Ryan laughed. "Trust me, you singing is a given."

Jon flipped him off, but there was no menace behind it. Just long years of camaraderie and taking care of each other.

"I say INXS," Cass said. "Vintage eighties cheese."

"No way." Jon had been up there before, plenty of times. *Tons.* But he'd never let anyone pick the song for him. "Not even close."

"Yes," Heather agreed with laughter in her voice. "Maybe 'Need You Tonight'? For me? That's something I'd pay good money to see."

Aw, hell. Like he could get out of that one.

"Fine," he grumbled.

Before he headed up to plug in the song, he caressed the back of Heather's neck. The kiss he stole was long and slow. Passing between their lips was a measure of tenderness he hadn't felt before. With any woman.

Drawing back, he fashioned one of his most dedicated smiles—the one he wore when he thought about her taste. "Sit back, Ms. Morris. You're going to love this."

Chapter Thirty-Five

Jon took to the small stage with his trademark slow-burn cool. Dressed almost as plainly as he had at the diner, he wore classic-fit jeans, a plain white T-shirt and a pair of Doc Marten boots. Everything about him, from his casual posture to his smug grin, said this was no big deal. She knew better. For every measured move, he concealed a hundred genuine impulses.

Nervousness twined with anticipation. She didn't just want him to sing; she wanted him to be fantastic.

A thumping chant of "Tin Tin" swelled from all around. Ryan, Cass, Leah, and a dozen other patrons, possibly more off-duty airmen, whistled and shouted along. Heather only clasped her hands around her knees to stop their jitters.

The instrumental track started up, and so did her pulse. That distinctive guitar riff ripped out from the speakers as Jon nodded in time. His wide grin reached out from the stage to find her.

Striking a pose, he started into the slinky, soulful lyrics. He didn't have the best voice on the planet, but he was by no means horrible. A wink here, a point there, he played to a crowd that obviously expected him to take the whole thing as a joke.

Heather laughed along, as everyone did, knowing what a good sport he was being. Only twenty-six years old, he'd probably been in diapers when the song debuted, which just made her head hurt.

Somewhere after the first chorus, he changed. Subtly. Gracefully. Heather couldn't name the moment when he began taking it seriously. She only felt it on her skin, heard it as the bar noise calmed. Hoots and shouts went silent, as did the drunken sing-alongs. Jon's playful gestures fell away, revealing a performance as earnest and sexy as the song.

After he'd claimed everyone's attention, he found Heather in the crowd. His eyes flashed mischievous heat. Every word seeped into her skin. Raw. Sweat. Need. Then even that awareness slid away as Jon closed his eyes. He gave himself over to the experience.

And owned every minute of it.

The bar shouted and applauded at the song's end. Jon made peace signs with his fingers and kissed them, but the return of his devil-may-care persona was à deliberate ruse. *Nothing to see here, people.* Don't look at how much he'd given, how much he wanted to be appreciated as the best.

Heather saw it all. His performance left her flushed and quaking with the crazy energy of a deep, delicious secret.

"Ryan," she said, tapping the officer's shoulder. "Is he always like that?"

"Every time, the foul-minded cherub."

"You're just jealous, Fang," Jon said, jogging the few steps down from the stage. "Admit it. My karaoke brings the chicks to the yard."

Leah laughed. "Watch it, dork, or 'Milkshake' will be your next assignment."

"Bring it on."

He flopped into his chair. Sweaty, a little breathless, he slid Heather a look. She caught it—the expectation. Her opinion mattered to him. In this, apparently, he was not one hundred percent sure of himself, unlike flying and sex.

She closed the distance between them. With one hand high on his inner thigh, she kissed his temple. "You turn me on when you mean it."

Jon blinked twice before blanking his surprise. "Glad you enjoyed it, Ms. Morris."

She didn't know whether to be thankful or disappointed when Cass broke the mood. "You're next, Ryan," she said. "Get your fine butt up there."

"Oh, c'mon. You know I suck."

"TMI," Leah said. "Please respect my delicate sensibilities."

Ryan laughed. "I would if you had any."

Heather observed the exchanges with a sense of longing that no longer surprised her. Their history was fascinating, just as she wondered if she could ever fit in so well. They held nothing back from one another—the insults, the laughter, the camaraderie. Such openness was as enticing as it was risky.

She glanced toward her flyboy, who was busy flicking mini pretzels, one at a time, at the back of Ryan's head. Jon laughed, full and deep, as if showing off his dimples on purpose. His smile held no pretense, and even his crafted calm slipped to reveal the young man inside.

"Come off it, Fang." Jon flicked another pretzel, completely unaware of how hard he was flipping her world. "You're not getting out of singing again. You're no better than the rest of us."

"Says the captain to the major."

"Bite me, Major Haverty, sir."

Leah finished the last of her soda and crunched an ice cube. "If you make me convene another jackass meeting, I'll find a gavel and bring the pain."

"Princess, I never knew you went for the rough stuff," Jon said.

She flipped him off.

"Come on, Ryan." Cass stood from his lap and tugged his hand. "For me? Please? I'll be your groupie."

Jon choked on a hard laugh. Leah only shook her head, eyes rolling to the ceiling. But Ryan took to the stage with unexpected resolve. His version of Springsteen's "Born to Run" was terrible—just *terrible*. Their table cheered anyway, like children on the last day of school.

An hour later, Heather's ears were ringing as they left Paulie's. She desperately wanted to be alone with Jon, if only to see which of her pinging emotions became reality.

Cass nodded toward the hot pink motorcycle Leah climbed onto. "Is that new?"

Leah grimaced as she fastened a matching helmet. "Nah. It's just hard to ride with your head between your knees. Nighty-night, kissy-faces."

With that she gunned the bike. Parking lot gravel sprayed out from the rear wheel as she sped onto the road. The men shouted their approval like a rallying war cry. After a few more goodbyes, Ryan and Cass hurried off to their truck, laughing, their hands clasped.

Heather came up behind Jon and folded her arms around his lean middle. "A good night," she said against his shoulder.

"Yeah, a really good night." He glanced back. "You were great onstage. The old blues tunes fit your voice."

"My voice?"

He turned, his hands low on her hips. "Very Lauren Bacall, all low and sexy. But I don't think you even realize it, do you?"

"Never thought about it."

God, he still terrified her—his keen mind and uncanny ability to dissect every detail. She'd enjoyed Jon being sincere onstage because that had been about looking into *him*. To have that same sincerity turned full-force on her was something she'd never be able to stand.

Being with him had come to mean too much. Impulses ricocheted between her heart and her brain.

"Come on," he said. "You look beat."

The DBS waited like a panther in shadow. Jon clicked his key fob to open the locks, then ushered her in. They sat side by side, silent for a moment. Heather recalled the peace and warmth she'd enjoyed upon waking up in his arms. She wanted that again.

Even more, their last sexual encounter—after the Air Force ball—had become a dark space in her mind. They shouldn't have ended it that way. After a shower and another quickie up against the bathroom wall, they'd called it a night. The bed, still perfectly made, had not even been touched. Memories of one of the best sexual encounters of her life now left her cold.

That evening contrasted so strongly with Friday, when he'd taken her to the clinic and made her drink Gatorade. From the start, his unexpected tenderness rubbed at all her insecurities. What did he want from her? What did she want from him, them, herself?

She wanted more.

The words flared bright in her brain, then filled her with a happy calm. "So, home then?"

"What are you asking, Heather love?" His face remained in profile, with his hand on the gearshift.

She laid hers over it. "Will you stay with me tonight? All night?"

After a tight nod and a slow exhalation, he gave her hand a squeeze. His side-eye grin made everything okay.

He revved that killer engine and powered the convertible top. The city sped by in a blur of neon and black. Heather settled into the

Inside Bet

sumptuous leather seat, her hand on Jon's thigh. The moment was, as always, sexually charged, but something deeper had taken over. She'd seen behind his mask. He had permitted entrance to a very exclusive sanctuary. The urge to reciprocate loosened her limbs and eased her breathing.

Jon pulled into her driveway and met her at the passenger door. He gathered her into his embrace. They simply held one another in the quiet. Heather's heart rushed and thumped.

"Thank you." She looked into his eyes. "I can see why they mean so much to you."

"They make it easy to care."

He led her up to the porch of her house then followed her in the front door. The lights were out. She took his hand to guide him through the darkened rooms. The intimacy between them was thick and slow, all honey-sweet.

They undressed one another in her bedroom. The streetlamp shone silver on their skin as they revealed each bare inch. A power built between them unlike any they'd shared. She wanted to shy away with a sexy tease on her tongue. Jon never gave her the chance. He smoothed every shiver with his palms, caught every unformed protest with his warm lips.

Until she didn't want to protest anymore. Only...be his.

The gentle pressure of his hands on her shoulders eased her onto the edge of the mattress. He knelt, his eyes lifted. Breathing became impossible as she realized the truth. Just like that moment onstage, he meant it this time. No dares. No masks and innuendo. Just Jon and how much he wanted her.

She was in love with him. So much.

With her heart beating furiously, and not knowing what else to do, she gave a little nod.

He spread her knees with infinite slowness and cupped his hands beneath her thighs. The hot brush of his breath touched her first, then the tender, delicious stroke of his tongue. The patient sweetness of his lips. The flexing caress of his trembling fingertips. Heather forced herself to be just as gentle as she petted the rasping hair along the back of his head.

Arousal built and built, with no end in sight. There was no hurry. No control to be wrested from one another. Jon leaned her back on the bed, and his kiss tasted of her own body. They learned one another by feel and sound. The smallest gasp became a guidepost—*more of that*—while each caress radiated between them like a shimmer of light.

Jon found a condom before levering above her. Classic missionary, just man over woman. Sharp shadows defined the muscles of his arms and chest. Heather slid her hands up, slowly up, to cup his shoulders. With his respiration labored, he pushed deep and filled her. Two low moans twined together.

No matter the almost reverent foreplay, their passion would not be polite. Jon's lean hips surged. Her slick softness yielded to where he was so hard, so eager. She pulled him close, her fingers splayed down past those twin divots at his lower back. He braced his weight on his elbows. Sweat-slicked chests pressed flush. Every slow groaning thrust rubbed her nipples against his skin.

Heather let her eyes close, lost to him. She crisscrossed her ankles around his ass, feeling it clench with each forceful push. The rhythm of desire and emotion that had intensified all night became a beat in her blood.

"I need you, my lovely girl," he whispered.

"I'm right here, Jon. Right here."

His mouth found hers, as intimate as where their hips met. Tongues slipped and pressed. Tight breath burst against her cheeks. With his hand at her breast, he drove her higher. Faster now. Endless grinding pulses were theirs to share.

When release shimmered over Heather in a long, hot shudder, he was there at her mouth, kissing, drinking in her sounds. He tensed on one last deep thrust. His gasping exhalation was her gift to keep.

Long after Jon had sprawled across her belly, fast asleep, Heather stared at the patterns made by headlights across the ceiling.

I can do this.

She could give herself to this incredible man—the man she loved. But even as Heather languidly stroked his warm, muscular back, her restless mind repeated the phrase. Over and over. Keeping her awake.

I can do this.

Not once did she believe it.

Chapter Thirty-Six

By Friday afternoon, even six straight hours of maintenance checks couldn't dim Jon's mood. The flight crew was on the top of its game and had his plane running smoother than ever. When Ryan suggested they all go home early, Jon wasn't about to say no. He left without even taking time to give his friends their daily ration of smartass comments.

The only thing better than an unexpected afternoon off was someone to share it with. He'd have to conjure some fast-talking to get Heather to leave early, but he had an inside track now. Something had shifted when she'd been sick. Or maybe afterward, at the karaoke bar and when she'd invited him to stay the night.

He made a swift stop by his condo to wash up and change out of his flight suit. Another stop at his favorite bistro meant lunch in hand. His Aston seemed to purr with anticipation as he drove toward Heather's office. Takeout bags dangling from his fingers, Jon held open the plate-glass doors to her building and allowed an older woman to enter first.

The reception area was swanky. His mother and father would have been proud. A touch of Southwest was apparent in the pale wood with purple and blue paintings, but not enough to be tacky. A seating area to the right was situated under a large bank of windows with a primo view of the city. A blonde receptionist sat behind a large desk of highly polished driftwood topped by glass.

"Can I help you?"

Jon smiled. "I certainly hope so. I'm here to see Ms. Morris. My name's Jon Carlisle."

"Is she expecting you?"

His smile only widened. "No, she's not."

"I'll see if she's available." Touching two fingers to the wireless headset tucked over her ear, she clicked numbers into a keypad. After a few quiet words, she returned his smile. "You can go right in. Top floor."

As the elevator swept him up, Jon whistled under his breath. The shining brass walls reflected his image. Damn, his smile verged on sappy. It'd be embarrassing if he didn't carry the memory of Wednesday night: the tremulous cast of Heather's silver-shaded mouth when she told him she was there. Right there with him.

Her office was at the far end of the hallway. The door stood open. A gold-tone plaque affixed beside it read *Heather Morris, Assistant Director*. She must be proud of that title next to her name. *He* was damn proud of her. She was a smart woman who'd earned every inch of the respect she garnered.

Even seeing her sitting behind her large desk gave him a thrill. Her charcoal suit jacket was almost militaristic with its stand-up collar and silver button fobs. The office was also impressive. A large bank of shelves to one side had been filled with company and personal awards.

The dark wood desk would conceal any multitude of sins. If he knelt between her legs, he could lick her pussy until she came without anyone being the wiser. He craved her taste more than he wanted lunch.

She pressed her palms flat against the polished surface and stood. "Jon," she said slowly. "What are you doing here?"

He quietly shut the door. The takeout plunked down on the corner of her desk, right next to a crystal award inscribed with her name. "I brought you Italian. Figured if I eat it too, you won't think it's laced with salmonella."

"That's sweet of you." But her smile had gone wary. Again.

He'd assumed they were past that. Then again, he'd never been to her office, much less uninvited. He'd taken a risk. Regarding anything beyond her sex life, Heather didn't take well to risks. He could sympathize, but he no longer wanted it to be an issue between them.

Easing around to her side, he tucked two fingers under the hem of her jacket. "Trust me, Ms. Morris. I had ulterior motives."

"Oh, did you?"

He made a quiet sound of agreement as he tugged her near. She'd loosely wound her hair into a knot at the back of her head. It held the sweetly sultry scent he'd come to associate with her. He gently kissed her neck, gratified when she curved under the attention.

"Remember the first time you called me?"

She swallowed tightly. "Of course."

"Do you know what I remember about that call?" He trailed a soft touch along the front placket of her jacket, circling each silver button clasp. His fingertips swept down and under her breasts.

Her shoulders tensed. "I bet I do."

He smiled as if putting on a mask. Something was off about her today. "I remember the quiet, breathy sounds of you coming in my ear."

A shudder took her over. She slanted her gaze toward him. A lick along her bottom lip left a glaze of saliva over her so-proper lipstick.

He caught the hem of her tailored skirt. "Want to try for a replay?"

"I..." Her voice had gone husky and breathy at the same time. "Jon, this is my office..."

A sweet flush of coffee sugared her lips. He kissed it away, delving deep with his tongue. Her fingers clenched his button-down shirt. He nestled his growing hard-on against the tops of her thighs.

She pulled back and shook her head so hard that a dark lock of hair slid free. "I shouldn't. Not...now."

Deep down, a twinge of frustration lurked in his gut. "Then we'll eat as I try to talk you into playing hooky."

She laughed, still sounding fairly tense. "I don't think I can do that, either. The quarterly reports for the Wynn are due in two days and I took that time off when I was sick."

"You'd be surprised at what I can talk you into, Ms. Morris." He slanted her an impish smile as he laid out the cartons, flicked off the covers and stacked them neatly back in the plastic bag.

Heather eased into her seat. "Plastic silverware? You're slumming it a bit, aren't you?"

"One makes do how one must." He drew the visitor's chair up to the other side of the desk and sat down. "There's an exhibit at the Hungerford Gallery that's quite remarkable. Where Cass works."

"What?" She paused in swirling up a forkful of pasta.

"When I get you to leave." He hitched one foot up on his knee, takeout carton in his hand. "In about a half hour, I think. We'll go to the gallery, and then back to your place. Once there, I plan on licking you from head to toe until you've come. Two or three times."

Her fork clattered quietly against the tinfoil box. She leaned forward, sucking her plump bottom lip between her teeth. "Is that gallery open late?"

"Until seven."

"So we could go later? Afterward?"

This time his smile came from somewhere deep inside. For a minute there, he'd been worried.

"We certainly could."

The door swung open before they could pack up the food. An older guy with salt-and-pepper hair stuck his head through. He smiled genially. "Oh, sorry, Heather. I didn't realize you had anyone in here. Am I interrupting?"

Jon waited four heartbeats for her to introduce him. Maybe not as her boyfriend. They weren't so much that type of people, but as something. A friend. Hell, even his name would do.

She only shook her head. "Not at all."

"Are you going to be at Mr. Quinn's tomorrow night?"

She'd straightened her shoulders—drawn back until she was a stiff board against her big leather chair. She threw out a smile that seemed like a picture of a picture of a real one—grainy now, and overly shiny. "Of course, Grant."

"Stupid question, yeah?" Grant laughed. Lines fanned out from the corners of his eyes and scored around his mouth. "Who wouldn't be going to the company's anniversary party?"

She dug the end of the plastic fork under her thumbnail. "No one I know."

Except Jon.

Because she hadn't mentioned it.

His muscles turned to rock under cold skin. Since his stomach had crunched down into a tiny pebble, he tossed his pancetta onto her desk. Her gaze flew to him, begging him for something. He couldn't begin to guess what.

Grant edged farther into the room. "Rumor has it Mr. Quinn will make his announcement about who's getting the promotion to director. You've got it in the bag, Heather."

"You'll jinx me."

"Do you have a ride yet? Because I could pick you up. I'd love to, actually."

Jon lifted an eyebrow, expecting Heather to turn the offer down flat. Instead she looked at her food. She pushed it away.

Shit.

He'd sworn he would never be here again, begging for attention from someone who didn't have it to give. He'd been a kid then. Defenseless. Now it was different. He retreated deep inside himself, sliding back along years of training—years of not giving a damn. The smile he aimed at Heather felt wolfish.

Grant flicked his gaze between them, perhaps noticing the sudden chill. "Um, maybe I'll come back later."

"Oh, by all means," Jon said, waving a hand. "Don't let me bother you. Heather, *do* you need a ride to the company party?"

Her cheeks went pale. The vein that dipped into the hollow of her neck fluttered wildly. "No, thank you, Grant." Although she spoke to the other man, she looked directly at Jon. "I was planning to drive myself."

"That's good." Grant's disappointment was impossible to miss. "I'll...I'll see you later, then."

Neither Jon nor Heather saw the door close. Both were locked too intently on one another. A quiet snick was the only herald that they were alone.

Heather let loose first. "You didn't even lock the door before you tried to get in my pants?" She put her hands to work sliding a white lid back over her carton and crimping the edges shut.

"I'd have locked it if needed, Ms. Morris." He whipped out the words like a harsh coil. "Don't try to distract me. Company party, is it?"

She nodded slowly, as if her neck had broken in increments. "Yearly thing. At the CEO's house."

"And you didn't invite me because...?"

Her hands dropped out of sight, beneath the table. "I didn't think you'd want to go. It's boring. Always is."

"I seem to remember making a similar argument about the ball," he said coolly. "What about this promotion?"

"Weeks of speculation. Nothing more."

"You've known it was a possibility for *weeks* and didn't say a word? What, you don't give a damn about a big promotion?"

"I do. I just didn't want to..." Her movements became jerky as she went back to cleaning up the lunch neither of them intended to eat. "You know what? Fine. Good for you. Jon Carlisle is right again. I didn't say anything because I was trying to keep you separate from work. I wasn't sure what would happen. Happy?"

Fuck, he was ice. All the way down to his bones.

"I'm a goddamned officer in the United States Air Force," he said. "I come from money, and you know good and well I can handle myself in company. So this is *all* you, Heather love. What the hell is your problem?"

Chapter Thirty-Seven

"*My* problem?"

Heather's head throbbed. Her face had gone hot the moment Jon arrived, and she hadn't been able to recover. The part of her touched by his thoughtfulness had been overruled.

"What if Grant had walked in on us?"

"Oh, I don't know," Jon said with a sneer. "Had you introduced me, he might've put two and two together."

"Introduced you as what, exactly?"

"Take your pick, Heather. I can be the guy who brought you lunch. Or the guy who makes you fucking *shatter* when you come."

She glanced toward her closed office door. "Will you please keep it down?"

"Horseshit."

"See? This is what I meant all along!" After tapping a pencil against the desk in an anxious rhythm, she forced herself to stop. The borderline hysteria in her voice had to go. "You come in here and act like my life doesn't have any foundation."

"If you'd let me in for just a goddamn minute, I might learn what that means. Forgive me for having trouble interpreting your mixed signals."

"You're exaggerating," she said, forcing the words out.

He leaned forward in the chair and ticked a list off on his fingers. "Let's see. You can tease me within an inch of my commission, but you sure as hell don't trust me to keep my dick in my pants around *your* boss. You like to hang with my friends, but God forbid you want to see where I live. And don't even get me started on your fucking career. I guess a pervert like me is only fit for anonymous hotel rooms?"

"You think you can smile your way in here and, what, assume I'd shove you under the desk to grab some quick head?"

His eyes flicked away.

"You did! Oh, God." Heather stood from the desk. The graphite dug into her thumb, but she only pressed deeper. "You have some nerve, Jon. Really. Maybe it's your money or your ego, but you assume the world just bends to what you want. Believe me, not everyone can walk through life that way."

"Right, because I'm getting exactly what I want right now. I love going in unprepared against an opponent I didn't even know I had."

"What opponent?"

"What's-his-fuck Grant. Are you sleeping with him?"

Face on fire, Heather could only gape. His words had become rougher and tighter, but Jon—the arrogant young playboy she'd met in July—was practically lounging on his chair. He was as unknown to her as that long-ago stranger. His familiar features had buckled around a deep scowl.

"No, maybe not yet." His scowl warped into a cruel smile. "But maybe you've got plans for him? A little variety, is it?"

"You're being absurd."

"Am I? Come on, then," he said, standing. "Let's go get him. I'm sure he'd take time off for a threesome."

"You sick little shit."

"We'd better go to your place, though. You don't even know *where* my condo is. I'll even give him first choice. Christ knows I've learned to be satisfied with less than all of you."

"That's *not* fair! Not even close! You act like we were ever going to be anything but a good time."

"Are you having a good time?" He looked her up and down. "Because all I've got left is wondering if you have *any* limits."

"You see what happens? I open up a tiny bit of myself and you use it against me."

"What? Do you think this has anything to do with what you did as a kid?"

She froze, toe-to-toe with him. "Why not? That's what you're thinking. Some guy in uniform drove me to Jersey and I let his friends crawl all over me. Must be the kind of girl I am underneath all this, right? Bound to happen again for the right sweet-talker."

"If you're comparing me to that jerk-off punk," he said with clipped syllables, "then we're not getting out of this one."

"Maybe that's for the best."

Her rusted joints creaked as she forced herself to cross to the office door. Outside there would be curious stares and reproachful glances. Unavoidable now. They'd been too loud. There would be no hiding this.

"You've been looking for it all this time, Jon," she said, opening the door. "So here's your panda. I'm done."

"*Fine*. I'm used to having it your way." There in the doorway, in front of everyone, he stared down at her. For a moment she caught a flicker of something ragged in his dark gaze, before he shuffled it away. "But I want you to do something for me when you get home."

Heather tightened her death grip on the doorknob. "Not here. Don't you dare—"

"Oh, nothing like that, Ms. Morris. I've think we've already done enough to embarrass you."

He leaned close, forcing his warmth and his scent on her. Heather swallowed a sting of tears.

"I want you to think about all the times you trusted me with your body. Everything we did and all that made you curious. Ask yourself why I never took more than you wanted to give, and how hard I tried to get it right." He pulled back. The naked pain in his honey-brown eyes shocked her to her soul. "You think about that, and then you try to look yourself in the mirror."

She stood stiff, numb, rigid, as Jon stalked away. He came to the end of the corridor and drew up short. With a rasping growl, he slammed his fist into the wall. Heather flinched. Tears smeared down her cheeks as he disappeared out of sight. Her hands wouldn't stop shaking.

"Heather?"

Her skin shriveled. She turned to find Mr. Quinn. "Sir?"

"I think you should take a few days, don't you? Kyle's accounts are up to date. He can finish up your numbers on the Wynn."

"Mr. Quinn, I—"

He shook his head, silently cutting off her protest. "Just take some time."

Everything she'd worked for...all in tatters.

And for what? Jon was gone and her heart was breaking.

Heather nodded stiffly. The eyes of the office burned into her back as she turned away. She threw the Italian food into the garbage bin as her stomach knotted around that cooled stench.

Even as she shut down her computer, she couldn't stop fighting to make sense of the grenade thrown into her afternoon. Jon had just been there. He'd brought her lunch. He'd kissed her. They were supposed to go to Cass's gallery for the afternoon.

Not to be. Any of it.

She found herself looking around in the vain hope he might have left something behind. Just a little something of him, of them, that wasn't tainted.

Wiping her flushed cheeks, she closed the office door behind her. Conversations stopped as she did. Heather no longer cared. The worst had already happened.

That evening, she stood in the shower and let the steaming water scald her back. For minutes and minutes, she pressed her forehead against the tile. Didn't wash. Didn't shave. Just stood there.

Her months with Jon became a movie she couldn't stop rewatching. As much as she didn't want to do as he'd asked, she pictured every audacious encounter and each moment when she'd placed her trust in his hands.

Not once—*not once* had he let her down.

Instead he'd given her a hundred little gifts. His caring and wicked humor, his restraint and daring. His unexpected laughter still teased in her ears when he dropped all of his disguises. With Jon she'd rewritten her own wild history, learning herself in ways she hadn't believed possible.

A fierce trembling took hold of her hands, so that turning off the water became a challenge. The faucet dripped its last in a quiet patter. She opened the glass door and groped for a towel. When she swiped away the condensation on the mirror, she couldn't lift her eyes. She already knew what she'd find there: a scared woman who'd let a good man down.

The last time she'd been unable to face herself, she'd been a terrified teenager in a sleazy hotel. And she'd called her father. Before she could second-guess, Heather grabbed her BlackBerry and crawled onto her bed. She hit the speed dial. Three long rings had her silently begging.

Please, please pick up.

"Hello?"

Heather closed her eyes in relief. "Hey, Dad."

"Heather, honey. Wasn't expecting to hear from you."

She swallowed. "Just wanted to say hi. Where are you guys?"

"Nova Scotia."

"In Canada? When did you get to Canada?"

"Early last week. The leaves in New England were gorgeous, and then we just kept driving north."

"What's it like there?"

"Chilly tonight. We're looking out over the ocean." She liked the sound of his voice, almost peaceful. Dragging it inside her fevered mind was a quiet medicine. "We might settle here if we run out of travel money. Be beach bums."

She flinched. Years of hard work had earned her the privilege of taking care of them—paying them back. She didn't feel like a competent, successful woman now. "You won't run out of money. You know I don't take my eyes off your accounts."

"I know, I know. Just teasing." He paused. The long-distance crackle filled her ear. "Heather, are you all right? You don't sound good."

The sob she'd held back for hours broke free. "Dad, I think I messed up. Bad."

"Are you hurt? Heather?"

"No, no—I, well, I am hurting. But I gave a lot worse than I got."

"You're gonna have to fill me in, baby."

Swallowing another sob at his endearment, she wiped her eyes. "I met a man in July. He's an Air Force pilot here at Nellis. Young. Smart. But...it wasn't supposed to get serious."

Her father offered a sympathetic chuckle. "It rarely starts out serious. And you got scared?"

So scared. Scared to trust what had seemed for weeks to be too good, too perfect.

"Yeah, I did."

"If he's worth a damn, then he was too."

Heather smiled despite herself. "I can't imagine that."

"Oh, believe it. Nothing more scared on this planet than a guy who has it bad."

She closed her eyes again, remembering the times when she'd seen Jon watching her, that expectant look on his face. Never anything overt. Just a certain...waiting. How long had he wanted to take their relationship deeper? How long had her determination to keep it crazy and carefree silenced him?

Yet, he'd never said a word. Silent, matching fears had amplified until nothing of them remained.

Her throat constricted. "Dad, what do I do?"

He was silent again, longer this time. Wet hair was giving her goose bumps, so she crawled under the covers.

"Honey, you have to know something about men. Young men. Maybe military men most of all. Our pride can be a helluva thing." He said that last with another rueful chuckle. "If you've hurt his pride, you're going to have to give him more than an apology. He'll need a leap of faith. You just gotta hope he catches you."

Heather's heart stuttered. She wouldn't have doubted Jon before that afternoon. Now she had even more to fear. The idea of opening herself up to a cold, remote stranger, with his emotions in deep-freeze, made her shake.

"But do me a favor, Heather?"

"Anything."

"Don't tell me if he screws up, okay? I don't wanna have to leave your mom in Canada so I can brain some dumb-ass throttle jockey."

Laughing softly—a break in the tension—she rubbed her wet nose on the sheet. "You've held yourself back from wailing on worse guys."

"You know, I'd do anything to save you some of the pain you've grabbed hold of through the years, but I can't bring myself to wish for it. I'm too proud of the woman you've become."

She buried her face in her pillow.

"Just be easy on that girl you were," he said. "I wasn't much older than you are now when we got through that time. Hopefully we're both a lot wiser for it."

She found herself nodding and shaking her head both. The idea that her dad took on board some of the blame for her wild years was almost too much. But he was right—they were both stronger and wiser, calmer with one another. Maybe she'd been hanging on too tightly for too long.

"You'd like him, Dad," she said with a sniffle. "You'd think he was an arrogant son of a bitch, but you'd like him."

"I won't hold it against him that he's Air Force. Not too much." He sobered then, his voice thick with an emotion Heather had rarely heard. "Does he keep you safe, baby?"

Heather let the tears flow, unable to fight them anymore.

No fear. Not here. Just admit the truth.

"He does, Dad. He really does."

"Then go get him."

Chapter Thirty-Eight

The last thing in the world Jon wanted was a houseful of people. But bailing on his monthly poker game with Leah and Ryan would be tantamount to admitting something was wrong. Then what would he say?

Gee, Heather and I are done and I have no idea what happened.

The next step would be tucking his dick between his legs, buying a carton of ice cream and renting *Bridget Jones's Diary*.

So he'd opened his door to the whole crew, which included Cass for the first time.

Jon smiled. Like he always did. Layered on charm and jokes. No hint that anything was chipping him apart from the inside. That was his thing. Giving and being there and treading through shit for it. He'd done it time and again and never learned his fucking lesson.

Heather's voice still hissed in his ears, calling him a sick little shit. Sure, he'd deserved that one. But what should he have done? Begged for what he wanted?

Needed.

Wasn't gonna happen.

Once the poker game hit a break, he ducked out. Alone in his kitchen, he poured a couple inches of scotch in a squat glass, tossed back a swallow and ignored the fine tremble in his hands.

"You okay, Tin Tin?" Leah stood in the doorway. Seeing a soda dangling from her fingers was still strange. She even looked more in control. The long brown hair scooped in a ponytail was much neater than usual.

Jon stuck his head in the fridge as if he really gave a damn whether there was enough guacamole. "I'm fine."

"Don't bullshit me."

Why couldn't he have gotten involved with someone like Leah? Not her, specifically, since they'd been friends so long it would be as disgusting as banging a cousin. At least someone who didn't have all the mile-high defenses? Leah lived with every response out in the open.

He knew why. Because he would've been bored inside of four seconds.

He crossed his arms and leaned against the kitchen counter. The same bloody counter Heather had never seen. She couldn't unclench enough to risk an encounter outside of her own territory. He should've known something was fundamentally broken between them.

"I said I'm fine."

Leah's eyes narrowed. "You don't want to talk about it, that's cool. But whatever happened to Mr. I Never Lie?"

He downed half his glass. The liquid burned like lava in his chest, but nothing could ease the sick emptiness there. "That line's easy to pull when you don't give a shit."

Thank Christ, Leah let him stalk by without saying another word. He couldn't take any of her usual smack-talking.

Out in the living room, he'd set up the green felt-topped poker table in the center. Cass and Ryan had migrated to the huge plate-glass window with the view of Las Vegas at night.

Heather would've loved it.

They stood with their fingers intertwined. "A hell of a place you've got here, Jon," Cass said.

"Sure." He finished the rest of his drink. Goddamned happy couples were nauseating. "We ready to play?"

They all resumed their seats. Jon leaned back as if he didn't notice the wary glances they traded. "Anyone up for higher stakes?"

Ryan shook his head. "No way, Tin Tin. Your pockets are way too deep for my blood."

"Fine, chicken out," he said, dredging up all the charm he could find. "You've got a shit poker face, anyway. I'd hate if you had to take out an allotment to pay me."

But a half hour later, there was no hiding the way he froze when the doorbell rang. His hand twitched on the deck he'd been dealing. Nothing moved but his gaze.

"I thought Dash said he couldn't make it," Leah said.

"Sunny was supposed to get in from DC this afternoon." Ryan

scooped a handful of pretzels. "Maybe she was delayed."

"Then I've got this." Leah hopped up to answer the door.

Heather stood there, with one hand tight around her purse strap.

On some level, Jon had known.

The smile he'd forced all night slid off his face. Only a cold clench of trepidation remained in his chest...and way underneath that, a single bright flash of hope—too quick to kill.

She looked as beautiful as always, despite the red that rimmed her pale blue eyes. Slim jeans clung to her hips. He'd never seen her in such a simple T-shirt because she never liked showing her true self.

Then again, neither did he.

Leah grinned. "Hey, Heather. Here for the game?"

Stepping inside, Heather wound her arms around her stomach. "No."

Even Leah managed to catch the thick tension filling the air. Her gaze slid between Jon and Heather.

He forced his hands to move. Cards flicked out across the green felt in a smooth arc. "Hello, Heather. Fancy meeting you here. I knew you could find my place if you put your mind to it."

"Can I talk to you? In private?"

"No. Don't think so." He smiled, ignoring how fucking painful it was to resume his crafted façade. After neatly stacking the rest of the deck, he leaned back. "Anything you need to say can be said in front of my friends."

She blinked as if noticing the others for the first time. Her cheeks hollowed. Resolve flickered across her features and firmed her mouth.

"You were right," she said tightly. "I couldn't look at myself in the mirror last night. Or this morning."

Jon's stomach plummeted. *Fuck.* He hadn't wanted to be right, not when it darkened her eyes with such naked pain. It wasn't enough either. He needed more.

Ryan clapped his hands on the table and stood. "All right, that's it. Our cue to leave."

Cass popped up beside him. She and Leah collected their purses as they made for the door. Heather barely shifted, moving aside only a step.

Inside Bet

One hand on the doorjamb, Cass paused. "Good luck, you two."

Ryan grabbed her by the waist. "Outta here now, woman." He pinned Jon with one last look. "You know where I'll be if you need me."

At least he hadn't misplaced his trust with some people.

Jon started cleaning up the mess they'd made of his poker table, stacking the chips in their case. When he turned away from Heather, he allowed his eyes to close. He dropped his smile. It had become such a relief to quit pretending.

"I think we're going to need more than luck," he said, biting out the words. "Don't you, Heather love?"

"Can you stop for just a minute? Look at me?"

He couldn't. Not without breaking. He kept straightening up, gathering all the red-patterned cards. At his back he heard her steps as she crossed the hardwood floors.

"Is this you?"

She stood next to his bookshelves with a framed picture in her hand. He liked seeing her touching his possessions. In his home. She looked right in the surroundings. He enjoyed finely made things with classic beauty. That was Heather, through and through. But priceless works of art couldn't be touched.

"Yes."

"And your sister." No question in her soft voice. She trailed a finger over the glass. "Curls, huh? I wouldn't have ever pictured you with long hair. But then, you've surprised me all along."

He clenched the edge of the table. The padded rim meant nothing to bite against his pain. "Made me look too young."

She carefully returned the picture to its place on the bookshelf. Wariness shaped her posture. She walked slowly toward him. Again, she crisscrossed her arms over her stomach.

"I'm sorry, Jon. I'm so sorry. For everything. I want to talk about it. Please? To end it this way, with our fight..."

He gripped the table tighter to keep from reaching for her. The twisted regret on her face tore him up. "I can't keep doing this."

A glassy sheen covered her eyes. "Will you hear me out? Let me try? You deserve the truth first."

"I'd have thought I deserved it from the beginning."

"You did. You *do*. But *I* didn't even know what was happening."

He waved a hand. "Explain away. You have my full attention."

She was near enough now that his bones tried to get to her. He fought his muscles, but nothing prevented a sweet inhalation of her scent.

"I was using you, Jon." She didn't look up at him from beneath her brows. Not this time. Instead, her pale blue eyes were wide and direct, lashes damp. Completely vulnerable. No hint of his playful, mischievous, wicked Heather to be found. Just a woman stripped of every defense.

"It wasn't the way you probably think," she said. "I didn't like what I did when I was young and stupid. No, that's an understatement. Those years have colored everything about me. I wanted to be successful, to repay the hell I put my parents through. I tried to play it safe with guys so that I wouldn't lose control. But it went deeper—so deep that I didn't see it until now."

How much longer could he stand there and look *her* in the eye? She was aching, nearly as badly as he. Jon resolved, however, to stand there forever if that's what it took. He needed to hear every syllable or he'd never be able to give this woman his heart, no matter how much he wanted to.

"Say what you think you need to," he said quietly, his voice nearly quavering with bottled-up emotion.

"I used you to make it better."

He frowned. And waited.

Nervous, graceful hands twisted at her waist. "With you, I got to do it all over again. All those crazy years, all the insane things I did. The chances. I loved dares, way back then. Any chance to prove I was fearless. Even a college psych major could see I was overcompensating. Lashing out. But with you... Every step along the way, you made old, dirty memories clean again. It wasn't just being stupidly reckless, and frankly, I don't think it was ever entirely about sex. *You* made it more. Special. Worthwhile."

Hope was a painful thing, sharp-edged and wild as it tore inside his chest. "So, free psychotherapy? With bonus orgasms? Guess I should be thankful I happened to meet you at the right time."

"No." She shook her head frantically. "It's not like that. It was you all along. Why else would I have gone with you that first night? Our challenges and risks—you made me feel safe from the beginning. As crazy as it was, I never had a doubt you'd take care of me. So it got to be terrifying. I was missing something, some flaw. I'd be proved blind and naïve all over again." She released her wringing fingers long enough to begin reaching for him, but his glare must have stopped her. "Jon, you made it work. You made me feel free."

"That's ironic, when you were making me feel pretty damn caged in. Your rules, your territory. Only."

A flinch. A nibble to her lower lip. He'd never seen her so rattled. Yet through it all, her eyes remained direct. She'd never looked at him without some hint of teasing or pretense.

"That wasn't my intention," she said. "Not consciously. I kept making reckless choices with you, sort of...purging them. As a grown woman now. I thought I could keep control this time—and that meant controlling everything. Any less and I'd spin out again." Her words kept coming in one long stream. "And all the time, you gave me everything. Even things I didn't know I needed. You've been wonderful. Through everything. Jon, please..."

Her voice broke. A tear ran down her pale face when she blinked.

The clawing inside of him settled. Only one thing remained true. He couldn't give Heather up.

"Damn it, don't cry." He curled his hands around her cheeks.

"I don't seem to be able to help it. I only want you. We trusted each other with the impossible, but we end it like this? Like scared little kids? We've been playing games and taking risks when it could be so much more. Don't you feel it? I think you have for a long time. I'm so sorry I kept looking away."

He swallowed. Might as well own up to his role in this train wreck. "I could have said something. Never did. It's hard to want something true and strong from people who can't return it."

"Your parents," she breathed. "Jesus. I did that to you too." Her cheeks were awash with fresh tears. Sky-blue eyes glowed like neon. "Have they ever begged you to forgive them? Because that's why I'm here, Jon. I'm begging you. Please give us another chance. A *real* chance."

He closed his eyes. "They've never even seen what I needed, let alone begged." Pulling their bodies together, flush and warm and right, he breathed the floral scent of her hair. "A real chance, Heather love."

The tension in her body released on a long shudder and another graceless sniffle. She buried her face against his shirtfront. She was the one crying, but they both held on for dear life. Brave. And so damn relieved.

"But..." She lifted her face and hesitated. "I don't want any of it without you. *Just* you. Not...not like what you said in the office."

His angered words about her coworker lodged between them—the only thing he regretted about their fight. He'd never been particularly against the idea of bending relationship boundaries, but this was Heather. He wanted her all to himself.

"I didn't mean it. You have to know that. God, sharing you would make me sick. I was...hurting."

She brushed a kiss over the reddened, raw skin of his knuckles. "We both were."

He focused on her mouth—her lush, trembling mouth. "But I can't keep playing these fuck-fuck games, Heather. It has to be all or nothing."

Her chest lifted on a fast, silent gasp. "Promise?"

Heather Morris had never been anything less than captivating. He'd been gone over her a long time, and now he could stay gone.

"Yes. If you can promise me something in return."

"I'll try. Whatever it is."

"Don't shut me out again." He laced his fingers into her hair. "I can't take it. I need you to let me in."

She pulled their foreheads together until skin pinched against skin. A soft pain, uniting them. "You too. I can't read your mind. Play how you want with the world. I know I do it too. But not here. Not with us." Boldly she wound her hands around his back, clenching tight. She nuzzled the bare skin at the open notch of his collar. "I'm so sorry. I love you, but I only made you hurt."

He froze. "You...?"

She nodded. A love he'd never expected to find shone clearly from her luminous eyes.

Exhaling, he pulled her more tightly into his embrace. His heart thumped. The glimmering tracks of her tears were drying on her cheeks. He kissed them away. She tasted like salt and all his best dreams. "I think I've been waiting for that. Needed to hear it from you first. Because I love you too."

She looked younger and happier than he'd ever seen. "That's... I don't even know what to say. Amazing. Can we be amazing?"

He grinned and kissed her lips. Half play. Half hard-earned emotion. "We already are."

"So, will you show me around your place? It's way past time I saw it."

The cinched feeling in his chest had loosened. This was where it would start. A real beginning.

"Well," he drawled. "The kitchen's a wreck."

"Living room?"

"You're looking at it."

"Do you have a den?"

His grin took on a devious feel. "Too far away."

"What does that leave? The bedroom?"

"Indeed. Right this way, Heather love." He hooked an arm around her shoulder as he led her down the hallway. "So...we were redoing your high school years, were we?"

Her cheeks went pink. "Yes."

That had certain possibilities. "You know, there were certain high school events I missed out on too."

"Surely not, Mr. Moneybags."

He nodded, but he couldn't keep his expression as solemn as he meant. He was too aw-shucks sappy happy. "For example, I never passed dirty notes in class."

"Would texting count?"

"We can improvise."

She twined her fingers with his. "What else?"

"I never passed the dutchie under the bleachers at a football game."

"Well, that's *definitely* out."

"Wait, I've got it," he said. "Heather love, how would you like me to tutor you in French?"

She giggled. Everything about her expression was bright and open, inviting him in. For good, this time. "That sounds lovely. But I'm not convinced. What is your teaching style?"

He couldn't stop touching her. Only touching made it real. "Hands on, Ms. Morris. Definitely hands on."

Epilogue

After completing her nighttime routine, Heather turned off the bathroom light and returned to Jon's bedroom. The polished hardwood floors were cool against her feet. Early December not only brought relief from scorching temperatures but made for gorgeous evenings. A breeze scented with desert sage filtered in through the open bay window where Jon sat in a leather recliner.

He was the same man she'd met during the high heat of July—her early birthday present—but he was nearly as changed as she. Nearly. He wore one of his customary dress shirts, bright white, the sleeves rolled to the middle of his corded forearms. Jeans tonight. And bare feet pulled up on the leather cushion.

The bare feet always got to her. An intimacy he shared with no one else.

With his head back on the recliner, he stared out the window. A wistful half-smile shaped his lips. She knew what gorgeous depravity those lips were capable of, which made his peaceful, faraway expression all the more endearing.

"Jon?"

He didn't shift anything but his gaze. A slinky sideways glance shivered anticipation down into her belly. "Hey."

"Who called?"

His iPhone lay on the antique writing desk next to the recliner. He eyed it with an amusement she didn't understand. "Come sit on my lap. It's been a long day and I've missed your ass."

"The ass you slapped last night?"

"Repeatedly? That's the one."

Heather smoothed a hand over the wrists he'd bound with a pair of suspenders the night before. Her body still hummed and shook.

He patted his knee, his smile gone from wistful to kinky in just a few heartbeats. She crossed the room with a sultry sway. Her nipples tightened under one of his plain white cotton T-shirts, in part because of the breeze, in part because of his heated appreciation.

She draped across the recliner and settled her backside against his groin. Strong arms circled her waist. He dipped his head between her breasts for a quick nuzzle.

"You're trying to distract me," she said. "It won't work."

"Give me a minute. I have more ideas."

Heather found his face, her hands flat on his cheeks. "Who was on the phone?"

He took a deep breath, his expression sobering. "My mother."

"Oh?"

"They asked if we would like to fly out for Christmas."

Something about his tone of voice, so dazed, made him seem even younger. A strong protective impulse took her by surprise.

"Let me in there," she said, rubbing her hands back along his buzzed head. "It goes both ways, remember?"

He exhaled again, then appeared to make a decision. "They've never... Fuck it, they've never *asked* before. It's been an imperial summons for as long as I can remember."

"You want to go."

Turning those dark eyes on her, he grazed her cheek with a feathery touch. "Maybe. Yes. I do. But only if you come with me."

"Jon, would this be us making plans?"

"I don't see why not. The odds have been good to us so far."

"Does that make you my inside bet?"

"Nah, *mon amour*, I'm your sure thing," he said with a slight smile. Heather touched his lower lip, overwhelmed, until he chased away the intensity by tonguing her finger. "So what do you say? Fly with me to Planet Hyannis for the holidays?"

She should have felt a slice of panic. What would his parents think of her? But that panic didn't come, only a determination to be strong for Jon as he accepted this tentative olive branch.

"I'd like that."

"The thing is..." He inhaled, let it go slowly. "Six months ago, I might've ignored the call altogether. You've changed me, Heather love. You said I could be better."

"And now look at you. Just bursting with potential."

He laughed and tucked her against his chest. "Don't I get enough trash-talk at work? I expect sugar from you."

Heather giggled against his throat, kissed him there. "There. Some sugar. Now, about this trip. Do I get to see your bedroom from when you were a kid?"

"With my No Doubt and Claudia Schiffer posters?"

"Hey, they're both blondes."

"Then I grew up," he said, brushing a lock of her hair. "Besides, Mother turned it into a respectable guestroom."

Heather unfastened one, two, three buttons. She playfully raked her nails down his chest. "Is it soundproof?"

"Hell, no." His soft laugh teased beneath her fingertips. "Are you going to be good?"

"For the sake of family harmony and new beginnings, I'll be *quiet*. I can't promise to be good."

"You've had a good run of wall-bangers, you know. I don't have much faith you can hold it in anymore."

"That sounds like a dare, Captain."

"It does, doesn't it?" His fingers began to work their magic at the apex of her thighs. "Don't you wonder? How slow we could make it? How quiet and tight?"

Liquid warmth flooded her pussy. She spread her knees, just slightly, to invite him inside. "Ah, right there," she whispered.

"We should practice, you know." Jon found the side of her neck and sucked—the lightest tease. "Otherwise my neighbors will start complaining. The Homeowners' Association will kick me out."

She giggled, no longer so embarrassed by the idea of other people knowing she had a passionate side. Jon had taught her the difference between running wild and having a wild time. Maybe come spring she'd buy a bikini to show off her tattoo. She had nothing more to hide.

"If they kick you out," she said, "you'd just have to come live with me."

Jon's hand stilled. "What was that?"

The hairs on Heather's arms stood up on a flush of gooseflesh. "You'd..." She swallowed. "You'd just have to come live with me."

He cupped her neck and brought her mouth down for a sweet, smoldering kiss. The strange thing about beginning their sex life with a series of dares was that kissing remained almost...novel. They went deeper every time, feeling, learning one another in a way that melted Heather's heart.

His tongue smoothed the seam of her lips, as if asking permission. She opened to him. Such a quiet burn. Such a honeyed tension. Her body was alive—wide awake and eager, and always so safe with him.

"That idea would be perfect if your place were as cool as mine," he whispered against her mouth.

"I'm sure we can come to some compromise."

He kissed her, just lip to lip. "*Je t'aime*, Heather love. *Je t'aime comme un fou.*"

Her heart squeezed tight, then burst into a fast, joyous rhythm. "And I love you. God, Jon."

She threw her arms around him and held on, believing in him, in *them*, more than she ever imagined possible. With every beautiful thing he did, he helped push her fears away until only their love remained.

Laughing now, she attacked the zipper of his jeans.

Jon leaned back, arms splayed on the armrests. His bemused smile returned, complete with those maddening dimples. "What happened to slow and sweet?"

"Save it for Hyannis. I have something else in mind." She stroked his cock, enjoying the thrill of finding him so ready.

Hissing in a quick breath, he claimed her unbound hair. "Oh, really? Do enlighten me, Ms. Morris."

"We're getting you kicked out of your condo. Let's make some noise, flyboy."

Author's Note

The 64th Aggressor Squadron is an active United States Air Force unit assigned to the 57th Adversary Tactics Group, stationed at Nellis Air Force Base in Las Vegas, Nevada. The pilots' objectives are as we've described: to fly as adversaries against allied pilots from around the world, teaching them to better counter enemy tactics. The unit dates back to WWII when it participated in multiple theaters of operation.

Now, the 64th and other "bandits" from the 57th ATG regularly conduct dogfighting simulations in the United States, known as Red Flags, and Maple Flag exercises in conjunction with Canadian Forces. They also add their expertise to the USAF's Weapons School syllabus and travel the country to provide training and test mission support to various units.

All individuals described in this story are fictitious. Research mistakes are entirely our own.

In the meantime, we enjoy assuming that at least one of these dedicated, highly skilled bandits can speak fluent French.

About the Author

Katie Porter is the writing team of Carrie Lofty and Lorelie Brown, who've been friends and critique partners for more than five years. Both are multi-published in historical romance. Carrie has an MA in history, while Lorelie is a US Army veteran. Generally a high-strung masochist, Carrie loves running and weight training, but she has no fear of gross things like dissecting formaldehyde sharks. Her two girls are not appreciative. Lorelie, a laid-back sadist, would rather grin maniacally when Carrie works out. Her three boys love how she screams like a little girl around spiders.

To learn more about the authors who make up Katie, visit www.katieporterbooks.com or follow them on Twitter at @carrielofty, @LorelieBrown and @MsKatiePorter.

A man with handcuffs. A woman with a paddle. Both fly F-16s.

Hold 'Em
© 2012 Katie Porter
Vegas Top Guns, Book 3

Daughter of a world-famous motocross champion, and head-on competitor with three brothers, Captain Leah "Princess" Girardi was born with a need for speed. No one tells her what to do, especially not men with chauvinistic "girls can't be fighter pilots" attitudes.

That's what ended her brief relationship with Captain Mike "Strap Happy" Templeton. Now, six years later, he's been assigned to her squadron, and whoa *damn*, he's filled out nicely. Plus he's cultivated a Zen-like chill factor that pulls at her hormones.

Even after four tours, Mike's the new kid in the 64th Aggressor Squadron. That's not the only thing new. Since he last saw Leah, he's learned a few things about himself. A female who outranks him still makes his teeth grind, but in the bedroom he craves the rush of pain inflicted by an adoring, powerful woman.

Their reunion is an explosive revelation. Leah is the beautiful mistress he's been searching for, and she takes to her new role like a natural. But Leah's aware one thing *hasn't* changed. Loving him is still an all-or-nothing proposition. She's not sure her reckless streak is wide enough to risk her career—and her heart.

Warning: This book contains a hot stud on his knees, a woman wielding a paddle, and filthy-gorgeous femdom sex. Also: dangerous rock climbing, two amazing motorcycles and some bad tequila.

Available now in ebook and print from Samhain Publishing.

SAMHAIN
PUBLISHING

It's all about the story...

Romance

HORROR

Retro ROMANCE

www.samhainpublishing.com